*The Death of
a Shenzhen Angel*

For Chris

徐啟源

12/10/05

Beijing
CHINA
Shanghai
Shenzhen
Taiwan
Hong Kong

The Death of
a Shenzhen Angel

David Tsui

VANTAGE PRESS
New York

Copyright © 2005 by David Tsui

Published by Vantage Press, Inc.
419 Park Ave. South, New York, NY 10016

Manufactured in the United States of America
ISBN: 0-533-15148-1

Library of Congress Catalog Card No.: 2005900176

0 9 8 7 6 5 4 3 2 1

For my parents, brother, and sisters

Acknowledgments

I'm indebted to the warm and responsive senior sales clerk working at the Borders Books in downtown San Francisco, who handed me a telephone directory (in which my publisher was found) in responding to my desperate croak, "How do I get my work published?" a month after I returned to the States from China with the written manuscript but had no idea where and how to begin in getting my book printed and delivering it to the readers. I regret very much my mindlessness at the time, which deterred me from finding out and remembering his name.

I'm especially grateful for the wonderful and professional help and work done by Vantage Press, Inc.

Author's Note

Despite the fictitious names, characters, firms and organizations, over half of this story is true. This book would have been written as a memoir had I not considered the risk of being blocked from entering my motherland again.

*The Death of
a Shenzhen Angel*

Prologue

The ten-year unprecedented and destructive Cultural Revolution—which had plagued and tormented the People's Republic of China—officially ended in 1976 with the arrest of the Gang of Four. These mighty individuals were Jiang Qing, the Communist party Chairman Mao Zedong's wife; Zhang Chunqiao, a member of the Communist party Politburo Standing Committee; Yao Wenyuan, a member of the Communist party Central Committee; and Wang Hongwen, the appointed vice chairman of the Communist party.

The gravest and most urgent agendas that Hua Guofeng, the Mao-appointed successor, faces now are the collapsing economy and the citizens' lack of confidence toward the government. However, neither he nor his government is capable to meet the challenge.

To rescue the economy and stabilize the government, Deng Xiaoping, the former Communist party secretary and the second main target of the Cultural Revolution, is released from the cowshed and reappointed as the first of the nine vice-premiers—in the request of many central government leaders. This is Deng's third comeback from being ousted in his half-century political career.

Within two years, Deng abandons Mao's class-struggle policy and rehabilitates millions of purged victims, many of whom are intellectuals or former government officials. Next he dismisses the ideological debate of whether what he and his followers have been doing is in line with communism or capitalism within the party, and points out: "It does not matter whether it is a white or black cat, it is a good cat so long as it catches mice." Then wielding his magic wand of power and charisma with pragmatism, Shenzhen and three other regions in southern China are established as the special economic zones in 1979.

These special economic zones are designed to attract foreign investments, technologies and management skills, to serve as the experimental base for both political and economic theories and policies, to play as role models for the rest of the cities in the nation, and to implement the strategy of "Letting the coastal areas become rich first."

Of all these economic zones, Shenzhen, bordering Hong Kong and enjoying the most advantages, is the biggest one. Whether it succeeds or fails will directly affect not only Deng's and his followers' political career, but the fate of the entire nation.

Can this cluster of fishing villages, with the population of merely thirty thousand at present, play such an important role in China's modern history?

Only time will tell.

**Book One
1979–1999**

1

Sailing back through the surging waves toward the tip of the triangular Dapeng Bay in the chilly breeze, Chen Yong stood on the bow of the shabby fishing junk, staring at the dilapidated villages scattered along the coast in the twilight. He couldn't remember how many times he had done the same in the past few years. Now he could see, as usual, the wives and children of the other fishermen standing on the protruding rocks, anxiously scanning the returning junks and boats, wanting to find out if their loved ones were coming back safely.

This will be no longer seen soon, he thought. Shenzhen, as they were told, would be a manufacturing base for both foreign and domestic firms instead of a fishing town. Their villages would be demolished to give way for building commercial towers, factories, schools, hospitals, highways and many other construction projects he had never heard of before now. Villagers had been given orders and the date to move out of their huts to the newly built eight-story apartment buildings by the newly formed Special Economic Zone government. Each family was provided with cash as an aid to start their training for new careers, such as a taxi driver, construction worker, salesperson, hotel clerk, janitor, waiter and waitress, even as a grocery store or restaurant or beauty salon owner.

What he wanted was to be a taxi driver and had already taken lessons for the written test. What a great career shift. He had only seen cars a few times in his twenty-year life, and often dreamed about riding in one of them. Soon he was going to operate one of those luxury foreign things. How fascinating it was for Chen Yong. Thinking of this life changing move made him feel so excited that he often had a hard time falling asleep most nights.

Chen Yong would no longer be a fisherman as his father and ancestors had been for thousands of years. His thought flitted back to present. He stared at the villages again, the sea, the fishing junks, and sighed; a mixed feeling with a sense of comprehension occupied him. His father had told him that they belonged only to the sea, that they could not live leaving the ocean behind—it would be as if fish without water. He remembered that his father had defiantly opposed the idea of shifting their career, but had finally given in after the village's party secretary talked with him several times. It was the government's order that he had to obey after all. He had no idea what his fate would be with leaving the ocean but hoped for the best.

"Ha, A-yong, help pull down the sail," his father yelled from the stern, where he was steering the helm, as the junk approached the wooden pier.

Chen Yong quickly released the ropes of the sail and pulled it down; the junk jolted to the left, then to the right, and slowed down immediately.

After anchoring the junk, Chen Yong and his father started unloading the sorted baskets of fishes onto the pier. His mother, younger brother, and sister were yelling happily and running toward them.

"Thank God, you are all safe back home," his mother rejoiced.

"We are lucky today, Mom, we caught more and bigger ones," Chen Yong replied, delightedly.

But his father's eyebrows were tightened and he didn't say a word. The contorted weather map on his face darkened. He and his wife were going to be janitors since they didn't have enough money to do business and were too old and had no skills to do anything else. Deep in his heart, he would rather die in the ocean catching fish instead of doing something else.

"We will be fine, A-ping, at least you will be safe and that is the most important thing for all of us," his wife discerned what was in her husband's mind and said.

"I understand," he muttered, griping one of the baskets, and started tumbling toward a cottage where their fishes were bought by the township government for a fixed price.

Chen Yong and his sister, Chen Jing, fifteen, and brother, Chen Song, thirteen, both high school students, were helping to carry the rest of the fish with their mother jovially.

Walking back toward their hut, they kept nodding, waving and saying "Hi" to the villagers—most of whom were old men or women or children, with occasionally a few young girls.

Chen Yong often felt lonesome because he could hardly find any young men about his age to talk and confide with in town. Most of the young men had escaped to Hong Kong seeking a better and more comfortable life.

Once in a while, he received letters written by his friends from Hong Kong, telling how wonderful Hong Kong was, how well they ate and dressed, and how much money they were making there. At the end of the letters, they seldom missed the opportunity to persuade him to escape.

At the beginning, he dismissed their encouragement because he had been influenced by his father and had decided to stay in his hometown to be a fisherman—as his father had been. He also felt that it was wrong to leave his socialist motherland for the decadent capitalist society.

But as his friends kept writing, sending him gifts and cash, Chen Yong could not resist the temptation and started to give in. Friends began providing information about his escape route and time. One night he planned to sail to an island, which belonged to the British colony in the Dapeng Bay, where his friends would pick him up and escort him to Kowloon, one of the major commercial towns of Hong Kong. But after he revealed his plan to his father and said goodbye to him, his father was furious.

"How dare you have such evil thoughts? You are no better than other decadent elements. My sons are going nowhere but staying here with me to catch fish," his father snapped.

So that was it. Chen Yong never thought about going to Hong Kong again.

2

An unprecedented scale of infrastructure construction in the nation started in 1980 within the newly-formed Shenzhen Special Economic Zone. Twenty thousand veterans from the People's Liberation Army joined the construction workers from all over the country. Bulldozers, cranes, trucks, cement mixers—all of the latest and best construction equipments the nation could provide—had moved in.

Within three months, many hills and mountains were made plain. Ravines and marshes were filled in while the deserted old villages were demolished and their debris removed: Major roads and streets had been paced, all the while new construction sites kept breaking ground.

After moving to newly constructed buildings, most of the fishermen and their families had nearly completed their new career training. Chen Yong had now started his road-driving lessons. He was determined to be a taxi driver.

On the first day of driving lessons, excitement was great for Chen Yong. He had had a restless night and arrived at the driving school before dawn—all the teachers were still sleeping! He was the first of thirty students to attend.

When the class finally began at 8:30 AM, Chen Yong felt over excited. Anxiously touching parts of here and there inside and outside of the car, he told himself one day he would own a fleet of them. That is, if the government allowed it.

He listened carefully and memorized every word the instructor had said. When it was his turn to practice operating the vehicle, the instructor was impressed by how orderly he performed. "You all should learn from Chen Yong," the instructor told the students.

But he was not moved by the instructor's praise. He knew there were so much to learn and so much to do in life, and no room for complacency. He took notes for the difficult parts of the lessons and reviewed them again and again after each class—even during his sleep.

Three months later, Chen Yong was the first student to pass the road-driving test, and with the highest score.

*　　*　　*

With the foundations being built in a myriad of construction sites, the configuration of a modern city next to Hong Kong began looming. With the help of advertisements in the western world, and especially in Hong Kong, many manufacturers, service providers, and real estate developers of foreign companies began swarming to Shenzhen inquiring and looking for possible cooperative opportunities with mainland state-owned and group-owned enterprises.

The central government stipulated that: foreign firms, including those from Hong Kong, Macau, Taiwan and all overseas ethnic Chinese, were not allowed to establish their own companies in China but to cooperate with both the state-owned and group-owned firms. Such combination was called "The Three-ownership Enterprise." Those enterprises were charged little or no-profit tax for the first three years, and they were allowed to import the needed materials and equipments in low tariff charge despite the country's tight foreign reserve policy. However, the main reason that appealed to the foreign investors was China's low labor and land cost. The salary of an average worker in China at the time, for instance, was around US $15 per month, compared to that with US $1500 in the United States.

Because of the geographic and language convenience, nearly 70 percent of the intended foreign investors were Hong Kongers. And most of them were labor-intensive industries, such as garment, shoe, and toy manufacturing and assembling.

The majority of them remained doubtful about the stability of China's policy and whether it could keep its promises and agreements. After all, the mainland was a Communist country that once prohibited capitalist activities. Hiring workers and making profit was considered exploitation and a crime. So many of them were in the early stage of inquiry, assessing and testing waters.

*   *   *

After getting his driver's license, Chen Yong rented an imported Japanese car from a rental company immediately. It was required, he needed to pay the rent daily.

His "taxi" had no fare meter or any taxi indicator on the rooftop. It was just a regular car, and every customer who entered it had to negotiate the fare—every time.

At the beginning, Chen Yong referred to the table of fares for different places given by the car rental company. But, later, he altered it and received higher fees from most of the riders because of it.

One afternoon, a well-groomed middle-aged man with a leather briefcase in hand, walked by and waved to him.

"How much does it cost to go to the Honey Lake?" the man inquired.

Chen Yong glanced to the fare-charging table, which indicated forty yuan. "Well, I usually charge others eighty yuan, but for you, master, I only charge seventy."

The man stared at him doubtfully, than slowly got into the car and said, "Go quick."

As he got more experience, he could judge whether a customer could be charged a higher fare. As a result, his monthly income increased as high as ten thousand yuan. That was an astronomical number considering an ordinary worker's monthly income was around one hundred yuan. He started accumulating a handsome fortune and was getting more ambitious as days went on.

I am going to be the wealthiest man in town, so that everyone, including the government officials, all of my former classmates and relatives, will admire and respect me, Chen Yong told himself. He remembered that he was often in the top-five list of his senior high school class, but had just a few points short in the college entrance exams. With the admittance rate of 4 percent, the competition among the students was so intense that only two of his classmates were able to go on to college. Still, he felt ashamed and humiliated, and he wanted to show that he was more capable than others someday.

He always encouraged his sister and brother to study hard so that they could both go off to the college of their dreams, and not to suffer the same sad feelings like he had.

"Jing and Song, work the hardest and be the best you can," he often urged them. "Don't be like me."

He had told them his experience and his feeling of regret, but they knew how bright their brother was and regretted that he just lacked some luck. They still admired and loved him very much and treated him as their role model.

"We will do exactly what you say, my dear brother. But stop putting down yourself. In fact, deep in our hearts, you are the brightest person, and if we are half as bright as you are, we are happy," Chen Jing once replied, and her younger brother echoed.

Chen Yong knew the fact was, as he used to be, his sister and brother were always at the top of their classes. He often felt proud of them.

Similar to himself, their looks and figures were not as great as movie stars but above average—a typical one that had double-lid eyes, big and straight nose, a nearly oval-shaped face with well-hidden cheekbones and smoothly curved jaw—standing five feet seven, tanned, a solid rock body with the trimming of physical work and consumption of marine foods. That was good enough, he often thought contentedly.

He had been feeling lucky in that he had a lovely mother who was pleasant, easygoing, caring, understandable, soft, and plain as a piece of fish meatball. She had never blamed any of her children for wrongdoing or receiving bad grades, instead she often encouraged them to strive in life and served as a safety harbor for all of them.

Although his father often acted as hard as a piece of rock, he was straightforward, honest, responsible and kindhearted. Everyone respected and adored him.

Eventually, Chen Yong stopped his parents from working as janitors, since he was more than able to support the whole family. But they did not seem happy with doing nothing everyday, especially his father. He often looked drab, bored, and absentminded.

"Just wait for another month, Mom and Daddy. I will have you both run a grocery store," he promised.

And he started to negotiate the rent of a shop nearby and make connections with several suppliers of goods.

3

As an experimental economic zone, Shenzhen was the first place in China to practice the theory of "socialism with Chinese characteristics." But it was virtually practicing socialism with capitalist characteristics. This had been the controversial subject that had caused conflicts between the reformers and the hard-liners within the Communist party and the central government.

To avoid the rest of the country being "contaminated" by the "evil spirit" of capitalism and to block off those who had criminal records to enter, the metropolis of Shenzhen was fenced off with three-meter-tall barbwire right at the start. People who wanted to come to Shenzhen would have to apply with their local governments to obtain the certificates of approval.

With intention of keeping the city vibrant, only the young people in their twenties or seasoned professionals were allowed to live and work there. All persons must apply for temporary residence permits once they have decided to stay. Then strictly enforced: those who violated the rules would be arrested, fined, and sent back to their hometowns. As a result, more than seventy percent of Shenzhen residents' were younger than age thirty, and the percentage of college-educated citizens in this new city soared several times higher than the national average.

Compared to the rest of the country, people in Shenzhen had more job opportunities, made more money, enjoyed more freedom, and had more contact with Western culture and customs as more foreigners stayed here. Shenzhen became the dream place for many people around the nation.

Due to the completion of more commercial and office buildings, roads and streets paved, phone lines installed, and sufficient electric power supplied, there were more taxis and buses and trucks and trains deployed. Many Hong Kong manufacturers—especially those who were on the border of bankruptcy due to the high labor and land cost in the British colony—started to ignore investment risks and relocated their factories into Shenzhen.

The mainlanders were reveled for the employment opportunities, flooding into Shenzhen in waves. Many of them sneaked in through the fence. Large numbers of them were young farmers or high school dropouts from the middle and western part of the country. The population in the city increased rapidly year after year.

Unexpectedly, the city started blooming, and all kinds of convenient stores appeared every where. More supermarkets, department stores, banks, and hotels sprouted everywhere. Restaurants, karaoke nightclubs, bars, discos, along with fashion shops, beauty salons, mobile phone and computer shops, and theme parks appeared. Roads and streets were jammed with automobiles instead of bicycles which were commonly seen in other parts of the nation. Commercial districts were always crowded with people walking shoulder to shoulder.

With the joining army of Hong Kong consumers enjoying the low-cost expenditure, Shenzhen's entertaining and catering industries were sizzling. At night all the bars, karaoke nightclubs, restaurants, and the streets were packed with various customers, hawkers and prostitutes.

At the same time, many people were hungry with knowledge, eager to upgrade and improve themselves. They wanted most to learn computer and the English language. Despite the abundance of training centers opening, they were often filled with adult students in all shifts with all ages.

Every now and then, the hard-liners from the capital visited and were stunned by what they saw. They attacked and accused their counterparts for practicing decadent capitalism and ruining the Communist party's revolutionary career and spirit. Their articles condemning reformers could often be seen in the party's and central government's newspapers and magazines. Every time it happened, the development in Shenzhen stagnated briefly; but quickly bounced back when hard-liners were counterattacked and suppressed by reformers headed by Deng Xiaoping.

The rapidly increased population and the booming economy brought more business for passenger transportation. Despite the considerable number of taxis in the streets, taxi business remained very lucrative. And taxi drivers' incomes remained stably high.

With a lump sum down payment, Chen Yong purchased his first taxi. Now his monthly payment was only one-third of what he had paid for the rental car. His savings, then, accumulated two times faster than before. One year later, he bought another taxi and rented it out. And, again, his income was getting even bigger.

One day, he picked up a passenger in front of a large state-owned bank. Looking at the man's appearance, Chen Yong knew from his three-year taxi-driving experience that this was an important person. He talked to him politely and casually and found that he was the finance manager of the Bank of Shenzhen.

He has the power to loan out money, he was elated. *I have to make friends with him.*

Getting to the requested destination, the gentleman pulled out a hundred yuan bill from his wallet for his taxi fare. But Chen Yong said, "Keep it, it is my pleasure to meet you and serve you, my dear master."

The man hesitated for a few seconds, then asked, "What do you want from me?"

"Nothing, just want to serve you and be a friend of yours, Master," Chen Yong replied humbly.

He put the money back into his pocket and got out of the car, heading toward a building.

"Ha, Master, how long are you going to stay there?" Chen Yong felt disappointed for not getting his phone number but grasped the last straw quickly.

The man paused and turned his head around. "Fifteen minutes," he grunted, then hurried into the building.

I've got it, he rejoiced, parking his taxi next to the building entrance, started fantasizing his plan.

But twenty minutes had passed, there was no sign of the banker. He began feeling despair. *What a fool you are. You are just a little taxi driver, a powerful person like him would not bother to talk to you for more than a minute.*

Another ten minutes had elapsed. "What a liar," he mumbled. Reaching to the key and turning the ignition, the car roared to life. He shifted the gear, and shot a last glance to the building entrance.

Right at that moment, he saw the banker coming out of the building. His heart started pounding.

The man was a bit surprised when he saw the same taxi still parked right where he left it minutes ago.

Chen Yong got out of the taxi immediately, greeted him and opened the door. "I am so happy to see you again, Master. Please get in," he muttered obsequiously.

When the taxi started moving, the banker groaned, inquiringly with a business tone, "Just what do you need, a loan? What project do you have?" He knew from experience that a person who was interested in him and did favors for him wanted to get loans from his bank. Although he had the power to approve a loan, the bank strictly required a borrower to have a workable project and have some sort of collateral as well. Yet banks seldom loan money to private citizens, since the number of bad loans had increased four fold in recent years.

"I want to have my own taxi company, and I need money to buy more cars," Chen Yong replied anxiously and humbly, feeling marveled by the banker's straightforwardness.

The bank knew how profitable a taxi company was because his bank had loaned to a state-owned one before and it had never had any problem of collecting the payments. He had really wanted to get his hand into this business too. Here came the chance, but he concealed his elation and remained composed. "Well, we don't lend out money to individual citizens," he said succinctly, wanting to make it sound harder so that he could make a better deal.

Chen Yong felt like being scooped with cold water on the head. He stepped on the brake pedal unintentionally and his taxi screeched to nearly a complete halt. A car following behind shrieked, almost hit his, and kept honking. He pulled his taxi to the street side and parked. Then he tilted his body around in the driver's seat and bowed, "Please, Master, help me. I promise to you that I will pay the loan back on time. To tell you the truth, the taxi business is very profitable and I will have no problem of paying my dues. You can charge me higher interest rate for that, Master."

But the banker pretended to be unperturbed. Bargaining and negotiating was his expertise in the banking profession. "How much do you have in assets?" he raised his voice to a high-pitched tone and asked sternly.

"I have three taxis, Master. They are worth about one-and-half million yuan," he replied quickly, detecting a ray of hope illuminating from what he heard.

That was a small asset compared to most firms his bank had loaned to. *But it's ok, it will grow, with my help, yes, with my help,* he mesmerized. He really wanted to make the deal now, but he reminded himself to be patient in order to catch a bigger fish.

"I tell you what, I will take your case back to the bank and discuss it with my colleagues. Here is my business card, you can call me in two days. Now, get me back to the bank quick," he ordered, pulling a name card out of his briefcase and handing it to Chen Yong.

"Yes, Master, thank you very much for your consideration," Chen Yong chirped happily, starting to shift the gear and glancing at the traffic from the mirrors.

Having had the episode of meeting the banker, Chen Yong got off from work early that afternoon and went to the temple. After burning some incense and sticking them onto the rectangular brass container, he knelt down in front of the gigantic sculpture of Buddha and prayed. "Buddha God and Guanying Goddess, please give me the luck and help me to get the loan," he mumbled faithfully while bowing. Then he donated some cash to the temple, wishing that it would bring him luck.

He did the same the following two days.

On the third day, right after 9:00 AM, Chen Yong parked his taxi in front of a payphone booth. Nervously, he dialed the banker's office number. He heard the clicking noise. A pleasant female voice answered after the third ring.

"Hello, Bank of Shenzhen, may I help you?"

"May I speak to Manager Tang Daming?" He replied immediately.

"He's in the meeting. May I know who is calling?"

"I'll call back later. But can you tell me how long Mr. Tang's meeting will last?"

"By eleven-thirty AM."

"Thanks." He hung up, disappointedly.

He called again after eleven-thirty, but he was told that Tang Daming had left the office with some customers. He called several times in the afternoon, receiving the same answer each time: Tang Daming was not in the office. Finally, after leaving his pager's number to the secretary of that banker, Chen Yong gave up calling.

Darting desperately in the streets and roads around the city, Chen Yong was in no mood to talk with the passengers. After dropping a passenger on Aiguo Road, he made a left turn to Shennan Road, where he picked up a beautiful girl. When the girl stepped into the car and slammed the door shut, Chen Yong felt choked by the strong smell of the perfume and make-up.

"Paradise Nightclub," the girl pronounced, shyly.

"What?" he cried, as he could not believe what he had just heard. He had had so many pretty and young female passengers who worked in nightclubs, such as the Three-accompanying Girls—accompanying customers to sing and chat and drink. Many of them had actually been prostitutes before, but this young woman looked different. With her small and egg-shaped face, tall and straight nose, big and double-lid eyes, small but thick-lip mouth, creamy skin, long straight hair with a tall and curvaceous figure, she was classically gorgeous and a feast for the eyes. Chen Yong adored her, but wondered why would she want to be a whore. He wanted to talk to her, but decided otherwise. This kind of woman, he knew well enough, could be the mistress of the richest or a powerful government official.

"A toad wants to eat swan meat,"* he condemned himself in a barely audible voice.

"What did you say?" the girl asked curiously. "Who wants to eat swan meat?"

"A toad."

"A toad? You?" the girl chuckled.

"Yes, do I look like one?"

"Very much," she chuckled again.

Now he felt a bit relaxed. This girl was funny and easy to talk to, and did not appear to be stuck-up like most of the other working girls.

"Where are you from? And how long have you been in Shenzhen?" he inquired curiously, wanting to find out her background.

"Sichuan province. I just came here three days ago."

---

* An unrealistic desire.

"Really? And you are working at that Paradise Nightclub already?"

"It's my first day to start working there."

He felt a bit relieved and a bit excited. *She is not quite a whore yet, maybe I can do something to help her out.* An idea came into his mind.

"Why do you want to work there? Can't you do something else?"

"Well, I have no college education and no knowledge of computer and foreign languages. What can I do?" she grimmed.

"I need a secretary in the very near future." Would you want to work for me?"

"A taxi driver needs a secretary? What a joke, you are funny."

"Believe me, I'll have my own taxi company soon," he pronounced with an assertive tone.

"Okay, tell me when you open it, I will think about it. Now slow down and park in front of that building," she said, pointing to the building next to the Paradise Nightclub.

"Can you give me your phone number?" he demanded, feeling the rush of adrenaline racing through him.

"I have no telephone yet. Bye, Toad," she smiled, getting ready to get out.

"What time will you get off from work?" he asked, grasping at the last chance.

"I have no idea. Bye."

Chen Yong watched her walk toward the nightclub and felt a sense of urgency. He wished he could help her out now. But how?

It was around 9:00 PM, the time for the foreign investors, the Hong Kong nouveaux riches, the local powerful people, and CEOs to make important decisions while being entertained in nightclubs and bars. From now until midnight was the busiest period of the workday for the taxi drivers in town—but tonight Chen Yong did not want to carry these passengers. He visualized one of them taking away that lovely girl as his night's mistress, resenting the ugliness of money and sex trade in this newly erected city.

He bought a pack of beer and parked his taxi on an unscrupulous side street and began drinking with fury. It was his first severe violation of traffic rules in his driving career, but he did not care. Feeling dizzy from the beer, he flattened the adjustable driver's seat and stretched out to relax, closing his eyes.

Awakened by the incessant beep of his pager, Chen Young got up slowly and checked his pager with bleary eyes. It showed a mobile phone number on the screen, one he had never seen before. He locked the taxi and walked to a nearby payphone at a corner store to make his call.

A familiar male voice at the other end answered, "Is this Chen Yong?"

"Yes, who is this?" He groaned into the phone with a drunken and raucous voice.

"This is Tang Daming. Where are you now?"

He couldn't believe what he heard and blared to the phone, "Who?"

"Tang Daming, the man working for the Bank of Shenzhen. Remember, we met in your taxi? Can you come to the Paradise Nightclub now? I am on the third floor, room 318."

Having gotten confirmed, his drunkenness faded away. He replied loudly, "Yes, Master, I will be there in ten minutes."

He ran back to the car and charged up its engine immediately. Five minutes later he was at the Paradise Nightclub, as he had not gone far after dropping down the lovely Sichuan girl. After parking his car, he rushed into the Paradise Nightclub. Squeezing ahead, he bumped to several people before finally arriving at room 318. The number 318, which many Chinese people believed to be a lucky number because the pronunciation of three resembled the voice of living—while the two digits eighteen sounded like getting rich for sure, unlike the bad luck number four which implies death when said—had been picked by the banker intentionally, he believed. Peeping inside, he was stunned. The banker was holding the waist of that lovely Sichuan girl sitting on a sofa while singing a song with her together.

A mixed feeling of anger and jealousy was burning inside him. He really wanted to barge in and beat up that old scumbag. But instead, he took a deep breath to calm himself. *I need to get a loan from him, let me not to screw it up,* Chen Yong told himself. He knocked on the door lightly and entered when he was told to do so.

"I am so happy to see you again, Master," he said humbly and nodded to the girl.

"I feel the same, Chen Yong. Sit down, please, let me call the Mother here to get you a beautiful girl and some drinks."

"Drinks are fine, but no girl, please, Master," he replied quickly. The one girl he wanted most in the world was the one embraced by that old scumbag now.

"Don't be shy, Chen Yong, and I will not talk about our business without seeing you holding a girl tonight," he threatened, "because you make me look bad."

Chen Yong hesitated, but decided to give in. Nothing should be on the way to stop him from getting a loan now. "Yes, Master, but may I ask you an embarrassing question?"

"What embarrassing question?" Tang Daming said, puzzled.

"May I have your girl, and you get someone else?"

"What? What the hell are you talking about? How dare you! This is the most fresh and beautiful girl here," he roared furiously.

"I am sorry. But don't be mad, Master, it's only for tonight, after tonight, she will be yours," he muttered nervously.

The banker was still mad, but the anger on him seemed ebbing. He reluctantly kissed the girl's cheek and said, "Honey, take good care of my friend."

Chen Yong was overjoyed. While the banker was out talking to the Mother, he held the girl's hand and mumbled to her, "What a coincidence, I am so delighted to meet you again. What is your name?"

"Oh, hi, Toad." She teased.

"Please be serious, I want to get you out of this rotten place. You do not belong to here."

She looked at him dubiously. "Are you serious? We just met today."

"Yes, I mean what I said."

"You're not the first one to say that to me. Anyway, my name is Lin Dan. I am happy to see you again. But what do you meet him here for? Is it the taxi business you told me about?"

"Exactly, I want to get a loan from his bank. Can I call you Dan Dan?"

"Sounds sweet, and that is what my parents call me, in fact."

"Dan Dan, it looks like I am going to get the loan. Will you work for me?"

"I really want to, but I guess that your company will use computers and I do not know how to operate them at all," she sighed.

"It really doesn't matter, I can pay you to go to the computer training center to learn while working."

"You're very nice. But how much do you pay me?" she was half serious and half joking. "I'm expensive."

"Well, it will not be less than what you make here," he promised.

"Why are you so nice and generous to me?"

When Chen Young was about to tell her that he had fallen in love with her, the banker returned holding a girl with huge breasts bulging out of her flimsy dress. A minute later, a waitress entered carrying a tray of drinks, snacks, and a gigantic fruit plate.

With his right hand caressing the girl's breasts and the left hand holding a glass of wine, Tang Daming toasted with Chen Yong and the girls.

After two rounds of drinks, Tang Daming said to Chen Yong, "Our staff in the bank have discussed your case and decided to grant you a two-million-yuan loan." He chugged another shot, then gazed at Chen Yong's rejoicing reaction and raised his voice another octave, "But the condition is, our bank wants to be rewarded with a 20 percent share of your company."

Chen Yong had heard before how bank finance managers were rewarded by their customers, but he had not prepared himself for what amount this banker would ask. He also knew immediately that the reward being asked by this greedy banker was not for the bank but for himself—and had to be given. Chen Yong loathed the banker more, but he remained composed and attempted to make a bargain.

"Of course, Master, I am always willing to give your bank some kind of feedback, but 20 percent is a bit too much. How about 10 percent?"

Tang Daming squeezed his eyebrows together and his face darkened. He finally twisted the girl's breast. She screamed. He sat down his drink and blared, "No bargaining, Chen Yong, you want the loan or not?"

Lin Dan pressed on Chen Yong's shoulder to signal him and said to the man, "Don't be mad, Master, he was just joking to you." Then she tilted her head back to Chen Yong. "A-yong, tell Master that you were just joking."

"Yes, Master, I was just joking. I have no problem with giving your bank a 20 percent share of my company," Chen Yong muttered, with an apologetic tone.

The smile resumed on the banker's face. He grabbed a bottle of champagne and shook it a few times, then opened it gleefully. The bubbles gushed toward the ceiling. He filled up everyone's glasses with champagne, announcing, "Let's celebrate our cooperation."

4

When she was in high school, Lin Dan was her male classmates' dream lover. It was because of her extraordinary beauty. With too much attention and courtesies, she was barely able to concentrate on her studies. Although she had dated in high school, after her graduation, she became the mistress of a local high-ranking government official. Her reason for this was the urgent need of money for medical treatment of her father's illness. For three years, she lived in a luxurious house and was given handsome cash, food, expensive cosmetics and clothes in exchange for sex—until her "lover" was arrested and executed for committing "serious corruption."

She was stripped penniless after her bank account was frozen and confiscated by the municipal government. She had become the laughing stock in town, and no company was willing to hire her.

Hardly enduring the shame and wanting to survive, she called her friend working at the Paradise Nightclub in Shenzhen. Her friend was surprised by her news and eagerly wanted her to come and promised that she would be the hottest "Three-accompanying Girl" there and would make tons of money, and eventually become a mistress of a local tycoon. Lin Dan hated he idea of becoming a mistress again, let alone work as a "Three-accompanying Girl." But she reluctantly gave in, as there was no other choice that would bring her quick bucks to continue her father's treatment.

Lin Dan refused to be the banker's mistress, at once, when he did ask her. Instead, she accepted Chen Yong's offer as his personal secretary. She liked him after meeting and talking with him. It was the kind of feeling that reminded her of dates in high school. She started to feel that the innocence as a young girl had returned and the nightmare of being someone's sex toy had begun to fade. She needed love—true love—the everlasting and ultimate happiness in life. But she had to be careful, men were not trustable—especially the ones with plenty of money.

The best way to avoid being hurt and vulnerable was to be financially independent. That was the simple but cruel recognition she had learned from her painful experience as a mistress and decided to make her own living without selling her body and soul. Now an excellent opportunity had opened for her. It was a good new beginning.

Since the first day of her new job, she worked hard and did everything the best she could. Soon she memorized all the names that her company had routine business with, such as the bank clerks handling their loan payments, insurance agents, mechanics, drivers, and everything being taught by her new boss. She learned to do the bookkeeping from reviewing old books with her boss and took a computer class after work. She had never been busier in her life. She felt good and solid and secure.

Although she could feel the affection and love of her boss from time to time, and they had dated often, she avoided being deeply taken by him. And she managed not to give any opportunity to her other admirers too. What she wanted to do the most was to concentrate on her work and career development, and to help the company to grow.

In less than a year, the taxi company expanded and hired more employees. Lin Dan became the general manager—a fledgling career woman.

*   *   *

It'd been a doubled pleasure for Chen Yong. He'd got his dream girl working for him and the badly needed loan. He couldn't be luckier. With the help of the loan, he bought ten new taxis first, then fifteen more—all this one half-year later after getting a bigger loan from the greedy banker. Chen Yong was no longer a driver anymore but stayed in the office doing bookkeeping, monitoring the pick-up services and other management work with Lin Dan. He was impressed how fast Lin Dan had been in learning the business, and how hard and diligently she had worked in helping make the company prosper. *She has got the look and the brain,* he praised her quietly.

He often recalled and savored an unforgettable incidence, in which they were taking a walk along the bank of the Shenzhen River after dinner one early evening, when they heard a baby crying inside a rubbish dump. Lin Dan rushed toward the pile of garbage and found a baby girl wrapped in tattered clothes and stuffed inside a plastic bag. She removed the baby and held it against her chest, comforting the child. Then she immediately stopped a taxi, and suggested taking the baby to an orphanage. From that day on, she went to see that baby often and donated food and money to the orphanage.

Later she named the baby Ling Ling. This loving and generous gift showed the genuine virtue of graciousness and kindness Lin Dan had possessed. Because of this, he loved her more, but he was never sure she really had the same feeling toward him as she always kept a certain respectful distance from him. She refused his kisses and was unwilling to hold his hands. They worked together and talked to each other every day and he had found out much of her past, but he did not quite understand this young woman. She often acted cordially toward him and others in the company, but when it came to intimate contact, she would turn cool abruptly. She always appeared to be a little bit overreactive, but maybe she was trying to protect herself from getting hurt again.

I am patient, I can wait. Time will prove my honesty and genuine love toward her, he told himself, *but I must be careful not to scare her or cause any misunderstanding.* He decided to put that sentimental thing aside and bury himself into work.

Chen Yong was able to explore other business opportunities while Lin Dan took care of most of the company's management work. He had, also, noticed the short supply of the diesel fuel and gasoline, and how easy it was to make huge profits within that business. He felt that was the time to wet his feet in such business. He talked to his banker who agreed to provide Chen Yong a five-million-yuan loan—of course, based on an estimation of the assets of his taxi company as collateral. He then spent a week traveling to northern China bribing his way through the diesel and gasoline suppliers to secure some commodity. With all the certificates of suppliers, a guarantee of the funds, along with expensive gifts and cash, the department of commerce and the department of transportation granted a business license to Chen Yong within three weeks. He was overjoyed. Those licenses, or tickets to riches—were extremely difficult to obtain.

He celebrated the company's success with Lin Dan at Guomao Revolving Restaurant, the most expensive restaurant in the city, located on the top of the fifty-story Guomao Commercial Tower downtown.

Most of the customers of Guomao Revolving Restaurant were domestic and international businessmen or politicians. One single meal might cost as much as the sum of an average local worker's half-year salary. When they arrived at the lobby of the Guomao Commercial Tower, Chen Yong and Lin Dan were greeted by two doormen clad in expensive dark western suits and ties. They were escorted into the elevator, where a young and beautiful girl in red, dressed as a servant, pressed buttons delivering guests going up and down. As she entered, they noticed the "50" button was immediately pressed.

As they stepped out of the elevator, four red-dress girls standing in front of the restaurant bowed, chanting, "Welcome to be here." A gorgeous-looking waitress stepped forward with a smile and asked politely, "Are you Mr. Chen Yong? And this is your—?"

"Yes, my partner, Ms. Lin."

"Welcome, Mr. Chen and Ms. Lin." She bowed. "Please, follow me."

They were taken to their reserved booths located behind a glass panel from which the whole city of Shenzhen could be viewed, slowly as the restaurant revolved.

Once seated, they were handed fragrant wet warm towels, and then snacks and an option of tea or coffee or juice. Two exquisitely designed Menus were placed before them. They ordered their favorite shark fin soup, Beijing duck, scallops, and abalone. Then champagne to drink. When the first dish came, Chen Yong raised his glass and chanted, "For our company's expansion, and for our love. Cheers."

Lin Dan smiled and clinked her drink with his and replied, "Yes, for our company's expansion and our friendship. Cheers."

After one sip, he laughed and responded, "Yes, for our friendship. Cheers."

They chatted while browsing the panorama of the city as the restaurant rotated. When facing west, they saw the newly-paved Shennan Boulevard meandered along the coast, clusters of buildings with various kinds of colors perching one after another along the forty-meter-wide road. There appeared many construction sites everywhere, thus, he couldn't recognize where all of the villages were located as before. As they were slowly turned to the north, more dramatic views came into sight: hills, reservoirs, lawns, groups of new towers, lines of newly paved roads, flyovers and footbridges, cranes and automobiles everywhere. Chen Yong marveled at the sight. Just a few years ago, he remembered, there were only desolate mountains and hills and ravines—and nothing else. Similar to the east side, all places were covered with a forest of concrete on and toward the west.

When the restaurant moved slowly facing south, the new territory of Hong Kong appeared. They could see the bay, hills, jammed highways and smog-shrouded skyscrapers in the British colony. It was a mysterious place for them. All the guests around them began pointing fingers and chatting excitedly.

"I will go there to take a look when it returns back to us."

"I wonder how many rich people will remain there until the year of 1997."

"Ha, I doubt it," one sitting behind Chen Yong raised his voice to a high-pitch tone, "if the British are willing to return it to us."

"I hope it will be as prosperous as what it is now after the handover."

Listening to their comments, Chen Yong and Lin Dan expressed their views and agreed that they should concentrate on what they were doing and leave the politics to the government to care about.

As the restaurant kept spinning, their talks went on. Suddenly, they noticed the waitresses were obsequiously caring for the tables where the foreigners were sitting more frequently and paying less attention to the Chinese customers.

"Why is that? It's because they admire foreigners and despise Chinese people?" Lin Dan raged.

"Well, it could be, but I know the main reason why they do so is that the foreigners usually give them tips and Chinese customers do not," Chen Yong replied.

"Oh, I see. We should learn to do the same as the foreigners then."

"Yes, indeed. What our country has been doing is learning to imitate the western world's way of handling things, especially in the field of market economy, I believe. I hope, one day, the foreigners will work and learn from us."

"Let's hope so," she echoed lyrically.

After finishing their turtle jelly desert, they left with a feeling of high hope and happiness. The waitresses were stunned when they saw the two twenty-yuan bills lying on the table left as the tip by these two Chinese customers.

After hiring more employees for the new business, Chen Yong and Lin Dan decided to move to a bigger office. They checked around the city and located several possible places. Like many other businesspeople, they hired a geomancy master to examine each one of them, in the hope of looking for the one that was the most suitable and propitious to conduct business. Finally, one in the downtown of Luohu district was picked. After the auspicious day and time were chosen, the grand opening ceremony began.

Many colorful red-ribbon floral baskets and bouquets covered the entrance of the office, each with the names of individuals or companies displaying their congratulations. Red banners were hung horizontally and vertically overhead and on both sides, with incense sticks lighted and placed before a bronze Buddha statue. A tray holding a roasted baby pig, boiled chicken, several steamed buns, mandarins, and grapefruit were placed in front as an offering to the Buddha. In family tradition, starting with Chen Yong's father, his mother, himself, his brother and sister, and then Lin Dan as the last, they all bowed to the spiritual icon and fortune god with their hands clasped and positioned in front of their chests. When the ritual was completed, the lion dance began with the beating of drums and gongs. It was a tradition to let off firecrackers during the lion dance, but the government banned the use of firecrackers. Explosions of cheering shouts and laughters echoed among the spectators as the lions rolled, leaped, jumped, crouched, and kicked in accordance with the rhythm of the drums and gongs.

As the celebration came to a close, many relatives, friends, and customers streamed in and greeted them with little red envelopes of lucky money, and they bowed to each one of them as a sincere form of thanks. Later, in the evening, they had banquets in a nearby seafood restaurant.

*　　*　　*

As the economy kept expanding, the demand for gasoline and

diesel fuel had been mounting up rapidly—especially in the coastal cities. Dealers and retailers often increased the prices dramatically as well. However, the demand had shown no sign of ebbing.

To respond to the demand and make greater profit, some greedy dealers added water to the fuel before selling it. This caused frequent "breakdown" on the road and engine damage for many vehicles. At first, drivers did not realize what had caused all this mess, and blamed the vehicle manufacturers. An owner of a seven-hundred-thousand-yuan Mercedes Benz slashed his car with a sledgehammer and paraded it in the streets with a cow hauling it. He advocated the public to boycott the auto dealers and demanded for compensation. Many others echoed his sentiment and took actions immediately. This farce went on for many months until the true facts were unveiled. The outrageous drivers and owners burned the dealers' offices and gas stations. Then local government stepped in arresting dealers and revoking their commercial licenses—the riot was ended and resolved.

Chen Yong was one of the few lucky dealers who could prove to the government that they did not commit such heartless commercial crime. His company remained untouched and business flourished. They hung banners in front of their office building that said, ONE HUNDRED PERCENT FUEL, NO WATER OR OTHER SUBSTANCES ADDED.

Soon he was not only in supplying, but also in retailing business by building and acquiring more new gas stations.

Chen Yong's fortune was snowballing as his business kept expanding. Now he was able to get small loans from other banks without giving out shares of his company or commissions to the corrupt bankers. But the greedy banker Tang Daming in the Bank of Shenzhen was still the only one that could loan them large funds. Although he felt being extorted, Chen Yong realized he needed him as much as the banker needed him. *Someday,* he thought, *I will sever the relationship with him and get rid of him.*

5

As a result of the modernization drive in China, the prevailing of machinery and modern farming techniques in the rural areas had left millions of farmers unemployed or semi-unemployed.

Many young farmers with little education and no skills sneaked into Shenzhen in search for employment and were unable to find any. The only way for them to survive was to commit crimes. These criminals began committing crimes individually or in small groups. Later, they grouped and organized into gangs in order to commit more and bigger crimes and to avoid being caught by the police.

Wang Qiang, twenty-eight, an unemployed farmer from the northeastern part of the nation, was dubbed the "Northeastern Tiger" due to his ferocious temper, rudeness and cold-bloodedness. He was the head of an organized gang, plotting and carrying out crimes such as prostitution, selling drugs, kidnapping, smuggling, robbery, burglary, pickpocketing, and even murdering. He also established all the rules for his gang members.

Recently, Wang Qiang had been boggled by the contemplation of taking over some beauty salons, which were actually brothels scattered inside a cluster of eight-story apartment buildings in the Futin district, and had been owned and controlled by a rivaling gang.

One afternoon, after having had sex with his beautiful "Three-accompanying" mistress, whom he had met in a nightclub, he was puffing cigarettes with her on the couch in the two-bedroom apartment near the roof. His pager flashed and buzzed loudly. He pressed a button and stared at the number displayed on the screen, and quickly dialed the number.

After two rings and a clicking noise, a familiar voice came on line, "Is this big brother Wang?"

"Yes, what's the matter, A-bill?"

"You know what, big brother Wang? A member of—"

"You goddamned idiot, say it quick, clear and loud," he barked into the phone.

"Yes, big brother Wang, I caught a member of the Human gang who had come to one of our salons. He did not have enough money to pay for the charge after having fun with a girl. Should we do as usual, that we cut off his balls?"

Hearing the news, he was elated. Here came the chance to straighten things up. He blared to the phone, "No, do nothing, just hold him. I will be right there in a minute."

Wang Qiang hurried out of the apartment and rushed down the stairs. When he got to the apartment next to a beauty salon, he recognized the man immediately.

"Devil Sam, just what the hell are you doing here? You know our rules, don't you?"

"Yes, I do. But they don't apply to me," he replied defiantly. "If you dare to hurt me, my big brothers will revenge it for me."

Wang Qiang gritted his teeth and snickered, "Really? But they will disappear soon when I finish dealing with them, no one can help you but yourself."

Devil Sam stared at him doubtfully and replied, "You are trying to scare me, my big brothers will never be defeated."

"Yes, without your help, Devil Sam," he admitted, nodding.

"My help? No way," he shot back, succinctly.

"Don't be too stubborn and stupid, your life is in your hands now, Devil Sam, no one can help you after our rule is observed," he warned.

Devil Sam looked around the room and saw the mad-looking men standing behind him with sharp butcher's knives in their hands—a feeling of terror chilled his backbone. He knew what they were going to do with him by the meaning of observing their rule. His eyes started to look frightened. "Just what do you want from me?" he muttered nervously.

"Very simple, just tell the exact address of where your big brothers stay," Wang Qiang said.

"What?" he croaked, the scenes of executing the traitors by his big brothers reappeared in his mind. He felt the chill going through his spine again. "No, I can't do this," he cried.

The men in the room shrieked, stepping closer to him and wielding their knives, while Wang Qiang gazed at him furiously.

"Devil Sam, you have a last chance to save your life. We will protect you, if you do what I tell you." He understood exactly what the man was thinking at the moment.

Devil Sam did not believe that he would be protected after giving what they wanted, because traitors were not tolerated in the criminal society. Either way, he would be a dead man. He sighed, closing his eyes. He regretted coming to Shenzhen and what he had done. He could have been happier living a simple life in his village. It all started with a wish of securing a better living, and then the greed. He couldn't remember how many innocent people had become his victims. He deserved to die many times over, and now the time had come. But he had missed his parents and really wanted to see them once more and say sorry to them for not being the successful and filial son they had expected him to be. Lost in a reverie for half a minute, he was interrupted by the roaring of his captor.

"Take off his pants and cut off his balls first," Wang Qiang ordered.

Devil Sam was knocked down on the floor immediately. Three men toppled on him, grappling his limbs and loosing his belt. The other one was holding a sharp knife, ready to proceed with the castration.

"Wait! Wait! Stop! I will tell you," he cried, wanting to earn some time before being executed so that he could seek a chance to escape.

"Yes, be smart, Devil Sam," Wang Qiang grunted, snickering.

After Devil Sam told them the address of his gang's headquarters, he was bound and locked up in a room. Then Wang Qiang informed other members of his gang around the area immediately. They gathered rapidly, each one carried a sharp knife and a home-made gasoline-bomb. Once arriving to the headquarters of the Hunan gang, they besieged it and ordered their rivaling gang members inside to surrender.

"I give you guys five minutes to come out with your hands up above your head, otherwise, we will bomb you all to death," Wang Qiang barked through the door.

Three minutes had passed, but there was no response. Wang Qiang ordered his followers to prepare for the attack. Then he howled again, "You guys are running out of time. Just one more minute, and we will take action."

When two of Wang's followers were approaching the windows and trying to break them, the door flung open and a mob of men rushed out with knives, killing all of them instantly. The gasoline-bombs were useless in such close contact. Two groups of gangsters were hacking and stabbing and chasing each other in the corridor and the stairway, the clinking of the knives, the yelling, screaming and crying were tumultuous—total pandemonium. Outnumbered, the Hunan gang members were in a defensive position.

The residents of the building were horrified, locking their doors and reporting to the police. When the police finally came, most of the Hunan gang members were either killed or seriously wounded, and Wang Qiang and his followers had managed to escape.

Returning to their own places, Wang Qiang counted his gang members and realized that it was only a small loss with few wounds. They celebrated their victory with champagne, catered food, and girls in his apartment.

Toasting around, Wang Qiang said, "My brothers, you all have done an excellent job. From now on, no one will dare to threaten us and take away our businesses. We will all be prosperous and happy. Cheers, everyone."

They indulged in a feast of wine and beer, eating, smoking, singing, dancing, and having sex. When it reached to a peak, some-one suddenly asked, "Ha, how are we going to take care of Devil Sam?"

"Just kill that traitor, as usual," someone suggested.

"Yes, kill that traitor," most of them echoed.

"No need," Wang Qiang said. "When the wind of what he did leaks out, he will be taken care of by his own people. What we need to do is just to chop off his hands and cut off his tongue. By the way, the police are looking for us now. For our safety reason, I have decided that we should stop doing all of our businesses for ten days, and travel to other provinces for sightseeing in small groups instead. What do you think?"

"Good idea, big brother Wang," they all agreed happily.

6

As the demand of educated employees continued mounting, and the nation was getting wealthier as the economy kept growing rapidly, the college admission rate had also been increased every year correspondingly.

Unlike their older brother before, both Chen Jing and Chen Song were admitted into the Shenzhen University with honors. Chen Jing was in her third year, majoring in business administration. Her younger brother, Chen Song, in his first year, was studying electronic engineering. They both were bright, active, outgoing, and easy to get along with, their classmates and teachers adored them. They both were expected to help their older brother to do business after their graduation.

Since their older brother was always busy, and that he seldom came home, they chose not to stay in the dormitory when most others did, because they wanted to be close with their parents every day. Although they wanted to go to school and come home together, they often returned home separately due to their different schedules, workloads, and activities in school. Chen Jing usually came back early with arranged pick-up rides by the chauffeur; while her younger brother, who enjoyed playing sports after school, was often late and returned home alone by bus.

Unlike many of their classmates, they did not date at all. They wanted to concentrate on their studies instead. After all, like all campuses in the nation, the school had advised the students not to date while studying. Yet they just wanted to be the best they could at school.

*   *   *

As the Reform and Opening policy being implemented in a larger scale drove deeper to the core issues of the society, learning from the western world continued gathering pace. The nation decided to abandon the Stalin-style planned-economy and adopted the market-oriented one. At the beginning, it was chaotic, as the price-control on goods was loosened. The inflation rate skyrocketed around the nation. At the same time, corruptions among government cadres were rampant. Complains and protests and uprisings were sporadically happening in major cities around the nation.

The chaos reached to the peak when the former Communist Party secretary Wu Yaobang died in 1989; and when college students in the capital took onto the streets to commemorate him and demand a clean government and political reforms.

The students' emotional protests were echoed by a large number of citizens in all walks of life, including the teachers and professors. When their protests were characterized as riot by a Communist Party's major newspaper, it rapidly developed into an uncontrollable demonstration that malfunctioned the city police system and threatened the function of the central government. The huge Tiananmen Square was half occupied by demonstrators, day and night, with a replica of the Statue of Liberty erected right in front of the castle facing the hanging portrait of Mao Zedong. A few days later, two divisions of the People's Liberation Army were ordered to enter the city from the west and the east to take control of the capital. The demonstrators blocked the unarmed soldiers from entering and got stuck. To break the impasse, the premier declared martial law and ordered the demonstrators to disperse. The premier's order was broadcasted repeatedly throughout the night until morning, but the stubborn demonstrators were unmoved until the armed soldiers drove them off the square and the streets by the use of lethal weapons.

This no-one-wanted and no-winner incidence badly battered the nation's image, setting backward and stagnating the economic Reform and Opening for nearly two years. It wasn't until Deng Xiaoping, the eighty-seven-year-old paramount leader and chief architect of the nation's Reform and Opening, visited Shenzhen and presented his opinionated speeches that the nation's modernization movement began picking up pace again and the economy started to turn positive.

In eleven years, Shenzhen's population reached three million from less than thirty thousand—a one-hundred-times increase. It still kept growing rapidly as the foreign investment continued pouring in. In fact, nearly the entire low-value and labor-intensive production industry in Hong Kong had relocated into Shenzhen, thus creating huge employment opportunities for both the skilled and non-skilled workers in the city. Citizens—especially the younger ones around the nation—continued swarming in, both legally and illegally. Consequently, its gross domestic product grew from fifteen to thirty-five percent each year, despite the last two years' stagnation after the Tiananmen Square incident. Deng Xiaoping's pragmatic policy had won the preliminary but significant success.

After Deng Xiaoping's visit, Shenzhen, the freest and most privileged city in the nation, was encouraged to attract both international and domestic hi-tech companies to relocate there so that it could be upgraded to the high-tech-based comprehensive production center. All along, the city government was working in full-blown scale toward this goal.

*   *   *

Chen Yong's gasoline business proved to be a moneymaking machine. His taxi company continued to grow steadily despite the new law requiring all taxis to have a fare meter installed and other competing taxi companies had opened. He supplied twenty gas stations and had fifteen of his own, and had become one of four major gasoline and diesel fuel suppliers and retailers in the city. Having owned more than a hundred taxis now, Chen Yong's firm was one of the five largest taxi companies in town. Although he had become one of the wealthiest persons in Shenzhen, he was not complacent.

Deng Xiaoping's visit and the local government's intention inspired him. He dreamed that one day he would have his own hi-tech company. Ever since then, he started to pay attention to the high technology field from reading related magazines, newspapers and governmental reports. Chen Yong had no idea what to do or where to start, because, not only did he lack the experience in this field, he had not been educated in science and technology.

One day, while chatting on this subject with his brother Chen Song, who was in his third year in college, he found how silly he had been in that the solution for his problem was right in front of him.

36

"What our country needs now are telecommunication equipment and their vast electronic solutions. But these are huge projects requiring lots of sophisticated talent and an astronomical number of investments, my big brother," Chen Song told him.

"Really?" Chen Yong was not faltered a bit by what he heard, instead he was confident that he could make it someday. That is, as long as he could find a way to do it.

"Do you have any knowledge in this field, then?"

"Yes, telecommunications is my specialty in what I have been studying in college, my big brother."

Chen Yong was excited. It was just what he needed, right at the beginning—to have a knowledgeable person whom he could trust and have confidence in.

"Where should I start, my dear brother?"

"I think you should start with working out the electronic solutions for the banks' and securities' automated systems first. They need them so badly now, especially the newly introduced securities in our country."

"Good, you will be my technical manager to begin with, Song."

"I love to, but let me finish school first, I have four more months to go."

"Of course, you can help me on a part-time basis right now. And I would like you to talk to your professors if they could work for us. Tell them that they will get at least two times higher than what they have been paid now, and they will get bonuses as well."

"That sounds attractive. I think we can convince them without any problem, but where are you getting the money? As I told you moment ago, this business takes up lots of capital."

"Don't worry, my brother. I will handle the financial problems, while you will just take care of the technical problems for me."

"Okay, my big brother, but I have to warn you that this business is very risky. You are facing tremendous competition from domestic companies, as well as from international companies. Also, our country has stipulated rules to prevent monopolizing. I believe, only the best ones can survive in the hi-tech field ultimately."

"We will make it, like what we have been doing. Don't worry about it. Besides, the government will help us out because the hi-tech field is our nation's strategic industry for the future."

"Yes, you are right, my big brother. Let's do it."

The following two months, Chen Yong started to sell the taxi company and talk with bankers about getting new loans by using his savings and remaining company as collateral. He also met with professors, scientists, engineers, and technicians, consultants and government officials.

This time, he decided to let the corrupt banker Tang Daming stay away from this business. He did not even talk to him about it, but he would inform him later that the taxi company had been sold and sent him his shares in cash. But the greedy banker got wind of what he had been doing and became furious, and called Chen Yong up immediately.

"Chen Yong, you are fledgling. Ah, you do not need me anymore?"

"No, this is just a small potato, you will have no interest in it, Mr. Tang." He had stopped calling him "Master" after the first deal eight years ago. "Besides, this is a very risky business, like gambling, your *bank* will not want to be in," he pronounced the word "bank" loudly to imply that he just wanted to deal with the bank, not him.

The banker knew the risk of the hi-tech business, but he also had found out that the government would help and support this industry. Once a company in this field succeeded, it would be a mega-moneymaking machine.

"Tell you what, our bank is very interested in this business and wants to have some shares of it."

Chen Yong had loathed this greedy banker for a long time, but he had needed him at the same time. Now it was the time to get rid of him, he must not give in.

"I think it is the time for you to stop taking shares of your bank's customers, Mr. Tang, before you get exposed. What you have got should be enough for you to spend for the rest of your life. You know, I am concerned about your safety."

"I hope you are just kidding. It will never get enough when it comes to making money. You know that," he sighed greedily.

Chen Yong knew then, it was hard to persuade him. He raised his voice another octave, wanting to end the conversation.

"Mr. Tang, I want to be on my own this time. I don't want to have any deal with you on this. Am I making myself clear?"

Hearing that, the banker wanted to explode.

"How dare you talk to me like this. Don't forget who has helped you to start and expand your business. Without my help, you would still be a goddamned taxi driver."

"Ha, I have given you what you wanted already. Our deal is half completed already, and when I sell the gasoline company, I will give you your twenty percent of shares."

"Chen Yong, you want to get rid of me? Not that easy," he roared to the phone and slammed it down.

*　*　*

Chen Song got the best three professors in the electronic engineering department to agree to work for his brother's company in the very near future. After classes, they worked together to make up a list of equipment their future company would need to purchase and what they would work on after the grand opening. Yet their preparatory work was approaching the end.

One late afternoon, as darkness hovered, after finishing classes and all the discussion with the various professors, he began his journey home by himself. Leaving campus on his way to the bus stop , he walked briskly along a path leading to Shennan Boulevard. When he passed a shrub in the middle of the path, three masked men came out from nowhere and toppled on him. Two of the men bound his hands behind him, quickly and deftly, while the other gagged his mouth and bagged his head to the neck. Together, they carried him, scurrying toward a minivan parked beside the path. After forcefully throwing him into the minivan, they hurried away.

Their minivan darted west onto Shennan Boulevard and smoothly passed through the checkpoint. It entered the freeway, continuing its way north. Once they arrived in the mountainous suburb of Guangzhou, the minivan exited. Driving along a bumpy and curvy road, it approached a thickly-bushed hill, then stopped on the hillside and shut off the headlights. It was completely dark now, with no lights nor any manmade noises around. Only the chirping of insects and the sizzling of the bush in the autumn breeze. It was as if they were the only humans on earth.

They pulled the bag off Chen Song's head and got him out of the van. Escorting him along, they climbed up a trail. Then they heard the van roar back to life and then the noise of the motor diminish away into the distance. Fumbling ahead on the bushed trail, with only a dim flashlight, they finally arrived at a hut half an hour later. They pushed Chen Song, motioning him to sit on the floor of the hut. Then one of them flipped open a mobile phone and spoke.

"Big brother Wang, we have gotten to the hut safely."

A few moments later, he answered into the phone, "Yes, we will take turn to watch him. Don't worry about it, big brother Wang."

*   *   *

Chen Yong continued to discover that Lin Dan was like a gem that kept on glittering while helping his business to grow. He noticed that her charm and wit were great assets and advantages on the negotiating tables and personnel management. With her help, he could win business contracts, get permits from the government officials, straighten things up and manage the company much easier.

In the move of shifting his business to the hi-tech field, he relied on her even more. Lin Dan was a gifted manager and organizer. She launched the talent hunting campaign nationwide to look for the top researchers, engineers, and technicians and arranged their meetings and interviews. She established the network of contacts with government departments, potential customers, equipment suppliers and installers. And she even helped to select the site for the new company.

He had been crazy about her and had proposed to her twice, but she still had no intention of getting married. She even refused the idea of cohabiting with him, as he asked lately, but she insisted on living in an apartment alone. Their apartments were not far away from one another and they often stayed together, yet she still refused to have sex with him. She had told him that she loved him but she was not ready yet to have the intimate relationship with him.

He was pleased to see that men who were either handsome or highly educated, or rich and powerful, and showed any interest in her, had been turned down. She had been dubbed "Icy Princess" by her admirers. Still, Chen Yong had worried that many of them would not give up and stop trying.

Although they could see and talk to each other every day, the more he loved her, the loneliner he felt. He had no idea when this ordeal would end.

40

                    *   *   *

At 7:00 PM, it was their usual dinnertime, Chen Jing and her
parents had prepared the food and waited for Chen Song to come
home for dinner. It was odd that her brother had seldom come
home so late; if he did, he would always call to inform them. But
tonight, there was no sign of Chen Song and no one had heard
from him. She called his professors and classmates, but none of
them knew where he was. *Where was he?* An ominous feeling struck
her. She informed her older brother about it immediately. Chen
Yong hurried back home and they went searching the whole campus
and the route their brother usually took to return home. But there
was no sign of him. Finally, they reported it to the police.

*What has happened to my brother? Why has he disappeared when I
need him the most? Did he have an accident? Has he been kidnapped?
Maybe he just went out somewhere with his friends,* Chen Yong wondered.

                    *   *   *

Driving through the jammed commercial district, Lin Dan entered a quiet and curvy street leading to her apartment building at
around nine o'clock in the evening. She usually went home with
Chen Yong after dinner. But tonight, her boss hurried home early
since his brother had disappeared last night.

She drove slowly, passing a curve, where thick and six-foot-tall
plants stood on both sides of the street. Suddenly, a large black
object rolled onto the street from the hedge, blocking her way. She
footed the brake and her car screeched to a complete halt before
hitting it. Trouble! She sensed trouble immediately and shifted the
gear to the back-up position. But it was too late. Three masked and
gloved men leaped out and smashed her car window and unlocked
the car door. A strange-smelling towel covered her nose and mouth,
she fainted at once. A van shrieked over and stopped next to her
car, pulled out and thrown her into the van. It took only a couple
of seconds, and then the minivan disappeared into the darkness.

When Lin Dan resumed consciousness, she could barely see
that Chen Song, with his hands bound behind his back, was sitting
next to her on the earth-smelly floor. Four mad-looking men were
crouched on two stools watching them.

"A-Song," she whispered, "your big brother and parents are looking for you."

"I know, A-Dan, soon they will be looking for you too. Who are these men? How did they catch you?"

"I have no idea who they are, they caught me—"

"Shut up, stop talking!" one kidnapper blared. "If you do it again, I am going to cut your tongues off."

The rest of the kidnappers echoed. One of them babbled, "I can't wait to have fun with that chick. She is classic. I have never seen such beautiful chick in my life."

"Oh, yes, I was on, while watching and touching her on the highway," another one confessed.

"Ha, you guys, remember what our big brother Wang told us? He will kill whoever gets on that chick, be careful," one fellow warned. "He doesn't allow us to touch her because he wants to enjoy her by himself," one pointed out.

"A-Sing, don't say anything bad about our big brother Wang. It's not because of that, it is what the big boss wants," said the one who had just warned them.

Hearing their conversation, Chen Song and Lin Dan pushed lightly to signal each other. They wondered who that big boss was and what he wanted from kidnapping them.

*　　*　　*

At ten AM, Chen Yong became perplexed, while sitting in the chair at Lin Dan's desk and wondering why his lover had not yet come to work. *This'd never happened before,* he thought, while an ominous feeling racked his mind. He called her home phone, but no answer; then her mobile phone; it said the phone had been turned off. He inquired several of his subordinates about it, but none of them had any idea what had happened to her and where Lin Dan might be. Wanting to check out her apartment, he started to hurry out. Right at that moment, the phone rang. He picked it up and heard a man at the other end of the line.

"Is this the Chen Yong Gasoline and Diesel Company Limited?"

"Yes, how can I help you, sir?"

"This call is from the police department. We want to know that if a girl named Lin Dan works for your company."

Chen Yong's heart was pounding. He responded nervously, "Yes, what has happened to her?"

"Her car was deserted on the street with the windows smashed last night. We towed it to our garage and found her ID card and some of your company's documents in a briefcase. That is how we could identify her as owner of the abandoned car. We want to know what had happened to her and want her to report to us once she returns."

Chen Yong wanted to scream, but forced himself to be calm. He sensed that his lover had been kidnapped. But why? He cried to the phone, "I believe she has been kidnapped, sir, along with my younger brother. I think these two cases are interrelated."

"We've guessed the same, tell you the truth. Could you come over to inform us more about her?"

"I'll be there in half an hour, sir."

Putting down the phone, Chen Yong got into deep thought. These two cases happened in two days, obviously, they had been conducted by the same group of kidnappers. But who were they? What were they after? As shown from the evidence, they were not professional kidnappers, or maybe they were novices in this crime. Otherwise, they would not have left Lin Dan's car deserted on the street. Another important cue was that right in the critical time of founding his high-tech company, two key members had been kidnapped. Now his plan had to be postponed.

Would it be the banker? He remembered his warning from the last time they talked on the phone that he would not be gotten rid of easily. *Yes, it must be him, that greedy son of a bitch had masterminded the whole scheme, wanting to get his hand on my high-tech venture.* Chen Yong picked up the phone, wanting to report it to the police to have him arrested, but he hesitated. *What if the banker got arrested and our previous business deals exposed? Would the government confiscate my company and prosecute me for committing bribery?* He took a deep breath, decided to make a deal with him. Dialing the number, he listened and counted the rings at the other end anxiously. After the receptionist transferred his call, a male voice came on line.

He muttered, "Is this Mr. Tang Daming?"

"Yes, Chen Yong, my brother, what can I do for you?"

Remaining silent for a couple of seconds, he said, "I want to make a deal."

"You are a wise young man, my good brother," he rejoiced but marveled on how quick his counterpart had given up. "So it would be the same old deal, twenty percent shares, ah?"

"Yes, if you release them immediately?"

"What? What are you talking about?" he queried. It sounded that his counterpart was accusing him of kidnapping or something. It was ridiculous. He would never do such a foolish thing for any purpose. All he had done was giving some financial information of his counterpart to some banks to persuade them from loaning funds to him. He barked to the phone, "Are you out of your goddamned mind? I have nothing to do with your damned people. Don't forget that I am only interested in handling the greens and reds and whites."

Chen Yong was puzzled. He then realized the banker was not the culprit in the kidnapping crime.

"I'm sorry, please forget about what I just said to you."

He hung up the telephone.

7

The police combed the nearby apartment buildings that evening, checking door after door, but found no sign and no cue of the kidnappers. What they had gained on the side though, as usual, were several hundred illegal residents who had not registered and paid the local government to get the temporary residential permits. But they had left the salons, the brothels, untouched. Li Ben, the deputy director of the police department who headed this operation, called off the search. Returning to the station, all the police vehicles jammed the already crowded street.

Li Ben reported the result of the operation to the director once back at the headquarters. Married and in his early forties, he was pudgy, with a fat nose perched on a round face just beneath a pair of bulging and ferocious-looking eyes. His keen and quick mind and snappy manner had won him the nickname ''Mad Dog'' among the criminals. Taking advantage of being the deputy director, he had promoted many of his subordinates who were obedient and loyal to him over the past few years. So he was actually the center of power in the entire police department—even the director had to listen to him, often. Under his leadership, corruption grew like a monster, eating up every healthy flesh in the department. The bad reputation of the city's law enforcers was notorious. Many citizens knew that to become a Shenzhen police officer, one must pay a quarter of a million yuan to the corrupt officials—an astronomical sum for an average employee making around an average of four hundred yuan a month. Becoming a police officer meant getting a ticket to wealth, as only the obscenely rich families could afford buying such position for their children. By the same token, if a police officer in another city wished to work in Shenzhen for the same position, he had to pay a fee from a hundred thousand to two hundred thousand in cash to the corrupt cadres leading the law enforcers in the fine city.

Since the police department was the most powerful department in the municipal government, Li Ben was, indeed, one of a few big heads in the city.

Once receiving reports, he wanted to be in charge of these two kidnapping cases. His department was about to launch a new round of "strike-hard" crackdowns against the rampant criminal activities in town, and in carrying out the central government's order. It would be impressive and bolster public opinion of him.

According to the current statistics and estimations, seven out of ten women in the city had their handbags snatched away at least once by looters; many men had their wallets stolen, and thousands of homes and offices had been burglarized in the past few years.

So the police department had been forced to launch the "strike-hard" crackdown several times in a year. Each time, thousands of murderers, robbers, looters, burglars, rapists, and an array of other criminals were arrested and sentenced to prison several times. Some of the most serious criminals were executed.

Still, waves of crimes continued surging. This was the negative effect of the Reform and Opening policy, all the while a treacherous tide drifted beneath the surface of prosperity. Once proudly claimed that the nation was free of prostitution, during the Mao era, after the communists took over, but now many women were selling their bodies for a living everywhere.

Shenzhen, a new immigrant city, the nation's largest experimental zone of the western-style market-economy, and the political ante of the reformers, unfortunately, was suffering the most from crimes.

However, the worst among all the crimes was the corruption within the government. Yet maintaining a clean government was the biggest challenge the reformers headed by Deng Xiaoping had been facing.

*   *   *

Since implementing the Reform and Opening, rice fields in the rural areas had been leased out to farmers by the town or village governments instead of with all farmers, lazily working together in the same commune, sharing the meager portion of what they grew. A farmer was free to raise or plant anything on the leased farms, as long as he paid the rent on time. With the similar policy, the hills and mountains had been leased out to fruit or lumber farmers by the local governments.

The hills and mountains in the Guangzhou suburb had been cultivated by the fruit farmers. There were many fruit trees, such as lizhi, Longan, peach, pomegranate, pineapple and plum, had been planted there. The farmers who leased the hills would often work them or patrol around. They soon discovered a group of strangers going in and out of their hut, which had been built for their occasional use for taking rests and storing tools. When they went to talk with these strangers, the kidnappers were nervous at first for being discovered. They blocked the farmers from entering the hut and wanted to proceed with the killing. But after reporting and consulting with their headman, they calmed down.

One of the strangers asked, "My farmer big brothers, sorry for using your hut without asking, but may we pay you to stay here for a few days?"

The farmers looked at each other, then gathered whispering and discussing. A few minutes later, an old man asked, "How much do you pay us?"

"How about one hundred yuan a day?"

The farmers murmured together again for a minute. The same old man said, "One hundred and fifty yuan a day."

"Okay, deal," one of the kidnappers replied curtly.

*   *   *

All the phones in Chen Yong's company were bugged by the two police officers on site. Nearly a day had gone, and they received no calls from the kidnappers. Sitting in his office in the afternoon feeling melancholic and having had not slept for nearly two days, Chen Yong drifted off to sleep. Soon the lovely face of Lin Dan appeared, and then all their happy times of being together: working, discussing, chatting, and dinning out together reappeared in his mind. His heart was beating fast when he said, "I love you, honey." He almost couldn't breathe when he heard her reply, "I love you, too." Although she refused hugging and kissing, being with her and talking with her had already made him feel happy. Tonight, he had prepared to propose to her again while dinning out to celebrate the founding of their new company. He would kneel down in front of her, showing his sincerity and love toward her with hundreds of patrons watching, so that she would have no reason to resist. He smiled happily. *Yes, after tonight, I will be the happiest person in the world.* He sang and danced jovially. But right at the moment, a police officer appeared, telling him that his lover had been kidnapped, that she might be killed at any moment. He yelled and screamed and went rather hysterical then fainted. He awakened, choking with nervousness.

Finding that he had just had a dream, he calmed down and struggled to clear his mind. But the cruel reality was, he remembered now, his lover and his brother had been kidnapped and he had no idea where they were and whether they were still alive.

Time was crucial, the sooner he could find them, the better chance for them to survive. He couldn't just sit there to wait for miracles. He got up and strode over to the cabinet quickly. Grabbing the tiny telephone directory, he searched on the private detective pages. One big-character title in red captured his attention. It read: GUARANTEE TO UNCOVER THE TRUTH, OR NO CHARGE. Avoiding being noticed by the police, he dialed the phone number with his mobile phone. A few seconds later, a female said at the other end, "Liu Ming, Detective."

Chen Yong told her what service he required. Two minutes later, a male voice came on line, "Master, your case is a criminal case, which is very dangerous and it should be handled by the police."

A feeling of despair struck him, but he didn't give up. He muttered, "I understand, but I just want you to find out where they are and who have kidnapped them."

Liu Ming hesitated for a few seconds then replied, "Okay. I'll try it, but I will charge you double."

"No problem," Chen Yong responded quickly and elatedly. He knew that although the private detective business was a new occupation in the nation, there were negative effects of it due to the lack of regulations. Most of the private detectives had connections with gangster-background informants and they work much harder than the police. So the chances for them to uncover the truth of many criminal and non-criminal cases were much better and quicker. He did not care much about the consequence, all he wanted now was to rescue his loved ones.

Putting down the mobile phone, he felt a bit relieved. He prayed there would be good news coming to him soon. A feeling of hunger struck him. He realized that he had not eaten anything since morning. Getting up wearily, he stumbled out of the office toward a nearby fast-food restaurant.

He was gobbling up a plate of rice with pork and vegetables when he heard his mobile phone ring. Pushing the TALK button, a raucous male voice came on line, eerily.

"Is this Chen Yong?"

"Yes, who is this?"

"Well, you would be very interested in talking with me, because your brother and your girlfriend are in our hands now. What is that noise? Is there any police officer with you now?"

Chen Yong's heart started pounding. He replied quickly, "I am eating in a restaurant by myself. But why do you kidnap my people? Have you done anything bad to them?"

"Why?" the man chuckled, "Because we need some money badly. We haven't done anything to hurt them yet, but, if you do not give what we ask for, they will be dying very soon and very badly."

"How much do you want?"

"Thirty million yuan. It is just a small potato for you, isn't it?"

Thirty million yuan? God! He only had fifteen million yuan in the bank and that had been used as collateral for a loan for his future hi-tech company. Where could he get the cash from? He muttered to the phone, "I don't have that much money."

"You are kidding. We know that you just sold your taxi company, and you still have the gasoline and diesel fuel company. Your combined asset would be worth around that much if you sell them all."

Chen Yong was struck dumbfounded. He would be stripped back to penniless again if he were forced to pay that amount. All these years of hard work would be wasted. Who were they? How did they know his financial situation so well? Would they be his future competitors that they wanted to strangle him to death financially before he would be able to compete with them? *That must be it,* he determined. "I tell you what, I will give you half the amount of what you ask for, and I will not get involved in the hi-tech business at all in the future," he promised.

"No, we want the exact amount of what we ask for, not a penny less. If you don't come up with that for us, you will never see them again. And remember never report to the police about our conversation. Do I make myself clear?"

Chen Yong slumped to the booth. He would have to do it, there was no way out. But it's okay, as long as he could save his loved ones. He could start all over again, he was still young anyway.

"How do I know that you have kidnapped them?"

"You don't believe it? Hold on for a second."

A few seconds later, he heard his brother pleading, "Big brother, come save us, hurry." Lin Dan was crying in the background, "A-Yong, help us."

"A-Song, Dan Dan—" he croaked, wanting to talk to them, but the voice had quickly switched back to the kidnapper's gruff voice.

"Now you have heard them. I give you three days to get the cash ready. Again, don't report this to the police. You know what the consequence is if you should do so," the man warned.

"Hold on," Chen Yong said desperately. "Three days is not enough. I need time to sell my company, you know. I need at least two weeks to finish doing it."

"I tell you what, I give you one week, that is all. I will contact you later," the man blared and hung up abruptly.

*　　*　　*

Detective Liu Ming sifted through the information Chen Yong had provided. He realized the complication of the case. It was obvious that the kidnappers wanted to drive Chen Yong out of business and get rid of all his money—something quite different from most of the kidnapping cases where they just wanted a bit of cash. Whoever masterminded this would likely be one of his rivals, he concluded. But who would that be? He investigated all of Chen Yong's business counterparts and rivals in the fuel supply industry and his future high-tech businesses, but found none of them had plotted and committed such malicious crime against him. He checked all the banks, which had loaned funds for his business development; and his loan payment records, no defaults had been recorded at all. Obviously,

50

there was no indication that the bankers had been involved in the kidnapping.

Enquiring over the gangster-background informants, by paying them handsomely through the underground channel, he finally got wind that a group of Shenzhen gangsters had appeared in the mountainous area of Guangzhou suburb. Why did the Shenzhen gangsters go there? It was likely that they had kidnapped Chen Yong's people there. He was delighted.

But how could he find them without being spotted? He decided to pay a visit to the villagers around that area to see if they had any idea about where the Shenzhen gangsters were. He took a long-distance bus trip there, then got a ride to a nearby village by a motorcyclist waiting at the bus station—who charged him three yuan for it. By paying each one of them ten yuan, he asked the villagers if they had seen or heard about the Shenzhen gangsters coming in and out of the hills there. But none of them could provide him any valuable information. He was disappointed. More to his desperation, he got the same result from visiting other neighboring villages. Why? Had he received the wrong information that was made up by the greedy informants?

When he was about to leave, he was informed that there was another village about five kilometers deep in the hills there. That was the last hope of his trip. He jumped on the back of a motorcycle and told the driver to rush him there. His last visit was fruitful after interviewing several villagers. He confirmed that a group of strangers had been using a hut of the fruit farmers on one of the hills. Guided by a fruit farmer, he sneaked close to the hut. Peeping through the bush, he gasped at what he saw there. He hurriedly took out a camera and kept taking pictures from different positions until the whole scene of what was going on had fully covered.

*　　*　　*

Being handed the pictures, Chen Yong was warned by the detective not to tell anyone from where he had gotten them. Otherwise, not only he would be forced to end his detective career, but he would be in a life-threatening situation. He thanked the detective for his quick and outstandingly detailed work and promised to keep it as a secret.

It was unbelievable. He kept wondering what had made such a prominent and powerful person to commit the crime, and how to rescue his beloved ones. He still had two days before the deadline, and had agreed to sell his gasoline and diesel fuel company to his competitor for an under-market price with the deal completed in two days.

"What can I do, A-Ming?" he asked the detective, with melancholy in his heart.

"Well, my job to uncover the truth of this incidence has been completed. I should not be involved any further."

"I know, but can you guess why this man wants to get rid of all of my fortune, since I have never had any grudge with him?

Having been in the crime-related business for a while, the detective knew what his client should do, but he was afraid of getting in trouble if his advice leaked out. After hesitating for a minute, he told him what to do and then hurried out of his client's office.

The next day, when Chen Yong called the detective's office to ask him if he could help him carry out his plan. He was told by the phone company's automated message that the phone had been disconnected.

Now he had to do it alone quick. But he was not confident if he could make it, because fighting against a powerful person was just like hitting a rock with an egg. He would be pulverized, destroyed, and not a slice of chance for survival. But thinking of rescuing his beloved ones, the miraculous power emerged inside him. It grew bigger and bigger and more powerful until it completely drove away his fear and despair. He drove out and darted in the streets to different places where his friends and relatives were and left the sealed envelopes of photos to them and told them what to do and what not to do. When he returned to the office, he was ready for the next move.

*   *   *

Lin Dan and Chen Song were horrified, they had been kidnapped to a remote mountainous place and detained in a filthy hut by the infamous mob. Listening to their kidnappers' conversations, they learned they had been kidnapped for a sizeable ransom. Also, Lin Dan would have been raped by the kidnappers without the order of the one who masterminded the scheme. It was odd that they had not been physically abused by these violent gangsters, and only occasionally suffered by verbal insults. They still did not know the reason behind their captors' restrains.

Chen Song felt sorry for his brother. Becoming successful in business and becoming a wealthy man was Chen Yong's biggest dream ever since the failure of not being admitted to college. Now he was about to be stripped penniless, and what a blow. Chen Song wished his brother could stand it and survive.

Consumed by the fear of their unknown fate, Lin Dan regretted being too cool to Chen Yong. She knew that genuine love existed between them. They could have been married and basked in the sunshine of love without her fuss and scruples. Now she realized that she had been too selfish in rejecting him, ignoring his feeling. Maybe the present situation was punishment for her heartlessness and rudeness, for ruining her first-time romance of true love.

Biting her lips, Lin Dan decided she would make it up to Chen Yong if she survived this crisis and would not pretend to be cool to him anymore. She would then release herself from this self-made manacle of love.

Struggling emotionally in this new-found reverie, she heard stamping feet approaching. She had been numbed to such noise previously. It was merely her detainees' stepping in and out of the hut. Yet her eyes remained closed, as nothing could make her more alert now.

"You goddamned son of a bitch! Why do you treat my lovely Dan Dan so badly?" a familiar voice roared next to her, "Unbind them right away."

Lin Dan and Chen Song had remained bound during their captivity, except for when they needed to eat and visit the restroom.

"Yes, Master," four kidnappers replied simultaneously, unraveling the hostages quickly.

Looking at the pudgy man standing in front of her, Lin Dan now realized who plotted their ordeal instantly.

It all started from the day they met when she went to the police department to register for the residency of the city a year ago. She was not qualified to be the resident of Shenzhen, according to the rules, because she did not own a house or an apartment in the city. Disappointedly, she argued with the clerks handling her case, stating that she had lived in Shenzhen for more than six years, and asked why she was not allowed to register as a permanent resident. Her loud argument perked the ear of Li Ben, who had just returned from an operation. Seeing her, the deputy director of the police department was stunned by her beauty. He consoled her in his office and ordered her case to be approved immediately. From that day on, he kept calling her out for a date, and was rejected each time. He became very angry—no girl had ever dared to reject him before. He checked her background and found out that she loved her boss more than any one of her admirers. He had tried everything including expensive gifts, cash, and even threats, but none of them worked.

Finally, he determined that the only man to force her to give in to him was to cripple Chen Yong financially and physically. At first, Li Ben wanted to destroy his company through the bankers, but he did not have good connections with any of them. So he decided to let the gangsters handle the job for him, since they were partners in illegal businesses. He had instructed them not to hurt or abuse Lin Dan. After all, forcing her to be his mistress was the purpose of his scheme. He decided to pay a visit to the hut to visit and persuade her. He didn't know that his stay in the hut had been photographed surreptitiously.

"You bastards, apologize to Miss Lin," Li Ben blared again. They apologized as he patted her head. "I am doing all this because I love you, please understand."

"Really? That's how you love a person? By kidnapping her and extorting her lover?" Lin Dan shot back.

"I am sorry, but I couldn't think of any other ways to change your mind. I love you and want to be with you, but you kept rejecting me. There is nothing I can do about it besides this."

"You don't know what love is," Lin Dan said with repulsion.

"Yes, I do. I tell you what, I will divorce my wife and marry you if you will change your mind. And, of course, I will never bother Chen Yong again, if that is the case."

She knew that he was lying. Although it had never been stipulated as a rule, but it was a fact: once a government official divorced, his position in government would definitely become jeopardized. Thus getting divorced would automatically ruin a government official's political career—anywhere in the nation. However, she would be willing to sacrifice herself if Chen Yong would be saved from ruin. That was the true meaning of love—always wanting loved ones to be safe and happy.

Lin Dan felt sad about her fate. Why did she have to be someone's mistress and not with the one she truly loved? Was it wrong to be beautiful-looking? For her, the familiar saying, "Beautiful women often have ill fates," was true. So that was the fate for a beautiful-looking girl like her. She couldn't avoid it, and had to accept fate at this moment.

"Okay, I can be your girlfriend if you call this kidnapping melodrama off and keep your promise not to bother Chen Yong anymore. You will have to allow me two work days to go back to his company and take care of the business first."

He couldn't believe what he was hearing. Li Ben was overjoyed. *Thank God, my plan worked perfectly,* he thought. *I am going to own this beauty.* "Okay, honey, everything is over, and your request is approved. But you have to keep your promise as well, if you try to break it or run away, the consequences will be very ugly. You know, Chen Yong will be destroyed first," he warned.

"A-Dan," Chen Song yelled. "You are destroying both yourself and my big brother by surrendering to this monster. You know how bad my big brother will feel if you leave him. Besides, this piece of human trash cannot be trusted."

"You'd better shut up, Chen Song, if you still want to get out of here alive," Li Ben threatened.

"Don't worry, A-Song, time will heal the wound. Your big brother will get over it one day."

"Okay, the deal is settled. Right, honey?" Li Ben smiled as he hugged her tightly.

Lin Dan pushed him away and said, "Not yet! I want you to call Chen Yong right now with your mobile phone and tell him that the kidnapping is over. And tell him that he will not need to pay the ransom at all and that we will be there shortly.

"No problem, let me do it now, Honey."

Chen Yong felt the sky had collapsed when he heard what Lin Dan had done. He screamed with pain. Crying, he hugged her the tightest he could, afraid that if he released her, she would go away. They cried together, mourning for their fate. They should have been married already. Why, suddenly, should they have to split? Why should their love end so tragically? Why? Where was the justice?

They kept crying and mumbling, holding each other tightly. They knew it was the fate they had to accept, as there was nothing they could do to change it. That monster, Li Ben, was too powerful to be conquered. Drying away her tears, Lin Dan said he should give up on her, that her body and soul would be soiled and stained. But Chen Yong insisted he would wait for her.

"You are my only love," he murmured.

"But I am afraid we will not have another chance."

"I can wait for ten years, twenty years, even the rest of my life until we can be together again, Lin Dan."

"I will become an ugly old woman then, and you will have no interest in me anymore. There are many nice and beautiful young girls out there, Chen Yong. Why do you want just one tree and ignore the whole forest?"

"Because this tree is worth more than the sum of the whole forest," he replied, kissing her.

"Oh, I love you so much, A-Yong. While detained in the hut, I regretted being too cool to you and wanted to make it up to you and marry you, that's if I had the chance to get out of there safely. I was cool to you because I did not want to get hurt. You know I had met and stayed with men who had no loyalty to their wives. Although I knew you were different from them and I loved you so much, I decided to have my own career first. I was too selfish then and rejected your proposals twice. It was a mistake. But since we have two days together, why don't we get married. We don't need to go through the tedious paperwork with the government, we are registered in our hearts. What do you think, honey?"

He hugged her tightly and cried happily, "Yes, honey, I have been waiting for this day for so long. Let's get married tonight."

"Okay, after tonight, we are wife and husband in our hearts for the rest of our lives, no matter where we are or whether we are together or not."

"Agreed, honey," he murmured and kissed her.

Holding hands, they went out to rent a traditional red wedding dress and gown, they bought a pair of wedding rings, a piece of red scarf, new bedding, red double-pleasure paper handicrafts, and some incense sticks.

After a feast in the revolving restaurant that evening, they went
back to Chen Yong's apartment. Locking the door, they started dec-
orating the windows, doors, living room, bedroom, dresser and bed
with the red double-pleasure paper handicrafts. With the wedding
dress and gown on, they each held incense sticks and lighted them
up. They bowed toward the sky from the patio wishing the marriage
god to protect them and give them happiness and long-lasting marriage. Then they helped each other to put on the wedding rings.
After that, the groom covered the bride's head and face with the
piece of red scarf, held her hand and led her back to the living
room. Setting up two chairs next to each other and pretending that
their parents were sitting there, they bowed to them three times
and served each with a cup of tea as a way of paying respect to their
parents, expressing affectionate thankfulness for having raised them
up while sharing their happiness. When the ritual was done, Chen
Yong and Lin Dan bowed once to each other.

Then the groom said, "I wish my dear wife well."

The bride responded, "I wish my dear husband well."

They then bowed to each other once more. He held her hand
again and guided her to the bedroom. After the bride sat down on
the stool, the groom unveiled her with a small stick. They gazed at
each other with happiness. They gulped a cup of wine with their
arms crossed and linked together. The groom blew out the candles,
carried the bride to the bed where they kissed and made love all
through the night.

Next morning, Chen Yong heard his lover weeping with her
back turned toward him. He immediately placed his arm around
her shoulder and pulled her close against his chest.

"What's wrong, Honey?"

"I feel sad because, after today, we are going to be separated."

"I feel the same, Honey, we will miss each other so much,"
Chen Yong mumbled and kissed her.

"Can we escape to somewhere, maybe to Hong Kong?"

"I've thought about that, but there are problems in doing so.
First, we are risking our lives in crossing the bay between here and
there. Secondly, the probability of getting caught and being sent
back by the Hong Kong police can be as high as eighty percent. We
will fall in the hands of that bastard again if we get caught and

repatriated. In addition, what can we do since we have no right to stay in Hong Kong, even if we successfully escape to there?"

"Then there is no way to escape," Lin Dan sighed, mournfully.

"Maybe there is one," Chen Yong muttered. "I have some secret pictures of that bastard taken when he was there at the hut with you and those gangsters. Imagine what will happen should those pictures become exposed in the media!"

"Really? How did you know that we were detained there?"

"I hired a detective and the pictures were taken by him."

"You think we can use these pictures to force Lin Ben to give up on me? Who dares publish these pictures? Who has the gut to offend this monster?"

"We can take them to the provincial government and the central government."

"But these pictures don't prove much, if no other concrete evidence comes with it," she muttered.

Chen Yong said nothing. He held and caressed Lin Dan as if it might be their last moments of being together, while knowing that their separation was unavoidable. Enjoying the sweetness of being with his lover, Chen Yong really wanted time to pause forever; no separations; and no sharing of his soul-mate's body with any other man.

Suddenly, a man's pride struck inside him and the male adrenaline surged forward. He got up abruptly and ran to the kitchen. Chen Yong returned with a knife, and yelled hysterically, "I can't take anymore. Let me kill that bastard!"

"Stop! A-Yong." Lin Dan leaped off the bed and ran toward the door, crying, "You will get killed."

"I don't care. I just want him dead," he screamed, brandishing the glistening knife.

"What about me? Who's going to take care of me if you were to die?" Lin Dan cried, while reaching for his knife.

Looking and breathing like a madman, he surrendered the blade and hugged her tightly. She caressed his head to console him, while they cried together. Kissing him, she mumbled, "Remember this saying, 'Revenging after ten years is not too late for a man with class'? You know, I can collect all the evidence of his criminal activities by taking advantage of being close to him. Sometime in the future, we can use this information to bring him down.

Chen Yong nodded in agreement, despite his emotional uneasiness about the approaching situation.

8

As was scheduled, Lin Dan was picked up by Li Ben's chauffeur in the afternoon. The BMW headed west along Shennan Boulevard, then south toward the beach and three kilometers west of Huang-gang customs, before stopping in front of an impressive villa. Two security guards standing by the gate spoke into their cell phones immediately. Seconds later, the wrought iron gate slipped to one side, allowing the BMW to slowly move toward the parking area.

Li Ben stepped out onto the porch, smiling obscenely. Ignoring the presence of the chauffeur and security guards, he raced toward Lin Dan and held her tightly against his chest. His tongue lapped at her face before thrusting itself deep into her mouth. She couldn't breathe, and tried to push him away—but she was too weak to budge him. He chuckled and lifted her off the ground. She struggled to break free with her little fists hitting at his back. He was amused and laughed, grabbing her like a hawk clawing at a baby hen. He strode into the house, carrying her to his huge bedroom with a king-sized bed. He thrust her onto the bed and began tearing off her clothes. He ignored her protesting, squeezing her big breasts and licking her nipples rather hungrily. After quickly undressing himself, Li Ben pressed on her and drove his penis into her. She screamed painfully. He became so excited, began aggressively thrusting in and out of Lin Dan who was crying hysterically.

When his cell phone started to ringing, Li Ben erupted in sexual joy. Panting, he grabbed the phone and barked, "Who the fuck is this?"

"Master Li, it is me, Wang Qiang."

"What the fuck are you calling me for at this time?" he blared angrily then switched off the phone. He pulled his dripping penis out of Lin Dan and held it to her face, then ordered, "Clean it."

His phone rang again. He glanced at the caller ID, then shut it off. Few seconds later, it rang again. He pressed the answer button and roared, "Stop calling! Goddamn you, Wang Qiang."

As he was about to push the off button, he heard the caller's urgent plea, "Help, Master Li, the 'flour' and the 'ice' got stuck in Guanzi Province." This was about the drugs they were smuggling in from Southeast Asia, and having to pass through Yunnan and Guanzi provinces to Shenzhen.

"Really? Why?"

"Our brothers are afraid of passing the two checkpoints there because the posts have been equipped with more dogs, soldiers, and more sophisticated equipment."

He wondered for a while, and then said, "I tell you what, I will straighten it up there and get them back down here safely, but I want sixty percent share of the profit, instead of fifty percent. Okay?"

Following a quick few seconds of hesitation from the other end, Li Ben exploded. "What are you thinking about? Without my help, you don't even get one cent from the deal."

"Yes, Master Li, I agree with what you said, sixty percent profit for you," he muttered, condescendingly.

"You sound like a partner now. Tell your men to stay right there. I will send a police van."

"Yes, Master Li."

Lying in the bed, Lin Dan listened to his conversation. She knew he was talking about an illegal business deal, but she did not know what it was about. She loathed him for his rudeness, insulting manner, and vulgarity. *I will make you pay for it,* she mumbled soundlessly. Then she heard another conversation of his on the phone.

"Liu brother, go up to the goddamned Guangzi checkpoint with one of our vans with two boys, now, and make sure you guys are fully armed and in uniform," he ordered to one of his closest followers in the police department.

"Yes, sir. Got it. We will be going in twenty minutes."

"Twenty minutes? I want you to start going in five minutes, and be sure to stick the search-exempted sign on the fucking windshield," he roared.

"Yes, sir. We are going in five minutes, with the search-exempted sign sticking on the windshield," Lieutenant Liu replied, curtly on the other end of the line.

Countless container trucks, cars, vans, long-distance and tour buses rolled on twenty-four hours a day, making the Shenzhen-Guangzhou freeway the busiest four-way freeway in the nation. A police van darted northbound, speeding along at a hundred kilometers per hour, with its siren on. The sluggish traffic was moving even slower than usual as vehicles jammed the slow-lanes to give way for the law-enforcers.

Two hours later, the freeway passed Guangzhou, the capital of Guangdong, and continued its way north. The freeway narrowed to two lanes and the traffic was surprisingly less, as it stretched deeper inland. Looking out from the window of the vehicle, one could rarely see the cement-forest that was ubiquitous in the coastal areas; instead the vast view was of the vegetable and rice fields with farmers and cattle, of villages with huts and little brick or stone houses scattered about.

Another two hours later, the freeway ended. The police van drove on in the narrow bumpy roads to cross the Guangzi provincial line. The siren was useless on roads jammed with cows, tractors, and small trucks. It was completely dark when the van passed the checkpoint and arrived in Guangzi, where the drug dealers and Shenzhen gangsters were. They recognized Lieutenant Liu at once.

After loading the drugs and having dinner, the four Shenzhen gangsters were handcuffed and locked inside the van. Then they started their way back. When they got to the checkpoint again, they were stopped by the soldiers. Dogs were barking and sniffing for the smell that they had trained to hunt for: illegal drugs. They showed the officers the search-exempted sign sticking on the windshield, but were informed that the checkpoint had been taken over by the Central Military Committee. The committee stated that no one or no vehicle was exempted from being searched.

The fully-armed soldiers besieged the van immediately. When the doors were unlocked, the soldiers were stunned. Not only did they see the handcuffed men and fully-armed policemen inside, but also the drugs in bags and boxes that occupied one-third of the van. The checkpoint soldiers pointed their guns to them at once, and the commander ordered the soldiers to unarm and arrest the policemen and confiscate their drugs.

"Wait, we came here to catch these drug dealers and to take them back to our court in Shenzhen," Lieutenant Liu explained.

"How do we know that you are not fake policemen?" the commander demanded.

"We have our own ID cards and the warrants issued by our police department to arrest these drug dealers," Lieutenant Liu replied, feeling great about himself for visualizing the need for the warrants—his boss did not tell him to bring them.

After examining them carefully, the commander said, "You can take the criminals with you, but you must leave the drugs here. No drugs can pass this checkpoint."

The policemen and the gangsters were startled, glancing at each other. But Lieutenant Liu remained composed. He said calmly, "We need to take the drugs back as the solid evidence against these criminals in our court. Once this case is closed, we will destroy the drugs there."

The commander hesitated for a few seconds, then decided to make a call to the Shenzhen police department. As usual, his call was transferred to the deputy director Li Ben by the receptionist.

"Thank you for informing me that my subordinates have successfully caught those wicked drug dealers, Commander Comrade Ma. Please congratulate them for me and urge them to return as quickly as possible, as I need to interrogate these criminals for bigger cases," he claimed.

"Your comrades have done an excellent job. Keep up the good work, Director Li. I will let them go now."

"Thanks, Commander Comrade Ma," Li Ben said, feeling relieved.

*   *   *

Having been robbed of his lover, Chen Yong suffered a hard blow emotionally. For months, he got drunk almost every night and was barely able to get up for work the next morning. He often stared at his wedding ring and then Lin Dan's desk, her framed picture in the office, and often got lost in quiet delirium.

One day, his secretary came into his office. He got up abruptly from his chair and said, "Dan Dan, honey, I have missed you so much." Then he hugged and kissed her. When his secretary woke him up and told him that she was not his lover, he was so disappointed and explained that he was dreaming about Lin Dan.

Yet with the absence of Lin Dan, he was unable to continue work on his hi-tech project, despite the support and encouragement of the professionals in the field and the investment bankers.

Knowing that their brother was unable to work effectively due to his often absent-mindedness, Chen Song and his sister Chen Jing joined the company to help him. Chen Jing had just received her master's degree in business administration, while Chen Song had received his bachelor's degree in electronic engineering. Their hard-working attitude and educational background had been extraordinarily beneficial and helpful to Chen Yong's company, and its plans ahead for the hi-tech industry. With Chen Jing in charge of the personnel and finance department and Chen Song managing the planning and engineering department, the company was ready to take off for the new direction.

Being his good sister and brother, they both understood the genuine love their older brother had toward Lin Dan, and how much he had been suffering since the incident and her departure. They grasped every opportunity to console him and cheer him up, and help to unearth the rationality that had been buried by his sentimental emotions.

Chen Yong, with the help of his sister and brother, finally realized there was nothing he could do to change the fact that he and his lover had been separated and that there was no reason to live in the past. In cherishing what his lover had sacrificed herself to save, Chen Yong felt he should keep on pursuing his dream and to be the best he could, instead of abusing himself emotionally and withdrawing from reality and his ambition. He was grateful to his sister and brother for giving him their helping hands in his darkest period of his life. He decided not to let them down by standing up again.

Together they resumed preparing to open the hi-tech company. Everyday they called or visited related companies, universities, banks and the government offices, and interviewed potential employees. Having compared with different locations and consulted with the geomancy master, they decided to set up their new company by renting rooms on the eighth floor of a commercial building in the Bell Tower area in the Futian district.

It was amazing that Chen Jing could handle the job as brilliantly as Lin Dan did—despite her banal look. Chen Song proved to be so keen and knowledgeable in the electronic communication business. Chen Yong, was, by nature, more mature and, thus, a good listener and decision maker. The three were the perfect team: working hard, playing hard, and laughing hard. They enjoyed being together as sister and brothers, colleagues and partners. They were happier now than ever before.

They registered the name of their new company as Octopus Telecom. To achieve the marketing purpose, they invited guests from the media, major companies in the information technology field, banks, and securities to attend their grand-opening ceremony.

Lucky enough, soon after the grand opening, they signed a big contract with the securities in the city to develop the electronic automated system for stock trading. That would enable them to stand firmly in the IT business and boost their morale, as well as their company's reputation tremendously. What a wonderful start. They were overjoyed and celebrated it with a dinner party in a local seafood restaurant. Chen Jing hosted the party. She thanked the guests who had supported their company right from the beginning and told them her older brother's dramatic experience in pursuing his dream of becoming a successful businessman. His experience, she said, was pretty much like, and related to, the development of Shenzhen: starting from zero, it grew bigger and stronger, and upgraded and shifted to broader and more glamorous fields. Chen Yong, in response, modestly said that his dream has far from fully come true yet, like the development of Shanzhen, and he urged their continued and concerted support for both the city and his company.

*　　*　　*

Since becoming the mistress of the city's police deputy director, Lin Dan functioned strictly as a live sex toy of the evil and powerful man. Often, he would return to the villa from his office in the middle of the day to have sex with her, and then leave for work again. There was no love between them, yet her irresistible charm and stubborn attitude toward him made him all the more insatiable and desirous of her. Unlike all the mistresses he had before, this one had class. She possessed stunning beauty and brilliant brain, and she was not after his money and power—but forced to be with him.

64

As days went on, he had lost interest in all other women but her, but his rudeness toward her, whether in bed or not, had not changed. That was the way a woman was supposed to be treated, he believed, for satisfying a man's sexual and dominating desires. One thing that had been bothering him, since the day she was carried to his villa was that he had never seen her smile. He was ready to offer her whatever she desired, but she had never asked for anything associated with money—only her freedom. Intending to keep her for a long time, he would not let her leave him or be alone. Without his approval and with the company of a chauffeur, she was not allowed to go anywhere or meet anyone. Neither could she call Chen Yong again. He checked the records of both the mobile and the home phone almost everyday to see if she had called him. He also warned that he would harm Chen Yong should she dare to call him.

Lin Dan would often call her friends to get her information about him, so she knew much about what was going on with her lover. She was happy to hear that his sister and brother were helping him run the new company. And she also called a well-acquainted government official working in the department of commerce to help Chen Yong win the contract, when she had found out that his company was bidding for the contract to build the automated system for the securities.

She deeply believed that making loved ones happy was the highest stage in love. She had never given up hope that the dark cloud shrouding them would one day be blown away, and that they would bask in the sunshine of happy reunion in the future. Yet it might be just a test, if that was the true love between them.

Lin Dan noticed her psychological and sentimental feelings toward Li Ben had slightly changed. Although she hated him very much at the beginning, the genuine pleasure from the daily sexual intercourse had been eroding her gradually. The man was rude and inconsiderate and ignorant. He did make great sex, she thought silently, as she had become used to it and was gradually learning how to enjoy it. That was the danger she was worrying about—the mixture of hatred and sexual enjoyment. She really did not know how long she could hold on to her lover before being totally trapped into the animal desire inflicted by her captor. The man was evil but he did bring her sexual pleasure. She was afraid that she would be turned into evil as well. Whether she liked it or not, it was the fact that she was unable to change as this monster's mistress or sex toy. How pathetic.

9

As the economy kept growing in double digits and citizens of the city got wealthier, buying new apartments had become affordable and trendy for many families. Thus among all other booming industries, the real estate in this newly-erected city became highly desirable. It all started with the foreign-invested property companies, mostly from Hong Kong, and then the local start-ups who extended their tentacles into the extremely profitable business—all with the advantage of getting loans from the domestic banks through both the legal and the corruptive channels. It'd even become the hot spot for the gangsters and corrupted government officials who wanted to launder their filthily obtained money for high returns. Although many people could foresee the burning of the overheated money-piling property business, people believed owning their apartments were good investments on a long-term basis, especially in a new economy just taking off. So hot money continued flowing in as the number of buyers grew steadily.

Observing the property market closely and greedily, Li Ben and other gangster heads eagerly channeled their money, through third parties, into property development. They set up the firm named "The Earth Dragon Real Estate Company Limited." They acquainted many obsequious and corrupt bankers who got them inflated loans, while wading in the river of greed in this field. It was that when one apartment complex was just halfway done, bankers would use it as collateral for bigger loans for another new project, always requested by the powerful customer. With this advantage, along with their powerful connections in acquiring lands and obtaining licenses, the Earth Dragon Real Estate Company Limited expanded rapidly. They built expensive twenty- and forty-story apartment buildings in Luohu, Futein, Dongmen, Nansan, Seikou, and even in Boian districts—all over the city. Their business was snowballing, and so few companies in the field could compete with them.

Tang Daming was one of the most corrupt bankers they had worked with. He was eager to make the connection and felt flattered to have the opportunity to provide services to such a powerful person, especially once finding out his customer's background. He often granted huge loans for him for small assets as collateral, and would get various favors and commissions in return. Along with a connection of the local prominent power, his desire for wealth grew insatiable.

One day, sitting in the office and calculating the commission that he was getting from a loan, he heard the receptionist droning on the intercom, "Manager Tang, you have a call from Mr. Wang on line-two." Mr. Wang was the biggest customer with the most commission. He was happy. It must be another new project.

"Master Wang, it is so nice to hear from you again. How are you today?" he said, happily.

"Don't say nonsense," Wang Qiang snapped. "We need a loan for an office building in the downtown area of Luohu."

"What? An office building?" he cried cautiously. Their real estate company had only developed apartment buildings, most of which insofar could be sold without difficulty. That could keep the cash flow running smoothly, as the mortgage payments being collected on time. He could also continue to make his filthy fortune without getting into trouble. But the office buildings had been over-supplied in the past few years, so it was too risky to loan funds for this sort of project. Hesitantly, he tried to persuade the gangster leader to change his mind.

"I tell you what, Master Wang," he said humbly, "why don't you keep on building the apartment buildings instead of the office buildings? They have been over-supplied already."

"What the hell are you talking about? Ours is in the downtown of the most busy commercial district, and is much different from all the other shitty places about the city," he retorted.

"Master Wang, you are wrong. The over-supplied problem exists everywhere in the city. Perhaps you should do a little survey first."

"Bullshit! Fuck the goddamned survey. You give me the loan or not? Or do you want you and your bank to get fucked up?"

"Don't be mad, Master Wang, I am just joking. Of course, you will have the loan for the office building," he said, condescendingly.

He could not afford to lose this big customer, nor did he want to get in trouble. This customer was a cold-blooded gangster head, and could do anything violently to him and to his bank.

"You sound like a partner now, just be smart, okay? I will bring the drawings and the building budget proposal over tomorrow, partner."

"Okay, Master Wang," he muttered, wondering how much trouble he would be in and what he should do about it if this loan defaulted. Anyway, it would be at least three years before any problems would burgeon up. He closed his eyes and calmed himself down, and began feeling much easier as he thought about the near-eight-digit savings he had saved in various banks under different names of his family members—his wife, son, and daughter, besides himself. He could buy citizenships easily from different countries in the western world, even if he quit working now. His son and daughter were going to study abroad soon, so most of his fortune would be shipped out secretly. They would get residential status by buying properties and registering a company under their names in another country like the United States or Canada. And, later, he and his wife would join their children and stay there for good. That was it—easy and clean—no need to worry about being caught and prosecuted in the future at home. Money is god anywhere in the world, and he possessed it in two full hands. No need to be worried too. What he should do now was to grab every opportunity to make more. Thus, the gangster's new project would bring him another handsome commission, and that was what counted. *Thank God for loving me.*

One thing that had puzzled him, he suddenly remembered, that little brat, Chen Yong, accused him of kidnapping. Later, he hurriedly sold his gas and diesel fuel company and delayed opening his hi-tech company. There seemed a lot of things had happened to Chen Yong since he decided to get rid of him. *Why? That brat,* he gritted his teeth, *a damned taxi driver before, got rich and became one of the wealthiest persons in town with my help.* Yet he had got out of the under-table-to-be-rich game cleanly by kicking his benefactor out of his business. *What a traitor.* He would make him pay for it. But he got wind that his girlfriend Li Dan had disappeared lately too.

Lin Dan, what a gorgeous creature, was supposed to be his mistress had that brat not come to the Paradise Nightclub that fateful night. That was the second debt Chen Yong owed him. He would make him pay sometime in the future. But where was that lovely Lin Dan? Why had she disappeared? He wanted to find out.

The next day, when Tang Daming looked at the drawings of the proposed office building Wang Qiang had brought over, he gasped.

"That's a terrible location, Master Wang. Have you consulted with a geomancy master?"

"What's wrong with the location?"

"Look. There is a street running right toward the middle of the building, it means that the evil spirit is always hitting right on it. Few people will buy or rent your building because they believe that the building will bring them bad luck and they will not do business successfully in that building."

"Fuck geomancy, I don't believe that shit. Are we not taught to be atheists by our high school teachers, many of whom are members of the Communist Party? Besides, it is our business, not yours, all we need is the damn loan from your shitty bank," he snapped.

Tang Daming knew he was just wasting time talking with this uncivilized and stubborn gangster. He would not understand that it would be his and his bank's business should this building's mortgage payments go sour. Anyway, he had gotten enough money to use for the rest of his life and would soon quit his job and live abroad. Why should he care?

"Okay, Master Wang, your loan application for this office building has been approved. We will work out the payment plan in detail and notify you to come back here to sign it in a few days. By the way, say 'hi' to Master Li Ben for me."

"Ha, watch your damn mouth. I have no connection with the deputy director of the police department," he said, rather madly. Tang Daming knew then perhaps this gangster leader had been warned by Li Ben not to reveal and admit their business relationships of any kind to anyone. Otherwise he would be ousted and prosecuted by his bosses both in local and provincial governments if it spread to the public. But it was not the secret for many who were in the real estate, banking, drug-trafficking, smuggling and prostitution businesses. His name had been linked to the illegal businesses and corruption, and was notorious in his way of handling deals.

"Oh, what am I talking about? Sorry, I am really out of my mind today, please forget what I just said, Master Wang."

"You could be nailed down for that, you know," he warned and strode out of the door.

He shuddered, knowing that the gangsters could do anything against anyone whom they disliked—and with the shelter of corrupted police bureaucrats. He told himself to be careful, as he started counting the days of staying in the nation. It was the ring of a warning bell that he should act now before it was too late. He called his son and daughter to register in the preparatory class for the Test of English as the Foreign Language (TOEFL) in an English language training center in downtown Luohu. TOEFL is a test designed to evaluate the English proficiency of foreign students contemplating to study in either American or Canadian colleges: The minimum score for admission was 550 out of 800 points. This test was so popular in the nation because it was the stepping-stone for making the dream of studying abroad come true, or a ticket to freedom and better living conditions, for many America-admirers among students.

In Chinese, the pronunciation of TOEFL sounds like "My happiness depends on it." So from time to time, since the Reform and Opening policy started fifteen years ago, TOEFL had been the hottest class in all available English language training centers throughout the nation.

For many of those who had no college education or were not wealthy enough to study abroad, the only legal way to get out of the country was to marry a foreigner or an ethnic Chinese. So many bars and nightclubs where foreigners or ethnic Chinese frequented in Shenzhen were often crowded with girls trying their luck at making boyfriends with foreign citizenship, regardless of their look and age. Taking the advantage of their alien citizenship, some foreigners or ethnic Chinese or Hong Kongers made several girlfriends at one time and then replaced them often. For them, girlfriends were like clothes that they casually replaced whenever they felt pleased. Many of them even had girlfriends in various cities around the nation.

Many who were not able to secure alien boyfriends locally would place personal advertisements in Chinese-language newspapers in foreign countries through a marriage agency, or surf the Internet in Internet cafes searching for their foreign boyfriends. Most of the marriages between foreigners and Chinese citizens, according to Chinese government's statistics, never lasted long and many ended tragically. There were reports or rumors that Chinese wives would disappear once they received the right to stay in their husbands' countries. Some men even complained that their Chinese wives were kidnapped by Chinese friends or their relatives from airports before they could even meet them. A large number of complaints of wives being abused by their foreign husbands were also reported or heard by authorities.

At the same time, many men who were unable to go abroad either through the education programs or marriage, would choose to place their fate in the hands of human smugglers—the so called "Snakeheads"—by paying them an astronomical amount of money. The human-smuggling activity was especially rampant in the coastal cities and villages of the Fujan Province. The fee for smuggling a person—a so-called "Snake"—to the United States was sixty thousand U.S. dollars, an amount of money the average farmer will never make in his lifetime. But since most of their customers could not afford that kind of charge, instead of requiring them to pay the whole fee for once, the snakeheads would usually charge them a few thousand U.S. dollars as the down payment, the rest would be made in payments on a monthly basis after a person was successfully smuggled into the United States. But unfortunately, many of them had never made it to their dreamland, because they were either suffocated or dehydrated or both inside the packed and sealed containers on the cargo ships sailing in the ocean for weeks before reaching their destinations.

The male "Snakes," who survived the deadly trips, were usually sent illegally to work in Chinese restaurants or sewing factories in the United States. Their living and working conditions were similar to those for slaves in past centuries. Their salaries were way below the minimum wages, a rate stipulated and required by the state governments in the U.S., and they usually worked twelve-hour shifts seven days a week. Most of their salaries fed back into the snakeheads' pockets, and this ordeal of paying back the smuggling fee often lasted as long as ten years. Not only that, whoever got caught attempting to escape would be severely punished both physically and financially—or killed. Those who did successfully escape, the snakeheads would track down their families in China and do horrible things to them, including crippling and murdering their family members. Thus, very few "snakes" dared to escape.

Many female snakes were usually forced to be prostitutes, so that they could pay back the smuggling fees much faster—often the snakeheads demanded because they wanted to collect their money sooner. If they did not obey, they would get raped and beaten up.

Sadly, however, few snakes would tell their relatives at home about what they had suffered in foreign countries where they were smuggled. They rarely called home or wrote letters. Amazingly, many of their relatives at home were able to build new houses with the little money they occasionally sent. Their neighbors and friends admired them so and soon followed in leaving the country. As a result, many houses in the region became empty—the owners were either smuggled out or died in transit.

Wang Daming always felt superior than most others. It was not only because he had a prestigious position making incredible amounts of money, but because none of his family members needed to go through such horrible methods to immigrate to wealthier countries. It would be no problem for his children to pass the TOEFL and get admitted by one of the American or Canadian universities, as they had studied English and accounting in college. Within a year his whole family will have moved from China and settled in the foreign country of their dream. *Thank God for giving me the wit. I deserve the fortune and happiness,* he mumbled to himself.

10

As the number of local start-ups kept increasing and foreign investors kept flooding in, there became a great demand for imported automobiles (especially the luxury cars). Wanting to protect the domestic automobile industry, imported vehicles were restricted to a small quota, and charged a one-hundred-and-twenty percent tariff. Although two times more expensive than the international market, imported vehicles were only allowed for the foreign-invested or partly foreign-invested companies or the hotel and travel industry. Hardly any were owned by local citizens as they are required to obtain a difficult-to-get permit from the government to buy them. Many private companies imported them by paying foreigners or ethnic Chinese to have them registered at their firms and listed as "fake" foreign investors. This was no secret to most people and known as "You have the policy, I have the trick." But it was difficult for those who did not have the foreign connections, despite of their richness. Issuing the import permits and smuggling in foreign-made vehicles had opened quick-to-get-rich channels for both the gangsters and the powerful and corrupt government officials.

It all began when Li Ben received a call from Wang Qiang asking for help. The gangsters were smuggling luxury foreign-made cars from Hong Kong to Shenzhen by hiding them in containers transported by trucks through Huanggang customs. There were two Mercedes Benz, two BMWs, and one Lexus. But they were discovered and sequestered by Chinese customs agents.

"Master Li, I need your help because I am getting in five cars from Hong Kong, but they are now stuck in Huanggang customs," he was begging.

"What? Cars? What the fuck else have you been doing and leaving me in the dark, partner?" Li Ben croaked.

"I am sorry, Master Li, I thought it was a small potato that you would have no interest in."

"I am interested in whatever lays golden eggs. You haven't told me what else you have been sticking your ass in."

"No, Master Li, nothing else. Anything new in the future, I will consult you first. But, please, help me this time as it costs me quite a fortune."

"I tell you what, I am not sure if I can help you this time because I have no idea if that particular customs director is interested in making some quick and easy bucks. But I'll test water." He paused for a second, then continued, "And I want sixty percent of the profit if I do succeed."

"Okay, Master Li, whatever you say. I have no objection," he said humbly. "You know, we can make it much bigger if you do succeed getting that baby to team with us."

"How big can you arrange?"

"Very big if we can make it by sea instead of over land by trucks," he assured.

"But how are you going to sell them?"

"Don't worry about that, I will take care of them. Did you know that there are several car dealers in town already? We can distribute our cars through them, or we can even open our own dealership."

"That sounds very interesting, to be a car dealer," he murmured. "Okay. I will try my best to get that customs boy in."

"Good luck, Master Li."

"I need no luck, simply because no one I have met so far can resist money. That boy should not be the exception."

"Yes, we need no luck. Money is our god," he echoed.

"We are the god, idiot."

"Yes, we are the god," he muttered. "No, you are the god, Master Li."

That evening, Li Ben called the customs director to meet at the Paradise Nightclub. He hesitated at the beginning, but quickly felt that he could not turn the powerful deputy director of the police department down as he was eager to make friendship with such important person.

Arriving at the Paradise Nightclub, Chang Bing, the director of the Shenzhen customs, was greeted in a luxury karaoke room by Li Ben. A few minutes later, a group of girls wearing light-pink and flimsy silk traditional dresses with two-thirds of their breasts exposed entered the room and lined up in front of him. Looking at them awkwardly and avidly, and pretending to be shy, he mumbled, "What are you doing, Comrade Li?" But his eyes and expression betrayed him, as Li Ben watched carefully. *He is an easy-to-be-baited fish*, he thought, feeling elated. *Yes, just what kind of men in the world could resist beautiful women? And money?*

"Director Chang, which lady would you want to be your honey for tonight? Or you want more than one?" Li Ben asked, alluringly and obscenely.

I want them all, if I could, they are all so gorgeous, he thought. However, he was a high-ranking government official and could not afford to appear as decadent as a capitalist in front of this equally important communism believer. Plus, he really did not know what was in Li Ben's mind for inviting him to such a place. *Is he testing me to see how I stand in resisting the decadent bourgeois lifestyle?* he surmised. It could be his preliminary corruption investigation? Since central government's establishment of the Central Disciplinary Committee, many government officials, ranking from managers of state-owned enterprises to governors and state ministers, have been purged, jailed, or executed due to criminal charges of corruption and bribery. Although it was only a very small number of corrupt government cadres, or as the saying goes, "Only a piece of hair out of nine cows." Still, to officials, it was disturbing and annoying. It was alarming enough that Li Ben, the vice chief of the police department, had invited him to this place to begin with. *I must be careful,* he told himself and then beckoned the girls to go away.

"Comrade Li, I have never been here before. This place is so decadent, we ought not be here. Let's go somewhere else." Li Ben was stunned from what he just heard. There was no mistake that Chang Bing had been enchanted by all the beautiful women in the nightclub. Why didn't he go for them? Staring at him, Li Ben could see that his face was slightly flushed and his hands moving awkwardly with nervousness. And sheepishly, he kept glancing at the girls. He knew the man was pretending to be a moral gentleman, as the saying goes, or he was careful, lest he would be nailed down, especially when hanging around with a not-well acquainted chief law enforcer.

"Relax, Director Chang. Have some fun here and experience the decadent Western lifestyle we have missed," he said. He beckoning a girl to sit down next to him. "Serve Master Chang nicely, sweetheart."

"Yes, Master," the girl replied. Wiggling her huge snow-white breasts toward his face, she sat down and held his hands.

He moaned deeply while burying his face into the soft mounds of the young woman's bosom. An explosion of laughter erupted in the room as Li Ben offered another girl and said, "Master Chang is my guest tonight, help making him happy."

With two girls for each man, the other ladies left the room. They started hugging, caressing, kissing and moaning, and indulging themselves with full body contact and lustful sex. A waitress knocked on the door and brought in their drinks. The men's hands never lifted from the girls' breasts, nor their tongues from the girls' mouths, faces, necks and chests. These gorgeous things were really a feast for the eyes and mind. How wonderful!

Glancing at the customs director, occasionally, Li Ben mumbled agreeably. "It is hard for a great man to pass the test of being enticed by beautiful girls."

After wetting their dry mouths with a round of drinks, Li Ben asked, "Big brother Chang, what do you think of this decadent bourgeois lifestyle?"

"Oh, I love it," he replied, putting his hands to the girls' breasts again, with girls on either side. He had no scruples about being investigated by the disciplinary committee now, since the deputy police chief absorbed himself in having fun with the girls. They laughed loudly, toasting each other. The atmosphere was romantic and exciting.

"Big brother Chang," Li Ben toasted with him and asked, "would you want to come here often?"

"Yes, definitely, big brother Li, but I am sure it costs a lot to have fun here. I don't think I can afford to come here often."

"Yes, you can. You can come here as often as you want."

"Are you drunk, big brother Li? If not, you must be kidding."

"No, I am not drunk and I am not kidding, either. It is very easy for you. All you need is to cooperate with me."

"Cooperate with you? On what?" he was puzzled. Chang Bing had turned down briberies before. Hong Kong merchants had tried getting him to allow them to import foreign-made products, such as cosmetics, jewelry, and mobile phones. But he had never encountered corrupt deals requested by local government officials—not to mention law enforcers. He was stunned after what Li Ben whispered to him.

He had remained clean and never thought about committing bribery or corruption, especially with being a cadre and a member of the Communist Party for decades. That was the reason why he had been appointed to be the director of the nation's, and the world's, busiest customs agency three years ago. Central leaders said that working as the director of customs, he was actually the security guard of the nation. He had to be able to resist the bombardment of money and beautiful women launched by bourgeois elements and international criminals as rewards for doing them favors. And he must be law-abiding, as he was told again and again by his supervisors. He had sworn on that doctrine. Now the one seducing him to commit financial crime was neither a bourgeois nor an international criminal, but a deputy chief of the police in the nation's newest and most dynamic city. How shocking. He couldn't believe it. His first reaction was to reject it at once.

"No, I can't do it, it is against the law."

It was within his calculation, and Li Ben posted no surprise and no anger. He knew well enough how the cadres of the old Communist Party believed in and abided by the doctrines of loyalty and discipline, the basic requirements for being a member of that political entity.

"Ha, Director Chang, how long have you been working for the Communist Party? Thirty years? Forty years? Look at what you have and how much money you are making. Your whole month's salary is not even enough to pay for tonight's expenditure, and you want to be here often? Don't be foolish, be realistic."

He was right. For decades, Chang had worked hard for what he believed. It should be time for him to enjoy life and be entertained, but what he was earning would not even afford one night of this bourgeois life. *How pathetic,* he thought. He hesitated, then took a large gulp of the drink, and then another.

"Fill up Master Chang's glass and make him happy," Li Ben instructed the girls.

"Yes, Master Li," the girls replied, with one filling up Chang Bing's glass, the other one unzipping his pants and stroking his penis.

Slowly sipping at his drink, Chang Bing moaned with pleasure. His body warmed with alcohol and lust. Unable to control himself, he kept kissing the girls and caressing their bodies. Finally, his hand massaged one girl's sensitive furry honeypot.

"What do you think of our cooperation, Director Chang?" Li Ben asked deliberately.

"Oh, I can't wait. Let's do it. Oh! Oh!" he moaned, reaching a state of ecstasy.

"That's wonderful. There's much more fun waiting for you, big brother Chang," he said excitedly.

Filling his glass, he bottomed it up at once. "It's time to celebrate the upcoming new fortune. Help Master Chang to go to the hotel room upstairs and make him a very happy man," he ordered the two girls.

Watching them exit the room, he chirped, "Big brother Chang, have fun up there."

"I definitely will," he murmured happily.

After paying the bill, Li Ben hurried out of the nightclub. He couldn't wait to get back to the villa and have some real fun with his stunning-looking mistress.

*　　*　　*

Octopus Telecom had been working on building the automated system for the stock market, the first of such system in the nation, and it was not an easy job. Although they hired a team of experienced electronic and computer engineers, professors and technicians, key technologies were needed to make the breakthrough. They consulted and hired experts from Hong Kong or elsewhere in the Western world, and major electronic components purchased overseas. And technological and equipment transfers had to be approved by the United States government, as they were sensitive about potential negative commercial and military uses. They waited months before designs could be conducted and completed. Testing was another painstaking and frustrating task, due to countless technical errors and malfunctioned components. But Chen Song's engineers and technicians worked diligently together. They often had quick lunches and dinners while working. They were dedicated. After many sleepless nights of testing and amending the system, the project was finally completed. They celebrated with a banquet and a dance party.

After the taste of sweetness of their first success, they decided to focus on manufacturing and selling telecommunication equipment, a business not yet dominated by foreign companies. Because of lacking competition in this new field, an applicant had to wait six months and pay four thousand yuan before installing a phone. It would open up a huge market with an extremely high return; that is, if a domestic company succeeded in designing and manufacturing a telephone exchange systems that matched the quality of foreign products of the same kind. But this business was very risky, and required huge investment without a guarantee the product would work. It was starkly a gambling game for a hi-tech dream pursuer.

Daring to take the risk and investing all of the money they could get, including loans from various banks, they started first with an eight-hundred-stationary-phone exchange system. It was considered to be very small and only good for use by a company or a small town or a village. They hired top engineers and scholars in the field from all over the nation. Still, there were core technologies of the central unit processor and routers that were new to most of them. With the effective management and the zeal of taking the challenge, they worked harder than ever.

In less than a year, the design of the telephone system was completed and built. A small town in Fujin Province was their first buyer of the new system. It was critical for their design to work there, if they could survive in the business.

Once the phone system was installed in houses and offices, next came the crucial part: the system test. Disappointingly, the phones could not get through at all. It failed the test! The rest of the company's engineers and technicians were summoned immediately. Examining the entire system, part by part, they failed to spot the problem. They thought maybe it was a wiring problem. With a shortage of wire, they searched the whole region and found the badly needed wires and replaced them. Despairingly, though, the problem remained unsolved. After examining every part of the system more carefully, they still believed the problem was caused by a defective wire or cable. Expensive new wires and cables were flown in from

Shenzhen and put to use at once. However, the system remained as dead as before.

That was it. They were about to admit failure of their design to their customer, and that their company was going to be closed soon. Everyone wanted to cry. How sad. Wanting to try his last luck, Chen Song tested the circuit connecting to the central processing unit at random. To his surprise, he discovered the malfunction of a little transistor and replaced it immediately. It was the magic touch, and the system clicked to life. They were overjoyed, laughing and hugging each other excitedly. Their hard work and bravery finally paid off, and Octopus Telecom had laid its solid foundation for the lead position in telecommunication equipment manufacturing.

Chen Yong and his brother and sister showed no complacence, after gauging their very first success in this business. There was so much catching up to do with the foreign giants or a small domestic company like Octopus Telecom could be wiped out by them easily. So they did two things immediately: they appealed to the central government to be protected from competing with the foreign company; and they immediately started developing a larger telephone exchange system. In responding to their request, the central government raised the tariff of imported telephone equipment and banned the foreign companies from manufacturing them in China.

By combining the smaller systems, they were able to produce the two-thousand-phone exchange system. Amazingly, it was as reliable as the foreign-made system of the same capacity, and only a fraction of the cost.

Synchronizing with its successful designing and manufacturing team, the company paid equal efforts on marketing its products. Its sales offices were all over the nation's media and in large cities, and their advertisements were often seen on TV, and in magazines and newspapers. As a result, the business of Octopus Telecom started to take off and expand rapidly from the rural areas to cities, from coastal regions to western, and southern and northern parts of the nation.

However, with the rising number of the domestic telecommunication equipment manufacturers, competition had never been keener. As a result of the competition, phone users benefited the most. The installation fee of a phone, for instance, had been dropped from four thousand yuan to only five hundred yuan. And it could be installed in just a few days instead of half a year.

More significantly to the nation, the telecom business had reversed from being dominated by foreign firms. This would ultimately benefit the country's economy and the defense system, because having its own national telecommunication system was almost as important as having its own armed forces—from a military point of view.

Willing to spend most of its profits on researching and developing new and larger and more advanced phone systems, they kept Octopus Telecom's competitive edge sharp. Designing and developing each new phone system required hundreds of million of yuan, and Octopus Telecom had never hesitated doing it. Now they decided to build a ten-thousand-phone exchange system, the largest phone system ever available in both international and domestic markets. This ambitious new project not only swallowed up most of the company's funds, but also required numerical technological breakthroughs. The company's toughest technological battle had just begun.

*　　*　　*

Hundreds of foreign cars without import permits and without being charged with a tariff passed through the Huanggang customs and entered Shenzhen every month. They had been sold privately or distributed to various auto dealers in town. It was the easiest money the corrupt officials and gangsters had ever made so far, but they couldn't allow too many in at one time because it was too conspicuous. They could make more money without looking suspicious if they could get lots of import permits, they figured. Due to the limited quota allocated for the city by central government, import permits were tightly controlled by the traffic and finance departments, and the vice mayor. It was easy for the gangsters to crack through the traffic and finance departments by recruiting corrupt officials in charge of approving the permits, but they had no confidence in getting the vice mayor to join their team.

They decided to test him.

Li Ben had learned much about the vice mayor. Han Fang was sixty-one and interested in buying a house for his retirement, which was soon. A recent decision by central government stated that provincial and city officials had to retire when they reached age sixty-three. So, then, Han Fang and his family could move out of the government apartment buildings and live leisurely in their own private home.

One Saturday morning, he invited the vice mayor to see a house. He and his chauffeur arrived in a black BMW and picked him up from the gate of the government apartment building. Once inside the car, the vice mayor was impressed by its luxuriousness. It was no comparison to the government-issued vehicle assigned for his use. The car rolled swiftly and smoothly along Coast Boulevard toward the east. The bay was on their left while the hills rolled skyward on their right. Well-shaped and trimmed flowers and trees and newly constructed buildings on both sides of the road appeared and receded rapidly. The early summer oceanic morning breeze made them feel good.

"You are very capable, Director Li," the vice mayor praised, with admiration.

"It's all because of your good leadership, Mayor Han," he replied, condescendingly.

Han Fang smiled bitterly. Compared with Li Ben's ranking, he was supposed to be his supervisor. But in reality, the deputy director of the police department was more powerful than he, because as a vice mayor he had no right to direct the police department. And because of that, few people would bribe him for favors. That was why he had remained relatively clean among the high-ranking municipal government officials.

"I feel flattered because I have never contributed anything or given advice on your work."

"That's not true, Mayor Han. I have always been influenced indirectly by your great leadership."

The vice mayor said nothing. He knew that the powerful police deputy director would not invite him to see a house that he badly needed if he had no usable value for him. But what was in his mind?

Their car climbed up a flyover and down south toward the sea. Turning a quick right, a cluster of newly-built villas appeared. They looked expensive and breathtaking. Li Ben had no intention of revealing it to his guest that the real estate company he remotely controlled had built them. The units were selling five million yuan for each.

"Don't waste time, Director Li, just take me to that house I want to see. I need to get back to work after this," Han Fang mumbled impatiently.

"The house is here, Mayor Han."

"Are you kidding? How can I afford it?" he cried.

"Yes, you can," he replied, succinctly.

The car stopped in front of the gate of a villa. Two security guards and a man in a suit and tie raced toward the car. Before the man could say anything, the car door flung open and Li Ben chimed, "Master Sun, I have brought a very important customer for you. Come to look at who he is."

The man got closer to the car and looked inside and cried, "Oh, what a pleasure, Vice Mayor Han Fang. I am so happy to see you here."

Han Fang got out of the car and shook his hand. "Nice meeting you, Master Sun."

Li Ben patted the man's shoulder and said, "Mayor Han is interested in buying this villa here. Can you take him inside to look at it?"

"Sure, my pleasure. Come with me, please, Mayor Han."

"No! No! It's a mistake, Master Sun. I can not afford this luxurious house," he shook his head and sighed.

"Don't be too modest, mayor Han. I am sure you can afford it," the man said.

"But how?"

Li Ben patted his back and said, "It's easy. Let's go inside and talk about it, Mayor Han."

Touring and looking around curiously, Han Fang loved the house very much and felt like he was dreaming. He had never imagined living in a five-million-yuan villa with his income of only two thousand yuan per month. And he was the second most powerful person in the city, theoretically. For his decades of dedicated hard work for the cause of communism, he now started to believe he deserved to own a house like this and have a comfortable living for the rest of his life. But he had been taught to believe in the doctrine of keeping a humble and frugal profile as a people's servant for as long as he remained in the current position. Was it necessary any longer? The society had changed dramatically. What is practiced now nationwide used to be criticized as the capitalistic exploiting system. As the society changed, people's thinking and belief had changed as well, he concluded. His reverie was interrupted when Li Ben patted him again.

"What are you thinking, Mayor Han?"

"Oh, nothing. I'm just thinking how lovely this house is."

"It can be yours if—" Li Ben paused for a second, stared at him and then continued, "If you cooperate with us."

"On what?" he marveled and his heart started beating quickly. If he could own such a beautiful house for just a little favor in return, he would not hesitate doing so.

"Well, thanks for our great leader Deng Xiaoping's policy of Reform and Opening, these days many people have become rich and they need new fancy stuff like foreign cars to play with. If we can help them to get what they are craving, we are doing a good service for the people. What do you think, Mayor?"

Now Han Fang understood what cooperation his counterpart wanted him to do—he had the ultimate authority to issue permits for importing foreign cars in the city. But it was against the law and the nation's interest to do so. As a high-ranking communist official, his reaction was to reject it at once.

"No, sorry, I can't do it."

Li Ben fully understood how his prey would react at first, and was confident in getting him. Yet this was the biggest fish for him to catch, and he must be patient.

"Mayor Han, don't you want to 'get two birds down with the same rock,' so that you may serve our citizens while helping yourself a bit?"

Han Fang hesitated and did not say anything. His mind was fighting fiercely. It was hard for him to abandon the decades-old principle of a law-abiding and devoted communist and leader.

"You know, Mayor, it is not fair for our citizens to just give out these permits to the joint-adventure companies, anyway. What I want you to do is to rectify it a bit while doing yourself a favor. Doesn't it sound wonderful?"

"Let me think about it," he said.

He knew that the vice mayor was giving in. Just one more little push, and the job would be done.

"I just want to remind you, Mayor, your power will expire in little more than a year. For your own benefit, you should take this opportunity and put it to good use now. Besides, someone is interested in buying this villa, I do not know if Master Sun could wait any longer. I can pay it for you now if you agree with our cooperation."

The police deputy director was right, he was going to be powerless in less than two years, as he would be retired. This was perhaps the last chance for him to get his dream house, with his power. *Do it,* he decided.

"Okay, Director Li, let's discuss it in details."

"Great, I am glad you have finally made the wise decision, Mayor."

11

Watching the stunning success of Octopus Telecom, Tang Daming was filled with awe and hatred. He could have been one of the shareholders of this skyrocketing hi-tech monster if he and his bank had not been kicked out as the major loan provider. *Without my help right at the beginning, this Chen Yong brat never could have had a chance to become today's nationally renowned hi-tech entrepreneur. What a traitor,* Tang Daming thought, raging with disgust. He would not let Chen Yong get off easily. He had to figure out a way to teach him a lesson, to revenge such action of ingratitude, and let him know the consequence of not abiding by the rule of business.

Searching news reports and bribing one of the Octopus Telecom's bookkeepers, he learned that Chen Yong often had good business sense, but also possessed the passion for gambling; he would use up almost all the savings and resources available for each new system's research and development. He was a mad gambler and this business, indeed, was a gambling business. Should the project fail, his company would be forced to close down; and at the same time, if the company stopped developing new technologies and new products, it would be rapidly beaten up by its competitors.

To carry out his plan of vengeance, he plotted two schemes. First he would bribe a technical person of the Octopus Telecom, the one person capable to cripple both the software and hardware of the ambitious ten-thousand-phone exchange system—the latest and largest phone system aimed to compete with foreign giants in the field. Then he would inform Octopus Telecom's loan providers of how Chen Yong operated his company and persuade them to stop lending money to his firm. Without sufficient funds to resolve the technical problems caused by the traitor, this project would be stranded and, consequently, ruin the company. That was it. He wanted to see Octopus Telecom ruined and closed, stripping Chen Yong to worthlessness.

Through the Octopus Telecom bookkeeper he had bribed, Tang Daming learned about a testing engineer badly in need of cash due to his wife's sickness. He arranged to meet him at a café the next day.

"A-Sun, I am so sorry to hear that your wife has breast cancer. These days, no one would share the pain and the cost of the medical bill with you. Our society has changed such that everyone has become indifferent and selfish, and the public health system has been abandoned. How terrible it all has become." Tang Daming sighed, sympathetically.

The man's face saddened, wanting to cry. He muttered, sadly, "What have I done wrong? Why do I have to suffer this?"

He patted the man and consoled him, "What has happened can not be avoided, you have to accept it and face it. You must be strong because you still have your wife, children, and parents—all to be cared for, by you."

The man was unable to control his emotions. "How can I be strong when my wife is dying and the medical bills keep piling up?"

"Don't worry about it, it's why I am here to help."

The man gazed at him tearfully, and in doubt. He questioned, "How? Are you trying to sell me the sky-high-interest loan, like sprinkling salt on my wound?"

"No, no, not like that at all. I am here to help you, sincerely."

"Really?" the man snickered, doubtfully. "There is no free lunch, just what do you want from me?"

He was right, nowadays no one would do favors for others for nothing in return. Tang Daming forced a smile and said, "I tell you what, it's very easy. If you can do me a little favor, I will give you one hundred thousand yuan in cash."

"What? One hundred thousand yuan for a little favor?" he couldn't believe what he was hearing. With that kind of money, he could pay off all of his debts and his wife's medical bills for years to come should she still be alive," What do you want me to do?"

"Simple, just tamper a bit the software of your company's new project and break a few parts of the hardware here and there. A piece of cake for you, right?"

"What? How dare you? No way will I hurt my company," he protested angrily. He loved what he was doing and his company. It was a challenging job in a vibrant company. In fact, he always felt proud and lucky to be part of it.

Now Tang Daming understood why Octopus Telecom could grow and expand miraculously. It had won the hearts of its employees. He was in awe of it. But, damn it, it was none of this man's business that Chen Yong had betrayed him, yet he had to pay.

"Good, I like you. I like your dedication and loyalty. I really want you to be my friend. But tell me, what would you do if you learn that a friend has betrayed you?"

"I would revenge it."

"Right, that's what I am trying to do. Your boss hurt me after his fledgling success began with my help. Should I let it go or do tit for tat?"

"Really? You helped him to do business?"

"Yes, he was a taxi driver fifteen years ago. I loaned him the money to start a taxi business. He agreed to give me shares, but later kicked me out after he shifted his business to the hi-tech field."

"But he and his brother and sister are very nice to us all, and we adore them and the company."

"Yes, nice veneer, but rotten inside."

"But I still don't want to hurt them or the company, because my career and my future are there."

"But do you think you and your family still have a future, if your wife's illness drags on and your debts keeps piling up? Come on, for you and your family and me, do it."

The man hesitated and said nothing, it was a painful decision to make. He muttered, "I can't imagine seeing my company get hurt so badly because of me, and I can't imagine getting caught."

"The worst they could do to you is to fire you, but with the money I am giving you, you don't need to work for a few years. You can move to somewhere else and start your new career."

The man raised his head and stared to the sky for several minutes and muttered, "How do I get paid?"

"I give you thirty thousand first, then pay you the rest once you finish doing the job."

"Okay."

"Good, I hope to hear your good news soon."

*　　*　　*

It was a dramatic shift for Lin Dan from being the extremely busy career woman to a full-time mistress to an evil man. She lived like a caged bird. Except at nighttime with the man, she was the only person in the huge and empty house during most of the day-time, and her meals were delivered to her every day. A part-time maid, who came every other day handled the housework. Staying in a little cottage in the backyard, the chauffeur was in on-call basis consistently. Taking turns of the day and night shifts in the booth at the gate, the two security guards were not allowed to go in the house without any security-related reasons. Although she had accepted her fate, Lin Dan couldn't get used to doing nothing every day, and she noticed lately that her belly was getting a little bigger due to the plenty of sleep and lack of exercise. She requested to go out shopping three times in a week, it was granted, but it had to be with the company of the chauffeur. She would buy novels and some other books, music cassettes and movie videotapes, clothes and make-up every time she went out.

Feeling bored and wasted, she started making some changes. First she got up early and did morning exercises. Then learned to cook from the cookbooks. She cooked not only for herself, but also for the man, and even the chauffeur and the security guards. The man especially liked the variety of long-hour soups she cooked almost everyday. Besides that, she asked to hire private tutors to teach her English, piano, and dance. All of the tutors the man hired for her were female, but that was fine for her. So her days were getting busy and structured again. Despite all of her changes, Li Ben liked her even more. She began to accept and like him more as days went on. Their relationship, unlike the form of angel versus devil at the beginning, began to shift toward friendship and intimacy.

Although their feelings toward each other had changed, deep in Lin Dan's heart no one could replace Chen Yong as her only lover. From time to time, she couldn't stop thinking about him, the marriage ritual, and the happy night they had on the day before their separation. Even though she was not allowed to see and call him, she knew from newspapers and her friends how successful Octopus Telecom had become. She really regretted missing the excitement of building up a hi-tech empire with her lover. She wished justice would be done one day, so that they could be together again. Lin Dan really didn't know if Chen Yong still loved her, now that her body and soul had been violated by an evil man. Maybe he had a new girlfriend already, which would be sad. Lin Dan wished him happiness. The ultimate meaning of life, she believed, was happiness after all. Jealousy and hatred would only destroy happiness. Man should never create hatred, but once it was created, be careful of getting hurt. She learned this knowledge from a philosophy book and thoroughly agreed with it.

Suddenly, she remembered the banker, who had a grudge with Chen Yong and his firm. He was as evil and wicked as the man holding her captive. Her instinct and sense of logic knew that he would do something to revenge and harm her lover and his firm. She picked up the phone and called her friend, Wu Ting, to warn Chen Yong about the banker and hoped that it would not be too late. She prayed.

Sitting leisurely after a cup of hot tea, Lin Dan recalled and savored what Wu Ting had told her about her hunting-for-a-mister-right story two days ago.

Wu Ting, twenty-six, a delicate and nice-looking girl, was still unmarried and without a serious boyfriend. She often read the personal advertisements in the newspapers. One day, she saw an ad which read, "Male, thirty-two, handsome, kindhearted and humorous, never been married, college graduate, owns an electronic factory, a luxury car, and several apartments. Looking for a pretty, tender, and honest girl for friendship first, and then marriage."

She was moved by the ad, and wanted to respond to it at once, but remembered that most of the personal ads in the newspapers and magazines were fake ads placed by the marriage agencies to attract customers. Anxiously, she picked up the phone and responded to the wonderful ad she had just read. She was instructed that she needed to bring four hundred yuan as the membership fee to the marriage agency, and then the address and direction to get there. Once there and fee paid, a clerk brought her into a room and had her wait. Sitting nervously for ten minutes, the clerk returned accompanied by a tall and handsome young man, then introduced him as the man from the ad. Her heartbeat accelerated and she fell in love with him instantly. The clerk left and closed the door at once.

The man spoke of how lovely she looked, and how lucky he was to meet her. With hands fidgeting and heart pounding uncontrollably, Wu Jing was barely able to speak. The man extended his hand and she slowly and shyly grabbed it. Her face flushed. They started talking fervently while holding hands and looking at each other like a pair of lovers. She was already crazy about him and regretted not having met him earlier. Fifteen minutes passed. The clerk came in and said that if they wanted to date each other they should exchange paper numbers now and then leave. Scribbling each other's pager numbers in a hurry, she said goodbye to him, involuntarily. She couldn't stop thinking about him on the way home and that evening, and smiled and kept thanking God for giving her such "A prince riding on a white horse." He was so perfect, my god.

She woke up early the next morning and paged him. Half an hour passed and there was no response. *Maybe there is a system problem. There is no reason for the man who appeared so sincere, gentle and classic not to return my call.* She kept paging him every twenty minutes until noon. Finally, her phone rang. With her heart pounding, she hurriedly answered it at once. At the other end was a man's magnetic voice. It was him, she suddenly had a hard time breathing.

"I'm so sorry to return your call so late. I have been busy the whole morning."

"It's okay, I understand. I wonder if we may have dinner together tonight."

"Oh, I don't know whether I will have customers to meet tonight or not. I will call you later," he replied before hanging up.

It was understandable and perfectly fine with her as he was a busy businessman. She could wait, just like the saying, "Fine things will take a while to get." For the rest of the day, she sat next to the phone and waited for it to ring. It rang a few times, but each time she was disappointed as it was her friend's call and not him. Into the evening, she still had no luck. *Probably he has been too busy,* she consoled herself, *or perhaps he has forgotten me.* She paged him again, then again half an hour later, and then every hour. By midnight, she still received no calls from the man, and started to realize that maybe she had been swindled, but she was unsure.

Feeling sad, she fell off to sleep. The next morning, she began paging him again and kept paging him the entire day countless times. Still she heard nothing from the man. She then called the marriage agency and shouted and screamed to them for cheating her. The clerk asked her to calm down and that she would ask the man what had happened and would call her back. Twenty minutes later, the clerk called back explaining why the man had not returned her call: he didn't like her. So there was nothing they could do except letting her return to the office and meet other male members periodically. She knew it was a lie, but there was nothing she could do against that marriage agency. Maybe it was true the man didn't like her. A man of that quality was too good for her anyway. Even if they had liked each other, dated and eventually married, she was afraid that he would have lots of mistresses. *Forget it,* she told herself. She would have to be down to earth and practical to find her mister right, as the one who was suitable to her ought to be a moderate and honest man.

Having been cheated by the agency, she was too ashamed to tell her friends. In the meantime, she kept reading personal ads in the newspapers daily, and one day found one that caught her attention. It read, "Male, 178 cm, 36, single, a returned scholar from America, owns apartment, marriage-oriented, looking for a pretty, down to earth and committed girl." So the man was a teacher with an overseas education background and a home—the kind of moderate man she was hunting for, and he was older—meant more trustable. She called and found out that it was from a different marriage agency, in a different district, and the fee for becoming a member was the same. She guessed that was the standard charge by all marriage agencies in the city.

Having paid the fee after arrival, she was told to follow a clerk to a room. Entering the room, through the dim light, she saw a man sitting on the sofa. Getting closer to the man before the clerk introduced her to him, she suddenly recognized the man was the same one from the previous agency she had met before. She screamed. Feeling sick and outraged, she yelled at them and demanded an apology.

After speaking with the man, the clerk said, "We don't care whether you have met him somewhere else before, it was his first time to be here. If you don't like him, you may come back to meet other male members another time." So no refund or apology were made.

And the man strode out of the room, saying, "I've never met you before, girl. You make me wrong."

There was no mistake about this man, she was sure. She could even recognize a mole near his earlobe on the left side of his face.

She shouted loudly, "Stop cheating people, you trash. I am going to report you to the police."

"Go ahead and get out of here before we get nasty, girl," a male clerk replied.

She ran out with rage. Wandering on the street, she called Lin Dan and told her the story, who felt sorry about her. "You are silly to trust those marriage agencies. Don't you know there are a lot of cheaters and swindlers in town nowadays? Before you do anything, discuss it with me first from now on, Ting Ting. There is no use to report it to the police. They don't care about this kind of thing, because many of them are cheaters as well."

Wu Ting used to be one of her subordinates at Chen Yong's company, and had become good friends. She had also become the messenger between her and her lover after their forced separation. Since becoming friends, Wu Ting had confided with her and told her many of her experiences.

One of the remarkable ones took place when she was walking with her friend on Foot Street, a car-free street filled with various fashion shops. The place was crowded as usual. A girl with a bag on her back was walking a few feet ahead of them. Suddenly, a young man came from nowhere, got in front of them, and followed the girl. A few minutes later, the man cut open the girl's bag, but the girl did not notice. She wanted to yell to inform the girl what was happening to her, but her friend stopped her immediately, telling her that there usually were other accomplices around with the man and would hurt anyone trying to help his victims. It was so terrifying and frustrating to see the victim being harmed and stolen from while other innocent pedestrians watched. There seemed to be lots of horrible news stories happening in the city and around the nation, Wu Ting told her, since being caged as the evil man's mistress. The fear of one of the horrible news stories still lingered in her mind.

An owner of a restaurant adjacent to a primary school in a city of a nearby province poisoned thirty-eight students to death. Many more people became ill by this owner, who placed poison into the water tank of his rivaling restaurant next door, all because he just wanted to get more business. How horrible.

Our society has changed so much since adopting the Reform and Opening policy. While people's material life had improved significantly, crime became rampant as people's greed and desire got unbound from the isolated and depressed society under Mao's leadership. *How sad and pitiful,* she sighed, being a victim of crime and a citizen who had to live in this kind of environment.

Once in a while, Wu Ting found some entertaining and controversial news rather than the usual sad and frightening fare. One was about a young man in a remote rural area who had been married for three years and queried a doctor as to why his wife had never been pregnant. After diagnosing his wife completely and carefully, the doctor discovered astonishingly that she was still a virgin. The doctor then asked if they had had sex in the past years, the young man said yes. The doctor was puzzled, asking them how. Embarrassingly, the young man showed him that he had made love to his wife's anus in all of these years. Hearing that, the doctor didn't know whether to laugh or cry, but calmly sighed. *How could such a thing happen in the twentieth century?*

Another news story Ling Dan found hard to accept was that of a twenty-year-old girl who, with the help of a journalist, had placed an ad in the newspaper. She stated that the man who could give her five thousand yuan for treating her father's illness, she would marry him. It was pathetic, startling and shocking for such a thing in modern society.

She really appreciated and felt grateful that her friend had kept her informed of what had been happening in the nation.

*   *   *

After receiving a warning call from Lin Dan's friend, Chen Yong felt heavy pain inside his heart. Despite that time had diluted the bitterness, pain, and despair caused by their forced separation, Chen Yong couldn't stop thinking about her. They had been apart for three years and he had met so many lovely girls in the hi-tech business circle who often expressed admiration to him. Some even flirted to him. He had no intention of making a new girlfriend because he still believed he was married to Lin Dan and had never lost hope that they would be together someday. From her friends' phone calls and, eventually, one or two of her recent photos delivered by them, he obtained her updated information, which was enough to sustain him with high hope. The call from Wu Ting was another proof that Lin Dan still cared very much about him and his firm. He would never mind her history of being a mistress, because she was coerced to sacrifice herself for the ones she loved.

Thinking about the warning call, Chen Yong agreed with his lover that the greedy and malicious banker, Tang Daming, would do something to retaliate and harm his business venture. He wondered what the banker would do, since nothing harmful toward him or his firm had happened in the past three years. Would he give up doing anything disastrous? But there was a saying that said, "It was not too late to revenge after ten years." Did this man possess such mentality?

What the banker could do the most harm, he thought, *is by persuading other bankers not to loan my company any more funds.* But his company had been making enough profits for future developments that it did not need to borrow money from banks anymore. So there was not much to worry about, he felt, because his company was shielded from vicious financial attacks.

He started to clear his mind and sort things out before getting back to work, and then the phone rang. It was his brother. "Big brother, something terrible has happened. We caught A-Sun trying to break the central processing unit of the new project, and the software of it has malfunctioned because of him."

"Really? Why did he do that? Have you questioned him yet?" he gasped. The software alone could take days or even months to repair.

"Not yet, big brother. Would you, please, come over to the research lab?"

"Yes, I'll be right there in a minute."

At the research lab, he saw the test engineer sitting in a chair with his head slumped down surrounded and questioned by his brother and several of his colleagues.

"We all have treated you like a brother, why would you want to destroy our company?" Chen Song asked.

"Yes, A-Sun, why?" another colleague questioned.

Shaking his head and keeping it slumped down, the man mumbled, "Sorry, sorry to you all. I didn't initiate doing it."

Chen Yong patted on the man on his shoulder and said, "A-Sun, we all know that you would not do anything on your own to hurt our company. You are our good brother and, I believe, you will still be, despite of what you did."

The man grabbed Chen Yong's hand and cried, "Please, excuse me, big brother Chen."

"I've already forgiven you, brother A-Sun, but would you tell us who convinced you to do this?"

"Will you fire me, if I tell you who he is?" the man worried.

"No. I told you I have excused you already."

"The banker, Tang Daming, who knew I needed money badly. He bribed me to do that and said he wanted to revenge you for getting rid of him from this business."

That was it. Tang Daming, the greedy banker, carrying out his malicious vengeance, was the perpetrator. But lucky enough, it didn't cause any lethal damage to the project and to the company. *But why would it happen just right after Lin Dan's warning?* Chen Yong wondered. *Did she know the banker's plot? Or it was just a coincidence?* Anyway, Chen Yong needed to defend himself from the banker's accusation.

"Well, he is a greedy and corrupt banker that I wanted to stay away from once I have the chance. I've always wanted to be a law-abiding businessman, if I can."

"We know you are a good businessman, big brother Chen. We love and support you and this company; no one can hurt us again," one employee said.

"Should we report this to the police?" another one asked.

"No, because A-Sun will be prosecuted by the police. We don't want to inflate the issue. We can solve it quietly by ourselves," Chen Yong said. He didn't want to expose his past under-the-table deal with the banker, which would harm his and the firm's reputation. He would never want to do that.

"A-Sun, you help clean up the software, and our company will pay for your wife's medical expenditures."

The man bowed to Chen Yong three times, with his forehead hitting the floor soundly each time, and cried, "Thanks so much for your love, kindness, and generosity, big brother Chen. I promise that I will follow you and be loyal to you for the rest of my life."

He pulled the man back on his feet and continued, "A-Sun is our brother. No one should discriminate him, ever."

Everyone shook hands and hugged with the man. Some murmured, "A-Sun, you've admitted and rectified your mistake. We are still brothers. There is no difference from before."

"Yes, we are supposed to care, help, and love each other as a harmonious and happy family here."

"Let's work together and harder to make our company the best in the country."

Seeing and hearing what his employees were saying, Chen Yong was touched. He declared, "I tell you what, our company is going to buy medical insurance for all of you and your family members. For those of you who don't know what medical insurance is as it is new to all of us, let me explain. If any of you or your family members become sick and need medical treatment, an insurance company will pay for most of your medical expenditures. This includes your salaries when you are absent from work due to the sickness. Our company has bought that benefit from that insurance company for you."

There was a rupture of excitement among the employees, and they praised to their boss:

"How wonderful!"

"We will no longer worry about being in the situation like A-Sun any more. Wonderful!"

"Thank you very much, big brother Chen."

Thanks to Tang Daming's malicious scheme, this destructive episode had turned from a negative effect to one of boosting the employees' morale. Chen Yong was delighted. He wanted to take this chance to further strengthen his employees' sense of belonging. The issue of letting employees be shareholders had been discussed for some time during the company's board of directors meetings. He beckoned the crowd to hush, then said, "Here I would like to take this opportunity to announce another bit of good news."

There was another thunder of cheers rumbling among the employees.

"Oh, good things come in pairs. How wonderful!"

"Big brother Chen, what is it? We can't wait to hear it."

"We should celebrate and remember this day."

Waving and urging them to calm down, Chen Yong pronounced, "Brothers and sisters, our company has decided to adopt the new policy of granting each one of you shares of this company as a reward for your loyalty, dedication, and hard work. We will distribute the number of shares to each one of you in accordance with your contribution to the company. So from now on, all of you are owners of this firm. Let's work the hardest we can to make our company the best world-class telecom company in the market.''

Right after his speech, a rejoicing commotion exploded. Everyone was hugging, dancing and yelling with joy. Chen Yong and his brother and sister were lifted up above the heads of the crowd and thrown into the air repeatedly.

Then another bookkeeper cried out, "I am so sorry, I have done some terrible and betraying things to our company, and am now willing to take whatever punishments required.''

A jumbled noise erupted, with the sudden change of atmosphere. Many were startled.

"Ah, another one?''

"What bad things have you done to our company?''

"I revealed our company's financial information to that banker and made the connection of A-Sun with him,'' she admitted.

A rumbling commendation and condemnation, and then appreciation began engulfing the room. Some expressed their anger, and others praised her courage. The rest had no opinions of their own and waited for Chen Yong's decision.

Listening to them and talking with his siblings, Chen Yong made up his mind. He pulled the bookkeeper over and said loudly, "Brothers and sisters, we really appreciate Miss Chai Ting's courage of admitting her wrongdoings. We should forgive her and reaccept her and give her the opportunity to continue making her contribution to our company.''

Applause began somewhere, and then quickly grew and spread through the entire group. The rumbling was deafening.

Tears rolled out of Chai Ting's eyes. "This can only happen at Octopus Telecom. I would have been given no chance to stay if at another companies. Thank you so much. I promise I will never do anything to hurt our company again.'' Another thunder of applause erupted.

12

The stock market, where enterprises in the Western world absorb investments for helping their growth and development by selling their corporate shares, was new to most of the Chinese population. Deciding to learn from the capitalist system since the beginning of the Reform and Opening, the nation had hired overseas securities experts (mostly from Hong Kong) and established a stock market in Shenzhen and in Shanghai.

To avoid being manipulated by sophisticated international opportunists and financial crocodiles, foreigners and foreign entities were not allowed to invest in either of these two markets.

At the beginning, no one knew what the stock market was all about. Very few people were willing to pull out their hard-earned savings from their pockets in exchange for stock certificates. But as the government placed the advertisements in the newspapers and magazines and TV programs explaining the benefits and the procedures of buying and trading them, as well as circulating a few stories about people who became rich from buying stocks, people started lining up in front of the securities offices with bundles of cash in their pockets and bags. Soon stocks became the hottest subject in people's conversation. For every company's IPO, people were lining up for days and nights to buy its stock. As a result, the stock prices soared, so did the index. In spite of the overheat warning given by the stock trading experts and the government, people just simply ignored the risk. The hot money continued to flow into the stock market from various enterprises, banks, and individuals.

Like many greedy bankers who had anxiously kept their eyes on the stock market every day, Tang Daming decided to get his feet wet. Amazingly, as the index kept rising, and whatever stock he bought, he made a great deal of money. To make more money, he was not only using his own money, but the bank's as well. However, this time, the stock index dipped for several days, and he had lost lots of money for getting out too soon.

Watching and trading in the stock market for a while, he had figured out an ambitious plan to make real big money. His plan required a huge amount of capital, but he could not use too much of the bank's money because of the bank's regulations. Instead he persuaded the gangsters' Earth Dragon Real Estate Company Limited, which was remotely controlled by the police deputy director Li Ben, to join his plan. They jumped in immediately, as they had observed the stock market for a period of time, but did not know which agent to be trusted.

Despite a few ups and downs, the overall index was on a rising trend. That was good for both the long-term investors and the speculators. And it worked extraordinary well for Tang Daming's plan.

Combining three parties' capitals, with nearly one hundred million yuan under his control, Tang Daming chose a relatively small and newly listed company to start with. He first paid a few stock commentators to write about how well that company had been operating and how bright a future it would have. Then he started to snap up the stock of that company. As a result, for every five million yuan he spent in buying that stock, more than a hundred million yuan followed in. The stock price soared like a skyrocket. When its price reached to an unbelievable high, he sold all of his shares quickly before others were able to do so. Doing that, he made huge profits each time. Tang Daming and his partners were overjoyed, and kept on investing all of their capital to make more and bigger deals. They got greedier as they saw more and more success and wealth.

"Great job, big brother Tang." Li Ben often called to praise him.

"Yes, Master Li, we are the god. The market does what we want it to do. How exciting!" Tang Daming boasted in reply.

"If it keeps going this smoothly, big brother Tang, we will be able to buy the whole city."

"You bet, Master Li, and we definitely will."

"I have no idea how to spend this money, big brother Tang."

"Well, we can have lots of beautiful women, buy properties around the world and, of course, travel as much as we want."

"Oh, you just reminded me. I have thought about opening a nightclub. It should be the biggest and most lavishly-decorated in town and, of course, we will only hire the most beautiful girls to work there. So doing this, we can have fun with a variety of beautiful girls every day while making a sizable profit. What do you think, my dear big brother Tang?''

It's too conspicuous, idiot. Too big a tree will often be attacked by the wind. I am going abroad soon, forget it, he pondered.

''It's a wonderful idea, but I tell you what, I am not interested in doing my own business of any kind. Why don't you open it and let me be your customer, Master Li.''

''Okay, no push on you. Let me do it. But you have to visit often.''

''I promise I will, and I will get a pair of your beautiful chicks there each time.''

''You're an nasty old man, I will remember now. And you will have lots of fun there, too, lots of fun.''

''Ha, I don't know a man who is not nasty, Master Li. There are three reasons for a man not want to have fun with lots of women: either he doesn't have money, he has a physical problem, or he is gay.''

''You are damned right, and we have none of those horrible things,'' he chuckled.

*   *   *

Located in the downtown Shenzhen, close to Luohu customs, the biggest and most luxury nightclub in the nation's largest economic zone called Happy Palace was opened four months later. With a myriad of colorful neon lights flashing about and a powerful searchlight rotating its giant light-beam in the sky, the grand opening ceremony started right in front of the nightclub. Hundreds of stunning and beautiful girls, recruited throughout the country from advertisements placed in major newspapers of every province, dressed in colorful silky costumes of all fifty-six races of the nation. Each held bouquets in their hands and stood around the vestibule where a scaffold had been erected. Well-groomed in suit and tie and in charge of the nightclub, Wang Qiang gave a short speech and announced the grand opening of the place. Immediately a thunder of beating drums and gongs struck away the quietness of the night, and then the lion dance. A huge lion rolled and jumped up and down with two baby lions following the masked-clown guide

102

and to the rhythm of the drums and gongs. There were explosions of laughter among the onlookers as the clown, with a fan in hand, danced like a drunken old man and the lions were trying hard to imitate.

After the lion dance, a group of nearly-naked girls came onto the scaffold and performed a voluptuous dance erotic enough for a man to have a wild fantasy. The girls standing around the scaffolding started passing out free drinks to the onlookers. Excited shouting, screaming and applauses exploded among the audience during each performance. The ritual ending with the girls, in groups of two, performing on the catwalk.

The onlookers were then invited to follow the girls as they streamed inside the nightclub. The building had five stories, with the ground and first floors designated as parking lots. The disco was on the second floor. There was a kidney-shaped stage with counters around which customers could talk and drink and play games with the girls, while watching the performance up on the third floor. The forth and fifth floors were private rooms. These were the dream places for karaoke and for the men to have fun and sex with girls.

For the first three days, it was fifty percent off for every customer's total expenditure. What attracted men the most was the night club's good-looking girls. It was crowded every night with men from Hong Kong, foreign joint-venture companies, local start-ups, corrupt government officials, and whoever had the money to afford being there. One wondered what the poor men or ugly girls would say. Maybe, cynically, "Beauty is only skin deep, the mind is more important." But the fact was that men were created shallow, and they would only go for beautiful women.

The nightclub was proven to be another moneymaking machine. Li Ben was happy, but as a high-ranking government official, he didn't go there often. He did not want to be exposed to the public. He let the gangster head take charge of it all. Once in a while, a violent event would occur if a customer did not have enough money to cover his expenses. Often, a victim would be beaten up, fingers chopped off, or an ear or a testicle removed—whatever punishment to cripple him. Rarely had anyone dared to report to the police due to the risk of being exposed to family members, friends, and colleagues. After all, although it was legal, it was not socially acceptable for a man to go to this kind of place.

As a special economic zone bordering the former British colony, Shenzhen had become a paradise for many Hong Kong men, especially truck drivers who helped move goods in and out of the mainland. They took the advantage of having a higher income, came here to have a sexual affair, to look for a wife, or find the mistress of their dreams. Although the law prohibited prostitution, police rarely enforced it. A fine of six thousand yuan was levied for each man got caught having sex with a prostitute. In fact, there were several notorious residential areas such as Bujy, Wasichian, Xanshachian, and Sashachian which were dubbed as a "red-light zone" or "mistress village."

Many beauty salons and massage houses were actually brothels. A large number of girls sitting inside in various new and old apartment buildings of these residential areas throughout the city were prostitutes. Amazingly, most of these girls were teenagers. The number of these shops in some areas, as some citizens described, were much greater than the shops selling rice and daily necessities. Also, many brothels were controlled by gangsters and protected by corrupt police officers.

The traditional saying, "Poor people are despicable but prostitutes," was yet truly applicable here. Perhaps it was the price a society had to pay for gaining material prosperity, in progressing from inhumane to humane, and from being economically depressed to being free.

*   *   *

Greed grew fast without limits. The astronomical income the police deputy director, the vice mayor, and the director of the customs received from importing and smuggling automobiles from Hong Kong to Shenzhen via land no longer satisfied their appetite of monetary greed. They got together in Lin Ben's villa to discuss the possibility of smuggling other commodities such as mobile phones, home appliances, diesel and gasoline over the sea. Before they arrived to the villa, Lin Dan was told to stay in the bedroom. Although they were working as a gang, Li Ben didn't want his mistress to be exposed. Shortly after arriving, they started the discussion in the living room. Being bored and curious, Lin Dan sneaked to the stairway to eavesdrop on their conversation.

104

"We can make much bigger deals with cargo ships through the sea, and avoid being conspicuous to the authorities," Li Ben said.

"But who will arrange the goods and shipments in Hong Kong?" Han Fang, the vice mayor asked with a concerned face.

"Don't worry about that. Wang Qiang and his brothers will handle them," Li Ben replied. "The most difficult and dangerous part is to avoid being caught by the customs patrol ships while at sea."

"I will take care of them since they are partly under my command," Chang Bing, the director of the customs, replied.

"Really? Make sure they are being taken care of, because it is the easiest part in our operation to be busted," Li Ben commented.

"Sure, I know how important it is, I will handle it myself, just don't worry about it," Chang Bing reassured.

"I trust you, big brother Chang. But our immediate concern now is where is the safest place for unloading our goods," Han Fang said.

"Let's look at the map," Li Ben suggested.

They moved to the library where a map of Shenzhen was posted on the wall. Studying the map for a while, Chang Bing pointed at Xeilmaisa, a fishing village in the eastern coast of the city, and said, "This should be a good place for us."

But Li Ben, who was looking at places along the western coast, disagreed immediately. "The eastern coast has heavy traffic, both on land and sea. With too many people watching, it's too dangerous. We should choose a place somewhere along the western coast."

"Big brother Li is right," Han Fang echoed.

"It must be somewhere in the suburban area," Li Ben muttered. His finger moved slowly on the map and stopped abruptly at a point and then asked, "Are you guys familiar with the Xixiang Pier?"

It was a little pier where fishermen used to unload and sell their catches, and used to belong to Xixiang village, which was about thirty-five kilometers west of downtown.

"Yes, I've been there twice before. It looks like a village in a rural area and is very quiet. An ideal place for our operation," Chang Bing said.

"Sounds good to me. What do you think, big brother Li?" Han Fang consulted.

"Okay, let's take it. I am going to tell Wang Qiang and his brothers the location and to arrange the pickups. By the way, it is more profitable and safer to smuggle diesel than any other commodity. Mayor Han, maybe you can borrow a oil tanker from one of the oil companies in Hong Kong to handle the job."

"It shouldn't be a big problem since I have met a couple of the owners of these companies there."

"Wonderful, let's get as rich as we possibly can," Chang Bing cried happily.

Listening to their conversation, Lin Dan became frightened. She had seen the vice mayor on the TV before and she didn't know who the other man was, but she knew he was as important as the other two. They were equally bad, like snakes and rats living in the same lair. *How could they claim to be the servants of the people?* She wondered. *They should be in prison or even disappear from society.* Suddenly, she felt that she should not stay with them any longer. Instead, she should leave this filthy lair of the animals as soon as possible, and stop being the sex toy of such human trash. She should fight with her fate, but she had no idea how to fight and how to get out of the situation, and her lover would get hurt once she escaped. A helpless feeling struck her, and she returned to the bedroom and wept.

It was her appearance's fault. It was her innate beauty that many girls would dream to possess that had repeatedly caused her trouble, she finally realized. Without being beautiful, her fate would be different. It was sad, a stunning face and figure ought to bring her own choice of romance and happiness, yet it worked the other way around for her. Pondering and pondering, she at last figured out a way, albeit a tragic way to get out of there without hurting her lover. But she didn't want to think about the consequence or whether she could face it, and if her lover would still love her after what she would do to herself—yet it was the only way out.

The next day, when she went shopping with the chauffeur, she stopped by a kitchenware store to buy a bottle of pipe-drainer. "The sink in the kitchen is clogged by the grease." Back at the villa, she poured out some draining solution into a big bowl. A sudden surge of tawny bubbles in the bowl with drops of water at the bottom scared her. Flinching, she wanted to scrap her plan. She couldn't imagine how painful she would feel and how ugly she would be if she followed through with her plan. Maybe she should abort it, just enjoy the comfortable life of being a mistress of a rich and powerful man—a living many women would dream to have after all. Hesitating, she stepped to the window, looking at the sky. A pair of eagles appeared, flying and gliding in circles, and twittering happily. She admired them, wishing that she and her lover could be as free and happy as the birds. Why did she have to be caged? Why was human life so grim and helpless? Since no one could help her, she had to help herself. She strode back to the table and plunged her face into the big bowl, and screamed with pain.

Hearing her scream, the chauffeur dashed in from the garage. He gasped at seeing what had happened. He held her up and ran to the bathroom. Rinsing her face with the shower head, he kept crying and asking why she had done such a horrible thing to herself. Her beautiful face was burned to a gruesome and unrecognizable mound of cooked flesh, and with small patches of blood and liquid. The chauffeur carried her to the car and rushed to the nearby hospital. The hospital refused to admit her, since the chauffeur did not carry enough cash for the deposit. The chauffeur told them she was the relative of the police deputy director, but they did not believe him. Not until he called Lin Ben and told him what had happened and threatened to take action against the hospital, did the hospital accept Lin Dan for treatment. After the implementation of the Reform and Opening, many profit-oriented hospitals would not admit patients unable to fully pay for their treatment.

She remained calm while lying in the hospital bed with her face all bandaged. Her mind kept thinking and recalling many things in the past, and thought about becoming a nun after finishing what she should do in the future. But she had to see justice served first, for what she had suffered and for the well-being of other victims.

Li Ben visited her once, but she refused to talk to him, and loathed him for causing all of her sufferings. Two weeks later, the doctor unraveled her bandage. She screamed, after looking into the mirror. She was much uglier than what she had imagined.

Returning back to the villa, Li Ben was frightened by her gruesome look. He was afraid to get close to her. What came into his mind immediately was how he could get rid of this gruesome-looking woman. He opened the safe, got out a gold bar and a bundle of cash. He put them into a bag and handed it to her.

"A-Dan, you have earned this, for your company and services. Take it. It should be enough to buy your own house."

"What? Company and services? Who do you think I am? A whore?" Lin Dan queried rather angrily.

"Whoever you are, whatever you did, you can't stay here any longer," Li Ben replied.

That was what she wanted to hear to be free, to get out of this cage. The price for freedom was almost her life, something more than she could afford. Why a gifted beauty ended up so tragic? Not fair! She wept.

"Get out of here, woman, don't play any woman tricks," he roared, pushing her out. He shouted to the chauffeur, "Take her out and drop her down in Futian."

"Yes, Master Li," the chauffeur replied.

*　　*　　*

The suspicious voyage of a ten-thousand-ton oil tanker, loaded with a few cargo containers on deck and the flag of a foreign country, was discovered by the Chinese naval patrol ship sailing off the bay between Hong Kong and Sheico, Shenzhen one evening. The patrol ship warned the tanker to stop, and then immediately notified the customs officials marine patrol unit based in Shenzhen. Twenty minutes later, a high-speed patrol boat with uniformed and armed customs officials appeared. It was illuminated with bright searchlights as it approached the oil tanker, urgently. With the naval searchlights beaming and the crew watching only tens of meters away, the customs officials climbed onto the oil tanker with guns and flashlights and began their searching mission. They asked questions and examined the ship's documents handed over by the captain. Then they began to check the cargo. Opening a forty-foot container, they saw two cars covered with clothing tucked at the bottom, and a wooden board on top of them supporting boxes of mobile phones and accessories. After checking two more containers and seeing almost the same content inside them, the officers nodded to one another. They opened the hatch on the deck and were immediately choked by the strong smell of diesel coming out of it. They replaced the lid back on position quickly. One officer informed the naval patrol ship captain that the tanker was just a regular foreign freighter legally carrying imported goods and sailing to

108

a nearby Chinese port. After the naval patrol ship left, the customs officials and the crew of the oil tanker congratulated each other.

"Good job, Master Chang," the captain of the oil tanker praised the director of the customs.

"It's a piece of cake, buddy, our first deal looks as smooth as a steering wheel," Chang Bing said, overjoyed.

"Are the trucks and boats waiting there to unload the goods?"

"Yes, they are waiting for you there."

"Good, we'll be there in less than half an hour. By the way, have you got your cash ready?"

"Of course, fourteen million yuan will be all yours, once we unload all the goods."

"Sounds wonderful. We should make bigger deals more frequently since it's so easy," the captain said.

"We will, but don't be hurried. See how much time we need to digest what we have this time first," Chang Bing assured him.

With the escort of the customs high-speed patrol boat, the oil tanker sailed into Xixian Pier without encountering interception by either the navy or the marine police. One of the head gangsters received them and directed the unloading at the pier. The trucks took turns unloading the diesel to the various gas stations, while the cars were driven to the auto-dealers in the city. It was past midnight when all the smuggled goods were finally unloaded at the little pier.

13

After being dropped down in Futain, Lin Dan called Wu Ting and told her what had happened to her. Her friend felt sad at first, but was happy about her being free finally. But when they met, her friend was shocked by Lin Dan's appearance. How could God punish an innocent girl like this?

Lin Dan was afraid to call her lover, and she did not want her friend to tell him. Their love would have to be terminated with no way to be continued, she decided. She really didn't want her beautiful image that had been implanted in her lover's mind to be ruined. With her present only-mother-could-love face, she believed she would scare away all men in the world.

Whoever destroyed her life had to pay, she thought, while rage and the fire of vengeance burned inside her heart. Whatever it took, how much it cost, she would keep fighting to the end. After discussing this with her friend, she wrote a crime-report letter. She wanted to complain to the provincial government about the corrupt officials in Shenzhen.

Departing from her friend the following day, she took a train to Guangzhou, the capital of Guangdong province. Her face was so ugly that the passengers on the train were afraid to sit near her. It was as if she had an infectious disease, a complete reverse from those eager to sit next to her before. What a change. She felt sad and embarrassed, and wondered how she was going to live the rest of her life with such constant mortification. She had suddenly become socially unacceptable. She thought of ending her life, too, as life had suddenly become meaningless to her. But she had to finish what she should do, first.

In Guangzhou, she wanted to take a taxi to the provincial government building located in the downtown area. The first taxi she had stopped ran away after the driver saw her face and suspected she was one of those penniless rovers. She had no luck for the second one either. Not until she used a handkerchief to cover her face, she got in one finally. On the way there, she saw many of the streets were narrow and crooked, and the buildings were old and ancient, unlike those in the brand new city of Shenzhen. And it was more crowded with people and cars.

Having got out of the taxi, she walked straight to the entrance of the building but was stopped by an armed security guard standing by the door. He asked what her intention was, and talked in a cell phone, and then told her to wait there for a minute. Half an hour later, a man came out to get her letter and told her to go home to wait for the government's reply. She asked to be received, knowing of the government's bureaucratic nature.

"I want to see the governor or the responding official," she demanded.

"No, they are too busy to care for this kind of thing. We have to do the investigation first," he snapped.

She knew it would be useless to fight with the bureaucratic official. "Can you give me your office's phone number then?"

He scribbled a number on a piece of paper and handed it to her and then headed back into the building. Feeling and sensing the arrogance of the man, she already knew the result of her trip. Nothing.

*   *   *

Chen Yong was feeling edgy. He had not heard from his lover or her friend for weeks. He kept calling her friend almost everyday, but the answer was the same: "Your girlfriend is as fine as usual, nothing much has happened to her, don't worry about it." He dared not ask for her phone number, lest it would cause her trouble, especially knowing how jealous and brutal the evil man was.

Although he had buried himself in work in the past few years since their separation, Chen Yong couldn't stop thinking about Lin Dan. Tonight was the mid-autumn festival, a holiday in which loved ones were supposed to get together to eat moon cakes and grapefruits and make wishes during the mid-autumn full-moon period. He had made many wishes alone during this holiday in the past years, but none of them had come true. Perhaps he had not been sincere enough. This time he wanted to make it as faithful as possible. He clasped his hands and bowed to the moon three times. Then he stared to it without blinking for ten seconds and began to make a wish: "Please, Love God, let Dan Dan be free and come back to me." And then he bowed toward the moon three more times. Eating the moon cake, he wondered what his lover was doing at the moment. Was she doing the same? Was she praying the same?

Thinking of his lover often made him exhausted. He didn't know when this ordeal would end. His siblings and friends had tried to persuade him to let go of the past and start a new relationship with one of his young female admirers. But he rejected the idea, wanting to wait as long as it needed to be with Lin Dan. No substitutes. He often reminded himself that without his lover's sacrifice, he would not have had today's success. And without his lover sharing in the success, what he possessed now meant virtually nothing.

To make his lover's sacrifice worthwhile, he wanted to build his telecom empire as big and as successful as possible. The tentacles of his Octopus Telecom had reached out across nearly the entire nation, making it one of the biggest in the field. Through many days and sleepless nights, the ten-thousand-phone-exchange system finally finished and tested successfully, thanks to his hard-working and dedicated engineers and technicians. The system was the most powerful weapon his company had possessed in fighting for their share of the market. Taking the advantage of being a domestic firm, Octopus Telecom was ready to compete and drive the foreign giants out of the Chinese market. In almost every business bid, Octopus Telecom was willing to go for the lowest price—but offer and provide the best after-sale services.

Unlike other tight-budget companies, Octopus Telecom encouraged its sales representatives to spend as much money as they could in conducting business activities and in satisfying the needs of their customers. It required them, for instance, to stay in five-star hotels during business trips and, of course, reimbursed for all of their expenditures. It would condemn sales representatives who wanted to save money and stay in inexpensive hotels, because it believed it would affect the company's image negatively. It wouldn't care if the company lost money in some business deals, so long as they could help increase its market shares. Chen Yong and his siblings had stipulated that occupying the market was the company's first priority and long-term strategy.

The ambitious Octopus Telecom was not satisfied in beating up both domestic and foreign firms within the nation. It wanted to extend its tentacles across the Pacific, Atlantic and Indian oceans to reach America, Europe, the middle-east, Africa, and everywhere on the planet. With its cheap labor-cost, advanced technology and effective marketing tactics, Octopus Telecom was positioned to conquer the world.

Where used to be one of the cradles of civilization of mankind, the liberated productivity of a private company in an open-door communist society started to release its boundless power. The world was stunned and frightened. And it all started in Shenzhen, in the experimental market-oriented special economic zone of China, by a young fisherman.

If true love could create miracles, then missing his lover and their separation had nourished the stimulant for such miracle making. Yet Chen Yong was never satisfied and happy with what he had achieved. The more successful he became, the more lonely and helpless he felt. With all the fortune he had, Chen Yong was unable to get back his lover. Drinking to escape from his sad and lonely feelings, an idea suddenly popped up in his mind. He stumbled to his desk and quickly flipped the pages of the phone book, and finally spotted the police deputy director's number and called him. He wanted to make a deal with the man.

* * *

As the economy kept soaring, petroleum had become one of the hottest commodities in the nation. The oil supply was getting extremely tight, while prices of its products were mounting higher and higher. To meet the demand, the nation started to import oil, shattering the once proclaimed national pride of self-help oil-sufficient nation under the leadership of the Communist Party. Due to the nation's scarce foreign reserve, the import was very limited and tightly controlled by charging high rate of tariff. This had made gasoline and diesel smuggling more profitable.

Taking advantage of being close to Hong Kong, Li Ben and his allied high-ranking corrupt officials indulged in digging the black gold mine, as they illegally shipped in the badly needed fuel without paying a cent of tariff. Distributing the fuels to gas stations from

113

ships could no longer meet the demand of larger and more frequent shipments. They surreptitiously built oil reservoirs around Xixiang. Then their supply expanded to other coastal and inland cities. Every day and night, formations of fuel trucks were running from Xixiang of Shenzhen to all nearby cities and provinces. Subsequently, these greedy corrupt officials' savings were growing and swelling. Indeed, they were richer than many corporate owners in the capitalist society, where the gross domestic product per capita was more than sixty times of that in China at the time. And they channeled out their money to various Western nations by buying properties, stocks and bonds, or simply just depositing them into banks accounts.

Li Ben was playing majiang with his smuggling partners when his cell phone rang. The number shown on the screen was unfamiliar to him, but it was normal since he was a busy-and-everyone-eagerly-wanted-to-be-acquainted important person. Pressing the answer button on the phone, he said loudly, "Hello, who's this?"

"Director Li, this is Chen Yong. Remember me?"

The name was familiar, but he couldn't remember right at the moment because he had met so many people every day.

"I'm sorry, who are you?"

It had been years since the last time they had talked. This evil man had extorted him and taken away his lover. He managed to suppress his anger and remained calm.

"I am Lin Dan's ex-boyfriend, remember? I wonder, if I were to give you the money that you asked for before, would you let my ex-girlfriend go free."

Li Ben paused for a while, assessing and calculating the situation. It was obvious that Lin Dan had not contacted her ex-boyfriend since her release. It was likely that she would not do so for a while since she would be too shamed to let him see her ugliness.

"Okay. It's a deal. But you have to transfer the money into my bank account before I change my mind."

"That was fifteen million yuan, right?"

"Exactly."

"We're going to do the exchange face to face: That is, I'll give you a check with fifteen million yuan, and you'll give me Lin Dan."

It just wouldn't work this way.

"No. How do I know that your check is good? You have to transfer the money to my bank account first."

"You know that I don't dare write a bad check to you, Director Li."

"Ha, I want to do it my way. Do you want the deal or not?"

Hesitating briefly, Chen Young replied, "Okay, give me your account number then."

After scribbling Li Ben's bank account number, Chen Yong could not conceal his excitement. Money did not mean much to him now. He was going to be with his lover again soon, that was what counted the most. Feeling overjoyed, he called Lin Dan's friend, Wu Ting, wanting her to inform Lin Dan immediately. To his surprise, Wu Ting croaked desperately on the other end of the line, telling him not to do so. When he mentioned that he did not care about giving the money to the man, so long as his lover could be free, she finally told him the truth. He screamed, feeling sudden pain in his heart. He demanded to see her right away. Wu Ting said his lover did not want to see him and wanted him to forget all about her. He told her he did not mind about her look: Still, she refused to talk to him. Wu Ting said goodbye after minutes of an impasse. Chen Yong went crazy.

*　　*　　*

One-and-a-half years after its completion, the new commercial tower, developed by Earth Dragon Real Estate Company Limited in the downtown area, still had an extremely hard time selling or renting out its units. Its bad location and market saturation was the problem. Although the company struggled to make several payments by dragging over some of the profits from building residential edifices, its large long-over-due payments were snowballing. The panicky bankers started sending out foreclosure letters to the company.

To make it worse, the real estate market became overheated causing the prices of apartments, houses, and office buildings to tumble. This horrible turn in the market, like an infectious disease, spread around the city quickly. While the bankers were hurriedly knocking on mortgagers' doors, the real estate developers stampeded, abandoning many uncompleted buildings throughout the city. The housing vacancy rate of the city had reached new record. This was the first painful experience investors had ever had in this field.

"Bad things don't happen single-handedly," according to an old saying. If the real estate market had become the pandemonium for many investors, the stock market turned into a hell for them too. Following the collapse of the real estate market, the stock market tumbled. As the stock investors dumped their shares in hurry, the index of the Shenzhen stock exchange plunged lower and lower every day of trade.

These were especially hard blows to speculators and bankers, especially with knowing that most of the capital used in the financial market came from loans provided by the banks. The large number of loan defaults almost closed several banks, and bankers who approved the loans were now in hot water.

Consequently, after losing their hard-earned savings, many small investors committed suicide while some became mentally ill. The entire financial market was in chaos. Yet citizens in this newly-turned capitalist with socialist characteristics society realized investing could be as risky as gambling. The financial market could not only fluctuate in an ascending pattern of big bull and small bear, but would slump and collapse abruptly in the atmosphere of fear. This was the biggest investment lesson these citizens had ever learned since the inception of Reform and Opening.

Earth Dragon Real Estate Company Limited broadly and massively invested in both real estate and stock markets with its capital loaned from the Bank of Shenzhen via Tang Daming, who was also in deep trouble with his bank. Earth Dragon was unable to pay most of its loan payments because of sluggish sales and price reductions. Tang Daming, the greedy banker, was like an ant in a hot pot, jumping, croaking and groaning around restlessly. He had been condemned and scolded by both his bank supervisors and the head gangster in charge of money laundering and investment for the corrupt police officer. While being threatened to be investigated and sued by his bosses, the gangsters demanded he compensate the money lost in the stock market and defer or cancel all their real estate loan payments.

Sitting in his office and pondering his fate, he regretted being too greedy which had delayed his plan for going abroad. His daughter and son had already gone to study in Canada, he and his wife should have already been there, according to his original plan. *It's all about greed, and fate,* he sighed. He could no longer go anywhere now, because he knew that the police department and the customs kept their eyes on him. He would be in trouble if he couldn't make the monsters satisfied. Tang Daming knew his fate.

*   *   *

In 1997, the British colony Hong Kong would be returned to China and begin practicing "One country, two systems." The proposal, mainly initiated and later made into a policy and law, was an agreement between Britain and China in which Hong Kong would remain with its political system and lifestyle for fifty more years by Deng Xiaoping, the nation's paramount leader. The news of this man's death shocked and saddened the country, especially Shenzhen, the nation's largest special economic zone which was created under his instruction.

This witty, visionary, careful and wholehearted man guided the nation as a whole for nearly twenty years after his former predecessor Mao Zedong plunged the nation's economy into ruin. Deng Xiaoping turned the financial situation around and jolted the economy back to life. In less than twenty years, the nation's gross domestic product had quadrupled. A country where everything such as food, clothing, soap, toothpaste, shoes, bicycle, electric appliances, construction materials, and so on, used to be strictly rationed was now in abundant supply. At the same time, citizens gradually began enjoying more freedom and a relaxed political atmosphere. Life had never been better despite the festering of the rampant crimes.

The enormous success of the special economic zone, Shenzhen, was one of the most magnificent feats of this man's work. Within eighteen years, this little fishing town had turned into a modern city. Its population soared from thirty thousand up to seven million. Its GDP climbed up to the fourth largest city in the entire nation. It also became a genuine manufacturing and hi-tech base for corporations.

This man, who once expressed a wish to visit Hong Kong after its return, died just five months before the colony would officially be handed back to its motherland. The huge poster displaying his photo with the background of the skyscraper of this new city, which erected a few years ago in the downtown of Luohu, had become a historical sight and a popular scenic spot. Many people knelt down in front of it, bowing, crying and mourning, while calling his name.

The greatest accomplishment of this remarkable leader however, was not to only rectify the wrong path down which the nation was heading but also pave the road for a bright future for his country for decades to come. The death of this man was a tremendous loss for the Chinese people, and especially the Shenzhen citizens.

*   *   *

Three months had passed and Lin Dan had never heard from the provincial government regarding her crime report, neither had any actions being taken against the corrupt officials in Shenzhen. She realized, suddenly, it had something to do with the vice mayor, a member of the provincial Communist Party committee. If that was the case, she reckoned immediately then, she was in danger. The gang of corrupt officials in this city had probably been hunting for her, or would hunt for her soon. She talked to Wu Ting and they both agreed that she should leave immediately. Wu Ting remembered receiving a strange call a few days ago that someone was asking if Lin Dan was there. But where should she go? She couldn't go back to her hometown in Sichuan because they would check her out there for sure, nor could she go to her lover's place because that would be the first place they would search. Besides, she didn't want to see her lover yet—perhaps they would never meet again. Pondering anxiously, she got an idea. She would go to the capital to make a criminal report to the Central Disciplinary Committee.

Covering her head and face with scarves like a Muslim girl, she left her friend's place after midnight. She took a taxi to a five-star hotel and checked in a double-room there and waited for dawn. Staying in an expensive hotel would be safer than lodging in a cheap and shabby one for her—police seldom checked these hotels, where most customers were either foreigners or important people.

Lying in bed, she felt anxious and didn't feel like sleeping at all. She wanted to be alert and wondering what to do next. She would never imagine that one day she would become a fugitive. She felt sad that her dream that someday she and Chen Yong would be together again had been shattered. Yet she really didn't know whether she was too selfish to deface herself without consulting her lover, but it would be of no meaning if they couldn't be together. Practically speaking, their relationship was severed the moment they were forced to separate. Of course, she still loved him very much and had craved to be with him, but in reality it had become a mirage to her. And she was no longer a dreamer.

Weariness drove her asleep. It was eight in the morning when she was finally awakened from nightmares. She struggled to get up and stumbled to the bathroom to shower herself with cold water to try and calm herself down and refresh her mind.

Again, for safety reason, she decided to fly to the capital instead of taking the train. She hurried to the Shenzhen Airport and was barely able to catch her flight at 9:45 AM. Three hours later, the airplane landed at the Beijing Airport.

When she checked in a five-star hotel nearby the airport, the receptionist spoke English to her. Only after Lin Dan presented her ID and reply in Mandarin did the receptionist apologize. She thought Lin Dan was from the Middle East. The receptionist was frightened after seeing her face, following her request to unveil the scarves to see if her features matched the photo ID. Obviously her look was starkly different from her photo, the receptionist rejected checking her in at once. Lin Dan realized the security check in the capital was more stringent than that in Shenzhen. She explained to them what had happened to her, but was still denied check in. Disappointedly, she took a taxi to the downtown area and tried another one, but the result was the same. Giving up in lodging in a luxury hotel, she decided to try the cheap ones in the run-down hutong area, the area where long and narrow alleys meandered between the ancient box-looking houses.

Entering a hutong, she saw it was packed with people. The snack, grocery and clothing vendors, with their filthy and shabby carts stood yelling, barking and touting. The air was a mixture of pungent, sour, and stinking smell. Squeezing through the crowd and rambling along, she spotted a sign hanging at the corner of a dilapidated house that said, "One bed, 20 yuan. Single room, 40 yuan. Double room, 80 yuan."

She entered and inquired if there were any vacancies. The stinking smell made her choke, she ran out at once. Strolling the crowded and smelly alleys again, she passed a couple of similar lodging houses but refused to go in. Until it was late in the afternoon when her legs were sore, did she see a better-looking one. Ignoring the unpleasant odor, she decided to be realistic and get settled. But she was told that there was no more vacancy. Disappointed, she returned to a run-down one she had just passed. No reason to be picky now. She asked to check in a double room, but was told that only one bed was available. Hesitating for a while, she pulled out her ID and a hundred-yuan bill and handed them to the receptionist. Observing the frowning expression of the woman after seeing that her face did not match the photo ID, she said, "Keep the change." The woman smiled and handed her a key.

Her room was in the left inner corner of a square-shape bungalow across a courtyard. The door was ajar. She pushed in lightly and the door bumped against the rack of a bunk bed. She gasped. Two bunk beds were positioned parallel and close to one another in a dim tiny room. Two middle-aged women were lying on the upper decks and staring at her. A stinking odor invaded her nose. She coughed. Barely able to control her emotion, she said "Hi" to them.

Putting her bag on the bed, she started to take off her scarves, getting ready to rest. The two women screamed and jumped off their beds, rushing out while yelling, "Ghost! Ghost!"

The receptionist ran in and said, "Don't be silly, she is no ghost. Her face was burned and scarred."

The two women, slowly and timidly approached Lin Dan, studying her face suspiciously. "How terrible. How did you get a burn like this?" one asked.

"It was an accident," she replied calmly, lying down to rest. She was in no mood to talk with these filthy slum lodgers. She just wanted to rest and wait for tomorrow to carry out her mission, as it was too late to do it today.

*   *   *

The vice mayor got wind that a girl from Shenzhen had submitted a complaint letter to the provincial government, reporting crimes committed by local high-ranking officials. Through his net of "ears and eyes" in the provincial leadership echelon, he found out that the girl was named Lin Dan. He got hold of the case and informed Li Ben and Chang Bing immediately. They all agreed the girl had to be hunted down and obliterated as soon as possible.

Li Ben quickly activated the informant system within the police force of the gangsters. Wu Ting was arrested and tortured and her

120

place thoroughly searched, but she revealed nothing about where Lin Dan might be.

Checking all the hotel records, Li Ben's men tracked down that Lin Dan had stayed in a five-star hotel for one night two days ago. *Why didn't she stay in that five-star hotel longer? Where did she go after leaving that hotel?* Li Ben wondered. He knew that luxury hotels were the last places his men had checked. She had no place to hide in the city, since his men were everywhere. And for her stubborn and ostentatious character, she would not have the courage to ask her ex-boyfriend for help, he knew it as well. Although his men had him and his place turned upside down, what he worried the most was that ghost-looking girl would report him and others to the central government. He barked to the door immediately, an officer replied and came in.

"Give my order to search all of the records of the travel agencies and airliners in the city, right now."

"Yes, Director," the officer replied and hurried out.

He had a hunch that Lin Dan had already left for Beijing. He knew very well the woman had the class and the brain. He picked up the phone and called the police department in Beijing. "May I speak to Director Guo?" he asked urgently.

"Yes, may I know who is calling?" a female replied.

"My name is Li Ben. I am the deputy director of the police department in Shenzhen."

"Hold on for a second, Director Li."

A minute later, a man's voice droned on line, "Director Li, I haven't heard from you for a long time. How have you been?"

"Not too bad, and you, Director Guo?"

"Surviving. But it's like the saying: 'you would not come to the temple if you were doing everything fine.' What's up, buddy?"

They had been acquaintances during the national police directors' meetings in the capital before, although Guo was not as corrupt as he.

"You're right about it, Director Guo. A female murder suspect from Shenzhen may have flown to your city two days ago. She is 167cm, 28, slim, her face has been burned unrecognizable from the photo of her ID. She has committed murder and other very serious crimes in Shenzhen. Please help track her down and bring her back here. I will fax her ID over, but I don't have her latest photo though."

"Sure, I will do it, Director Li. It's our job to get all the criminals arrested and punished."

"Thank you very much for your help, Director Guo."

"Don't mention it, maybe I'll need your help in the future."

Anxiously stamping back and forth in his office, he wondered the consequences if they failed tracking down Lin Dan. She may have already submitted her report to the hands of the nation's top leaders. He regretted letting her go and yet realized why she had defaced herself. She ultimately had no feeling toward him after years of cohabiting with him and wanted to destroy him now. She was the most gorgeous girl he had ever seen and she had been his mistress. He was crazy about her and willing to share all the fortunes he had with her. Why hadn't she moved and accepted him? He recalled all the great sex with her and how she had enjoyed it as well. Why did she suddenly want to ruin herself and him? Women, he still did not understand them at all, even after having had so many. Now he had to hunt this woman down before she destroyed him. He raced to the door again.

"Little Su, tell the grand-team leader Lu to bring two brothers to fly to Beijing to help Director Guo there to catch that crazy woman."

"Yes, Director Li."

Having finished organizing and deploying his hunting party, he felt much better and more relaxed. That woman would not slip out the net of his hunting forces, he believed. Lying down on the couch, he closed his eyes to relax himself more. But seconds later the phone rang, he jumped up abruptly and answered it. A man's voice was cracking at the other end of the line.

"Director Li, we have just found out from a travel agency that Lin Dan bought a one-way air ticket to Beijing yesterday morning. The flight was at 9:30 AM."

"Okay, call off the search then."

He was right, that woman wanted to report him to the central government. He prayed she would be captured before she finished it.

*　　*　　*

Chen Yong was questioned with threat by the police officers;

122

and the offices of his company, including all branches, had been thoroughly searched. His heart was broken, not because he was insulted and abused by the police, because he worried so much about his lover. He really wanted to know where she was and why that monster was looking for her so urgently. He had released her a few months. Since the day he knew she was free, Chen Yong called Wu Ting everyday trying to talk to her and persuade her to come back to him. But she refused to answer his calls, not to mention about going back to him. Her friend declined giving out her address to him at her request and kept telling him that Lin Dan wanted him to forgive and forget about her. He had been feeling so frustrated these past few months for not knowing what to do to change her mind. Now it suddenly came to this. He didn't care about the mortification inflicted on him and his company from the action taken by the police, but he did care about the fate of Lin Dan. He decided to call detective Liu Ming, since he had reopened his firm in town recently.

Detective Liu Ming had continuously paid attention to the development of his special client Chen Yong and his girlfriend, and the police deputy director. He knew the deal very well that was between them. He was surprised about Lin Dan's sudden release, but did not know the story behind it. Now he was puzzled to hear the same girl had been urgently wanted by her former kidnapper. He decided to find out why. His profession had made him curious about things happening around town, especially an important case like this one. Someday, he thought, he might write a novel about it.

When he was about to leave for the day, his phone rang. Listening to his receptionist's dialog with the caller, he knew who was calling.

"Hello, Master Chen, it is Liu Ming. Long time no see. How have you been?"

"Not very well. I need your help, Detective Liu."

"How can I help you, Master Chen?" he asked, in a manner that sounded like knowing nothing about what had been going on with Chen Yong.

"It's the same old headache I have always had. You know what I am talking about?"

"You mean your girlfriend has been kidnapped again?" he pretended not knowing any recent development of the complicated relationships between the deputy police chief and him and his lover.

"No. It's a long story. But let me make it short, since you found her last time, my girlfriend was forced to live with that damned police deputy chief until recently. Wanting to free herself, I guess, she damaged her face and the man deserted her. But she suddenly disappeared a few days ago. That son of a bitch and his running dogs have been looking for her so badly now. I have no idea what is going on between my girlfriend and that man. Can you find out for me?"

"That sounds terrible. I am sorry to hear that and deeply understand how you feel about it. I will definitely find something out for you."

"Thanks. If you need any help, just call me."

"Sure, I will."

*　　*　　*

Having receiving Li Ben's call and the copy of the girl's ID, the director of the Beijing police department organized a hunting operation. The information provided by the Shenzhen police chief indicated that the suspect preferred to stay in a five-star hotel. He ordered to check on the luxury hotels first.

Holding a copy of Lin Dan's ID, each of the two-officer teams started questioning the receptionists and examining records of lodgers of the luxury hotels in the downtown area. After they finished checking all of them, they found no record or clue if that girl had been to any of the hotels. Now the only five-star hotel remained unchecked was the one near the airport, two police officers rushed to it.

They examined the lodging record first, and were disappointed after finding no record of Lin Dan. When they began to question the receptionists and show them the copy of Lin Dan's ID, the photo of the ghost-looking girl was immediately recognized. They told them that she was refused to be checked in because her look was starkly different from the photo of her ID card. This indicated that she was in the city, and that she had to be in one of the hotels in the capital as she was just a visitor there. They would find her eventually. They felt excited and reported to the director at once.

Taking the order from the director, the police officers immediately began searching all the less-expensive hotels in the nation's

124

capital. There were hundreds of less-expensive hotels ranging from four-star ones in downtown to the rental houses in the slums of the precinct areas within the city. It was one of the largest hunting and pursuing operations in recent years in the capital.

They started with the four-star hotels, and then the three-star ones, and worked their way down. But after the exhausting day search, and night, they had covered most of the hotels and found no sign of the suspect, only caught some prostitutes, drug-addicts and drug-dealers. Nevertheless, making shifts and taking turns to rest, the search went on.

*   *   *

Despite of sleeping in a hard bunk bed and a strange environment with stinking odors, Lin Dan slept soundly. Her roommates, frightened by her look, marveled on how easy the ghost-looking girl had fallen asleep.

As she slept deep into the night, dreams came incessantly. She was having a wedding ritual in a huge restaurant, marrying to her lover, Chen Yong. After bowing and putting on wedding rings to each other, the ritual was about to end. Suddenly Li Ben appeared with a gun in his hand. He pointed his gun to her lover and ordered her to follow him. To save her lover, she obeyed. But once stepping out of the restaurant and into the crowd on the street, she ran. Ignoring Li Ben's warning, she kept running and passing street after street until reaching a foothill in some suburban area. She turned her head around and saw that the man was approaching. She was frightened, dashing onto the hill and then up the mountain. Missing a step suddenly, she fell and rolled down into the man's arms. Holding her tightly, he chuckled obscenely. Suddenly, a huge tiger appeared, jumping down on them while roaring fiercely. She screamed and was awakened. Her entire body was wet with sweat. Sitting up, she was panting. Her roommates were awakened and terrified, screaming, yelling and running out. The whole house was up. Running, scolding, inquiring and shouting. It was pandemonium in the middle of the night. She felt ashamed for causing the panic for all other lodgers and decided to leave after dawn.

She was unable to sleep again for the rest of the night, just lying in the bed and recalling the past and pondering what she would do after the trip. What a joke fate had been making of her, she sighed. Just got out of the shadow of being someone's mistress, she developed her own career in corporate management in her boyfriend's company in the new immigration city, and then suddenly she was forced to be a mistress again. But now, she was a fugitive. Knowing that Li Ben and his men had been hunting for her, she could not return to Shenzhen after this mission, nor could she go back to her hometown. Although her life had been ruined, she had no intention to end her life yet. She still had her parents to look after. Yet, still determined, the best place for her to go would be to the famous Shaolin Temple in the Song Mountain, located in the middle of the nation. She buried her emotions, no more dreams, no love, no happiness, and no pain. She was dead psychologically and emotionally, just a walking carcass. She really needed a quiet and reclusive place for the rest of her life, although she really did not like the idea of being a nun.

The hutong resumed its boisterousness in the early morning. The loud and jumbled barking of hawkers touting and cajoling with customers, the incessant ringing of bicycles and the honking of vehicles from nearby streets resonated. It was time for her to get up and leave for her mission.

With her veil on, she checked out and stepped into the hutong and was about to mingle with the crowd when she noticed two police officers entering the lodging house. She had a hunch at once these officers were looking for her. Curiously, she peeped in the reception room through the window and was stunned. One of the officers was holding her enlarged photo while asking the receptionist if she had seen the girl.

Lin Dan took a deep breath and squeezed into the crowd. Her heart started pounding. She had to run away quickly before more police officers came into block to cordon the hutongs. But the narrow and crowded alleys slowed her pace. When she got to the exit of a hutong, a couple of police officers were scanning the people coming out. She retreated and made a detour to the other exit, but it was being cordoned as well. In panic, she kept crossing hutong after hutong to the more run-down and smaller ones. Finally, she ran into a garbage dump at the end of a filthy alley. Struggling to get through the grisly filthy rubbish, she was barely able to control herself from vomiting. Trying to trudge over it, she fell into a pool of rancid dark and thick liquid up to her waist. She screamed. Feeling horrified, she tried to climb out of it, but was pulled back by the silt-like thick liquid. Desperately, she tried to free herself, but with no luck. She felt weaker with each attempt. With no hope of getting out, she cried for help. Crying and yelling was useless as no one came to rescue her. She would end up dying in a stinking pool. What a nightmare. She screamed hysterically.

Suddenly, a strange man appeared and extended his hand to her. Staring at him she hesitated. The man whispered, "I have come to rescue you, Lin Dan."

"How do you know my name? I guess we haven't met before," she queried dubiously.

"I will tell you later. Let me help you out of this cesspool first."

She grabbed his hand, and the man pulled her out of the pool.

"Now tell me who you are," she demanded.

"My name is Liu Ming. I am a detective. Chen Yong wants me to find out where you are because he worries about you so much."

"How did you know I was here?" She was curious.

"I got wind that you had flown to Beijing, hence I came to the capital immediately. As a detective, I knew that you would not have checked in at any of the registered hotels due to the tight security management in the capital since your damaged face does not match up with the photo of your ID card. So I came directly to the hutong area. There are not many lodging houses in this slum of the city. I was able to locate you without much trouble. And I had checked in at the same lodging house as you did. What had happened last night puzzled me. Did your roommates know how you looked like before they went to sleep?"

"Yes, they did. But I had a terrible nightmare. I screamed and they were wakened up and were terribly frightened."

"I see."

"How did you know that I would check out that early?"

"I really didn't know. But I was afraid you would do that, so I got up before dawn and sat on the bench in the courtyard and kept watch of your room. I saw you come and check out. That's when I followed you. I worried about you the moment I saw the cops. Since you had been alerted about the police, I wanted to approach you but was afraid of scaring you. I kept following you all the way but got into a wrong alley after you disappeared into this garbage dump. I was looking for you desperately when I heard your screaming.''

''Thanks for saving my life.''

''I didn't actually save your life, but Chen Yong did. He sent me here.''

Her eyes wetted with tears. She was deeply touched by her lover's dedication and persistence. She was probably wrong about him. He had not stopped loving her simply because her look had changed. But how could she face him and see him suffer staying with such an ugly woman. No, she would never let that happen. Their love should not be smeared. She mumbled, ''Please say thank you to him for me.''

''Perhaps you should see him once at least.''

''No, just tell him to forget me, please. My life is still in danger now. Let's get out of here.''

Together, they got out to the street. Her clothes and body were soaked with the nasty smelling dark and sticky liquid, and her bag contained her important belongings and the letter of crime report. All remained intact. She thanked Liu Ming again and suggested he should go and let her alone. But he insisted accompanying her to a safe place, the nation's anticorruption organization, because not many people knew where it was located. She finally agreed.

They stopped a taxi. When the driver started shaking his head to refuse giving them a ride, they said they would pay him double, even three times of what the riding fare was. The driver's attitude changed immediately. Liu Ming instructed the driver how to go the headquarters of the Central Disciplinary Committee. The driver stared at them again and said he had been there once but made no further comment, just shifting the gears and starting the car rolling.

Once there, the detective handed the driver a hundred-yuan bill and told him to keep the change for the fare for less than thirty yuan. They rushed to the entrance of the building. When the security guard stopped them by the door, Lin Dan said she had a very important case and needed to see the director of the committee. With his hand covering his mouth, the guard hesitated for a few seconds. Then he talked to the cell phone. A few minutes later, a serious but warmhearted-looking man came out to receive them. She pulled out the letter from her bag and handed it to him. After reading it, the man praised her courageous move and told them to follow him in. It was time for the detective to leave. They said good luck and goodbye to each other.

Getting up to the office by an elevator, the man instructed a female clerk to buy some girl's clothes from a nearby shopping mall. He told Lin Dan to go wash up in the ladies' room and wait there for the female clerk for her fresh clothes. After washing and dressing up in the new and clean clothes, Lin Dan went back to the office. The same man handed her a cup of hot tea and asked if she were hungry. This was the first time she had felt real warmth after days of a fugitive life. And she was told to stay there until the case was taken care of—it was for her own safety.

14

The news of a gristly-looking girl having jumped into a river was in several major newspapers in the capital. After hours of effort a team of divers were unable to recover her.

That was the suspect the entire police force in the capital was looking for in the past two days, Director Guo concluded. He called the police deputy director in Shenzhen to inform him of the news, telling him that the suspect had committed suicide by jumping into a river.

Li Ben thanked him for his effort to help, but he doubted the news was true. He called the team of his men in the capital to do the investigation. They were unable to locate the divers in the news report, so they aborted their mission and returned to Shenzhen.

Li Ben discussed the dramatic result of their pursuit with the vice mayor and the director of the customs. They all agreed that the news was too good to be true, and they should refrain from conducting corruptive activities for the time being and should keep their eyes on any move taken by the Central Disciplinary Committee. Although they expressed their worry, Li Ben reassured them that Shenzhen was their kingdom of power and it was too hard for the CDC to break into their operations.

The occasional news of a high-ranking municipal and provincial government official getting caught for committing corruption and sentenced to death or to serve long terms in prison often haunted them daily and gave them psychological shocks. It was especially frightening to them when a governor of a southwestern province was executed because of a large amount of money involved in his grafting and bribery activities. The money they gathered from this kind of criminal activity was much greater, and they knew their fate once caught.

One of them suggested that they should consider immigrating to the western countries. The money each one of them now possessed was enough for them to spend for the rest of their lives. But to do that, they needed connections with highly trusted friends in those nations to help them get settled down. This had been neglected right from the beginning of their power-fortune converting game, even when they possessed the financial capability to do so. They should have sent their children to study abroad as the stepping plank for their emigration. It was the same mistake the three of them had made. In their frustration, the name Tang Daming came in their minds. They knew he had two children studying in Canada and the man had expressed his intention of joining with his children there with his wife. They decided to let go of his mistakes, in both real estate and stock market, and become friendly with him again. He was the last straw for their future.

*   *   *

Tang Daming marveled at how the police deputy director's and his followers' attitudes had changed toward him. He had been threatened and bullied by them in the past few weeks, since the biggest slump in the financial markets. He wondered what had caused this change, but had no idea until Li Ben called him to have dinner at the revolving restaurant. During their dinner, Li Ben showed extra concern about his children and his plan for leaving the country, if any. He encouraged Tang Daming to join his children as soon as possible. Then told him that he and his friends wanted to emigrate to Canada if they could obtain Tang Daming's help there. And if he agreed to do so, not only the losses caused by his blunders be forgiven in the disastrous financial market, but also he would receive a certain amount of cash from them. Tang Daming knew instantly his only option was to do what he was told, so he thanked him at once and promised to help. At the same time, he was happy about being able to survive the crisis and had another opportunity to escape. With the help of this corrupt officer, he would have no problem to get out of the country to start his new life in Canada with the rest of his family.

As was expected, he picked up his and his wife's passports from the police department a few days later. Now they had to apply for visas from the Canadian consulate. It should be easy with their qualifications: they had a huge amount of savings and their children were studying there. They could even buy green cards simply by purchasing houses or setting up a business there. He had the savings to do so. He was no longer worried about being fired and prosecuted by his bank before leaving the country, especially with the protection given by the deputy police department chief. How wonderful.

He started selling off his properties and stocks in a hurry, and did not care much about their prices. Through the help of the customs director, he made a trip to Hong Kong and deposited most of his savings in a Canadian bank there. Everything had gone smoothly—now, just waiting for the visas.

*　　*　　*

Clandestinely, a team of four people checked in the Shenzhen Hotel. They started working immediately and independently like detectives. Within three weeks, they visited beauty salons, brothels in various places, car dealers, gas stations, the piers in Xixian areas, the storages and parking lots nearby the customs, the securities, banks and real estate companies around the city—playing different roles as customers, investors and investigators. Lin Dan had provided the information. They also visited detective Liu Ming and Chen Yong to confirm and collect more information. Chen Yong gave them pictures taken when Li Ben was in the hut, where Lin Dan and Chen Song were hidden during their kidnapping.

They did not contact the local disciplinary committee, lest they were involved in corruption and revealed their mission. From the bug which was installed in Wang Qiang's office, they got wind that the gang of three high-ranking corrupt officials planed to smuggle fuel a few more times before quitting. They decided to take action and catch them red-handedly.

They deployed a fully armed contingency of disciplinary policemen around the Xixian Pier to ambush the oncoming oil tanker that evening. They caught the director of the customs and the head gangster and their followers. They interrogated them overnight, immediately.

The next day, headed by the CDC officials, the disciplinary policemen stormed both the vice mayor's and the police deputy director's offices at the same time. The corrupt officials were arrested and their offices were searched thoroughly. In one week's action, hundreds of low-ranking corrupt officials, bankers and gangsters were nabbed. It was like a strong earthquake that had struck the local bureaucratic and outdated system. The operation almost closed the entire municipal government. In order to keep the offices running, many important positions had to be quickly filled by reviewing qualified personnel as acting roles from nearby cities and provinces.

Unfortunately, a big fish slipped through the net: Tang Daming, that one of the most wanted corrupt bankers, had gotten away from Hong Kong and was headed for Canada.

*　　*　　*

Listening to Liu Ming's report and recalling the recent explosive news of smashing the corruptive gang of the high-ranking officials of the city by CDC, Chen Yong fully understood why Lin Dan had defaced herself and her activity afterward. He loved her more for her heroic and unselfish acts and did not care how her features had changed. He really wanted to see her now. They hadn't seen one another for more than three years. And, of course, he wanted to be with her for the rest of his life. She had sacrificed herself to save him from bankruptcy, which would have utterly shattered his dreams. It was now time for him to rescue her from self-destruction and self-isolation, and resume her self-esteem and their intimate relationship.

The detective suggested he should fly to the capital to meet her. He told his secretary to order an air ticket for him immediately. He called the CDC in the capital, demanding to talk to his lover, but he was told that, for her safety reason, Lin Dan was not allowed to answer any calls. Then he asked them to inform his lover that he would be there to meet her tomorrow.

In the afternoon, he went out to buy some snacks that he remembered she would enjoy eating the most, the brand name of her favorite dresses, and the cosmetics and jewelry that she had used most often. And, as Liu Ming had reminded him, some various kinds of silky scarves that she might need to put on her face when she went out.

The next morning, he got up three hours earlier. He took a shower, washed and dried his hair, then styled it the way she had praised. Then he shaved again and again, and put on the wedding ring, the traditional wedding red gown, hat and shoes that he had used in the wedding ritual the day before they were forced to split. Finally, he packed up his luggage carefully and rehearsed the words that would persuade her to come back to him.

On the way to the airport, his chauffeur giggled once in a while at his boss. He had never seen him in such a strange appearance and hearing his embarrassing mumblings.

After claiming his luggage at the Beijing Airport he hurried to a floral shop and bought a bouquet of red roses. He jumped in a taxi and instructed the driver of the address for the Central Disciplinary Committee building, from a piece of paper given by the detective.

Once there, he couldn't help singing a song. In just a few minutes, he would meet his lover again. How exciting. He had so much to talk to her after all these years of separation, and he was sure that she would be touched after seeing his appearance and listening to what he had to say. It was time for their unification after such a long ordeal. Yes, he muttered, it was time to end their emotional suffering.

But after being received by the official who was in charge of Lin Dan's case, he was disappointed to be informed that Lin Dan had left the capital yesterday, after hearing that he was coming. She refused to tell where she was headed. Feeling the world collapsing on him, he wanted to cry. Why was he not given a chance to do what he was supposed to do, to be with a girl he really loved?

Having returned back to Shenzhen, he urgently called the detective to find out where his lover was.

*　　*　　*

She felt nervous when she learned that Chen Yong was coming to meet her the next day. The news disturbed her. It was as if a rock thrown into a quiet pond, then causing the surging of ripples. She really didn't want him to see how ugly she was now, and to let her beautiful image that had remained in his memory be ruined. She had to stay away from him, away from the secular world forever.

Although she was advised to stay in the CDC building for her safety, she insisted on leaving before Chen Yong came. There was nothing they could do but let her go.

Having packed up, she took a taxi to the train station, then bought a ticket to Henan province, an administrative region in the upper middle part of the nation. After a twelve-hour uneasy ride during the night, she got off at one of the stations in Henan in the crisp early morning air. It was still dark, there was no bus running that early, so she bought some snacks from a store as her breakfast and stayed in the station until dawn. Then she walked to the bus station and got on a bus that would carry her to that world-renowned scenic spot and the mecca of martial arts lovers.

After two hours of bumping up and down on the ragged road and looking at the huge mountain that emerged in the cloud at the summit, she was in awe. Song Mountain was listed by the United Nations as one of the world's greatest cultural heritage sites. Its value was not only the distinguished beauty created by nature, which was about five thousand feet tall with seventy-two peaks meandering along the east and west for about sixty miles. It also had various carvings on rock and wood, and ancient constructions such as temples, schools, towers, pagodas, bridges and stairways. More importantly, the Shaolin Temple, the sanctum and mecca of kung fu, the Chinese martial arts was there. It attracted numerous kung fu lovers and tourists throughout the year from all over the world. Indeed, many kung fu movies with the background of Shaolin Temple and its monks had been made in the past decades. And the stunning and marvelous Chinese martial arts performed by the monks of the famous Shaolin Temple had impressed the audiences around the world. There were monks and nuns stationed in the temple, living reclusively for hundreds of years throughout different dynasties. They did nothing but pray, recite Buddhism litany and practice martial arts every day. Their living relied mainly on the donation made by the kung fu lovers, tourists, Buddhists, religious organizations, and local governments.

There were hotels in various locations of the mountain. Those who wanted to see the stunning panorama of sunrise and sunset, to appreciate the real beauty of nature, to worship Buddha, or wait for admission results for entering the martial art schools, would choose to stay in the hotels there.

Briskly, Lin Dan started to climb on the rock-carved stairway. Smelling the sweetness of the ancient earth, she felt relieved and rejuvenated. Yes, this would be her home from this moment on; all the pains in life, desires, despair and unhappiness would be forgotten.

Climbing on, she saw various huge ancient towering trees all around, strange-looking rocks that resembled the shade of animals or humans protruded or perched here and there. Eagles were hovering and gliding up and down the ravines and mounds and peaks. Rays of sunlight shot down from spans of tree leaves, while tourists ahead and behind her were snapping shots of various sights.

Passing through small and narrow bridges built with logs or stones, the intestine-shape path attaching on the cliffs and bushy ditches and ravines, she arrived on the ridge. Looking down, while heavily panting, she saw the huge red sun, veiled with a flimsy, cloud-turned fog, perching on top of the ancient trees. It was breathtaking. She regretted missing the opportunity to see the beautiful sunrise. It didn't matter, she would make it up thousands of times for the rest of her life. Struggling for hours, she finally spotted a temple looming among the trees on a peak of a ridge. It looked awesome and sacred. *This is my home,* she was elated, mumbling.

15

The ambitious Octopus Telecom began stretching its tentacles overseas. Starting with selling phones and their accessories to the precinct nations, it had set up offices around the world to market its most advanced phone systems. Its goal was to conquer the world-class telecommunication giants, and to take up a certain market occupancy rate global-wide.

As the company expanded rapidly, Chen Yong had become an internationally renowned entrepreneur. He was often on business trips between China and nations around the world. The country he often traveled to was the United States of America. It not only had a huge market potential, but it also had the most advanced medical technologies in the world—especially in plastic surgery. He would often consult and inquire information about hospitals that conduct plastic surgery through interpreters, and would visit the best ones once in a while. From the information he had gotten and had been told by doctors, his lover's damaged face could be healed to as good as her original look. He was so excited, wanting to share this good news with his lover at once.

With further thinking of it, he frowned and his mood plummeted. He hadn't gotten any clues about where his lover had been hiding. He hired more detectives and had almost turned the nation up side down in trying to locate her. None of the detectives had come up with any hint or productive results. He had also placed advertisements in major newspapers and magazines to handsomely reward those who could provide information leading to helping find his lover. Except for a few prank calls or imaginary calls made by those who wanted to become rich instantly, no useful information at all had been received. He had also checked with her parents, relatives and friends. Their answers were nearly the same—they had lost contact with her. Although he had called them almost every day, the negative result remained unchanged. All methods in his imagination had been used, but none of them were working. He was so desperate, but didn't know what else he could do.

In his office one day, an idea of visiting a fortune-teller came into his mind. But where could he find one, a good one?

Even though fortune-telling was illegal because of the communists' atheistic belief, such activities commonly existed both publicly and privately throughout the nation since the nation adopted the open-door policy. It was not difficult to find fortune tellers who conducted such activities as a way of making a living in quiet places both in urban and rural areas. But at the same time, many charlatans who knew little or nothing about fortune-telling often mingled with the knowledgeable ones. Thus, it was hard to distinguish them apart. People in southeastern China who wanted to find genuine and good fortune-tellers would refer to the advertisements posted in the Hong Kong newspapers and make contact with them.

After a few days of arrangement conducted by his secretary, a Hong Kong fortune-teller came to his office. He praised and congratulated Chen Yong's good fortune after doing all the complicated calculations with the data of "the eight elements," or his birthday and the exact hour he was born, reading his palm, and conducting the physiognomy observation. He also told him that he would be a dedicated lover, husband and father, and that he deserved to be rich and successful. Then he asked for "the eight elements" of his lover. Mesmerizing in calculations for twenty minutes, he frowned but told him that his lover was a lovely, kind and gracious person and that she would have good fortune after suffering all the misfortunes before the age of thirty. She was in a safe but remote place, possibly in a temple or church; a temple was more likely since she tended to believe in Buddhism. It shouldn't be too difficult to find her if she was in a temple somewhere within China since there were not many temples left after all the past political movements, especially the Cultural Revolution. Chen Yong thanked him and paid him handsomely.

*   *   *

Getting closer to the temple, Lin Dan saw some monks sweeping the front vestibule leisurely. Not many tourists or kung fu lovers or Buddhism believers were there yet. The temple had four edifices and a cemetery: one stood in the front, the other guarded at the back with the cemetery right behind it, and the remaining two were being sandwiched between them. Positioned on a relatively low slope, with a two-meter-high compound surrounding it, there were many ancient trees within the compound and around it. Suddenly, she heard the dull and deafening chimes of the familiar brass bell she had heard in a temple located on the famous Emei Mountain near her hometown when she was a child. The rumbling noises reverberated between ridges and peaks. The reason why she chose not to go to that temple was she was afraid of being recognized by her parents, relatives, and villagers. The chiming of the bell reminded her of the happy days of her childhood. Being a child, she often went up to the temple with her friends. Sometimes, they followed the adults to kneel down in front of the giant Buddha and pray, but often didn't know what to pray or what wishes to make. Sometimes, they imitated adults to play marital games, bowing to each other and then to the Buddha and mumbling, "We will love and care each other and stay married forever." Other times, they sat next to the monks, repeating what they recited from the Buddhist sutra, or helped them to fetch water and clean the temple. But the most exciting thing they did was to strike the gigantic brass bell with a log hanging next to it, and each time it rang it was so loud that the children stuck their fingers into their ears and giggled. That memory was still so vivid. She smiled, feeling like a child again. But she would never imagine that someday she would belong to a temple, living, and doing the daily routines with the monks she was so familiar with.

She stepped calmly into the front yard of the temple and said to a monk who was sweeping the leaves on the floor, "Good morning, Teacher."

"Good morning, Benefactor."

"I would like to see the abbot. Could you help me, please?"

"Benefactor, may I ask what you want to see our abbot for?" the monk asked mildly, gazing at her, and frowning a bit.

"I want to be a nun here."

"Really? Have you thought it over? Not many people can endure the life here. We have had some quit after staying here for just a few months, even days."

"I am different from them. I will commit myself to be here for the rest of my life. Please, let me see the abbot."

"Okay, follow me, Benefactor."

Following the monk closely, Lin Dan entered and passed the first building and then climbed onto the rock stairway to the two edifices in the middle. She heard the familiar chanting of the Buddhist sutra when she stepped into the building where many monks sat in rows with their legs crossed and hands clasped in front of their chests while reciting the religious litany.

Ignoring the scenery, they continued their way on and exited the rear door to the last building. When they got up to the threshold through the marble stairway, she smelled the sweetness of incense burning. She hurried in and saw a huge brass rectangular container with a myriad of incenses sticking on the top standing right at the entrance. Behind it, there were rows of wooden benches in front of a gigantic Goddess of Mercy statue, which was sitting at the back of the roomy baldachin. She guessed the baldachin was big enough to accommodate hundreds of people at one time, if not thousands. The smiling, exquisite and plump Goddess of Mercy statue looked gracious, warm, tender and classic. She knelt on the wooden bench and bowed to it at once. This was the goddess she would worship and pray to from now on. She would, no doubt, devote herself doing it for the rest of her life.

Having finished praying, she got up and was surprised to find another monk standing behind her, smiling and nodding to her. He was taller and bigger with a bulging belly; and he was introduced to be the abbot of the temple. Clasping their hands and positioning them right in front of their bosoms, they bowed to each other.

"Benefactor, I heard that you contemplate to join our temple here, is it true?" the abbot asked mildly.

"Yes, Priest."

"We believe that it is good for you to think it over for three days, and we will observe how you behave as a test during these days. After that we will decide if we should arrange an admittance ritual, which is the tonsure ritual, for you."

"Okay, I agree. But is there any suggestions that you would give to me?"

"I don't usually give out suggestions to applicants, but since you are a female benefactor, I suggest you to forget about the outside world completely."

"Thanks."
"Take care, Benefactor."
"Take care, Priest."

*   *   *

Right after the fortune-teller had left, Chen Yong called the detectives to check out the temple located in that national-renowned Emei Mountain near Lin Dan's hometown, the two in the capital, and then the other two in the adjacent provinces of the capital. There were only a few more left in the entire nation to be checked, if his lover were not in one of those five temples. But he had a hunch that his lover would be in the one on Song Mountain, because she admired the kung fu masters there and loved the beauty of nature very much. She often climbed up to the Emei Mountain when she was a child, as she had told him; and she had mentioned about how she had been craving to visit the more beautiful Song Mountain someday.

The thought of putting away his work for a while and take a trip to visit the nation's hot scenic spot and, more importantly, to a place where his lover was likely to be hiding in, popped in his mind. He called his sister in and talked to her about it. His sister, Chen Jing, was concerned about him and his lover. She often consoled him and gave him suggestions. Once hearing what her brother said, she agreed with him immediately and wanted to go with him as well. It would be helpful to have his sister to go with him because the two girls were good friends. Chen Yong was delighted and instructed his secretary to book the air tickets and hotel rooms at once.

Sitting alone after his sister had left, he wondered what he should bring and how he should dress to persuade his lover to come home with him if she happened to be in the Song Mountain. He decided he would bring the pictures that they had taken before and, of course, their traditional red wedding gown, the photos of the American hospitals and the ones taken with the plastic surgeons were a must, along with the brochures (both in English and Chinese) telling and showing how patients with more severe conditions were healed with their modern medical technologies under the intensive care of the professional doctors and nurses in the sophisticated American hospitals. He would take the tape and recorder to

141

deliver the words of the American doctors in both English and Chinese to her, telling her that her face was absolutely fixable and that she would be as beautiful as before after the face-altering incident.

The next morning, after telling his brother and his subordinates to take care of the business, he hurried to the airport with his sister. His instinct kept telling him that his lover was there. He was a bit nervous, but couldn't wait to be there.

Landing at the airport there, they got in a taxi immediately. The driver was stunned when they told him they were going to the Song Mountain. It would take at least three hours to get there and cost them hundreds of yuan. He advised them to take a long-distance bus, but Chen Yong refused at once and promised they would pay him double of what the meter would show.

It was late afternoon when they got there. They were so hungry and tired, and decided to eat first before the climbing trip. They entered a restaurant named The House of Mountain Treasures and were amazed to find that most of the dishes were either fresh herbs or wild animal meats and organs. And they found that it served several kinds of long-hour-soup, the soup that cooked with both herbs and wild animal meats and bones, besides the famous snake soup. Lastly, they had the mountain fruits for desert. The taste of the food was so different from what they had in the coastal metropolis where restaurants usually served seafood, cattle meat, and planted vegetables. They enjoyed these mountain treasures very much. It was a feast. And they agreed that they would spend some of their vacations there in the future.

It was sunset now, the thin and scale-shaped clouds hanging on the sky were tinted pink and orange and white. It was time to go. They started climbing upon a foothill. They were told by the restaurant owner that there was a hotel on the lower ridge of the mountain behind the foothills. It was too late for them to climb on to where the temple was, so they decided to stay in a hotel until the next morning. Struggling on, his sister kept appreciating and praising the beauty of nature very much, but he had little mood for it. He really wanted to see his lover tonight if she were there, but he doubted if the temple would allow any of its disciples to meet with people from the secular world during the night. It was completely dark when they reached the hotel.

He was not used to the chirping noise of insects, nor could he calm himself down. He was restless for the whole night. When dawn finally came, he took a cold shower. After having breakfast in the dining hall next to the lobby, he hurried back to the room and put on his traditional red wedding gown. His sister was astonished and giggled at his funny appearance and asked if they had already married secretly.

After hearing the story of their episode, Chen Jing was touched and adored them more. Now she believed the true love between a man and a woman did exist. The doubt and precaution that had prevented her from accepting dates in the past years might be unnecessary, as she used to think that she was not very beautiful, because whoever wanted to date her must be a fortune hunter. She might be wrong about them, or at least some of her admirers. She had had many of her admirers since becoming the chief accountant and then the general manager of the Octopus Telecom. But she had rejected them all, feeling insecure while burying herself at work. Sometimes, the successful feeling inflicted from work could not fill in the emptiness of her loneliness. She really admired her brother for his dedication, commitment, devotion, and persistence in pursuing true love. She wished she could have met a good man as her brother. Now she would do all she could to help him.

*   *   *

The first thing Lin Dan did after talking with the temple's abbot was to destroy her mobile phone. She would have no connection to the outside world. At first, she wanted to call her parents to inform them of her decision of staying in a temple for the rest of her life, but the abbot's advise wiped away her very last thought of the secular world. Her new life should be absolutely reclusive and isolated, none of her relatives and friends should know where she was living.

In the following three days, except helping the monks to do the cleaning, she knelt in front of the statue of the Goddess of Mercy and prayed and bowed. She behaved exccllently. The abbot had often watched her secretly and approved what she did. Her admitting ritual began on her fourth day there.

At noon, the gigantic brass bell was struck five times to summon all the monks and nuns to the baldachin at once. Lining up on two

143

sides and facing each other in ten feet, the monks and nuns were clasping their hands up above their bellies. The abbot, wearing a special orange dress, stood between the two lines at the very end and faced the statue of the Goddess of Mercy, and announced the commencement of the tonsure ritual. Two monks stuck a bundle of large incense sticks onto the huge brass container and lighted them. Immediately the monks and nuns turned around and knelt down and bowed to the statue of the Goddess of Mercy three times and then chanted. Minutes later, still chanting, they turned back facing each other.

Then Lin Dan, with her straight hair loose on her back and shoulders, and her hands clasped, was instructed to step slowly between the two lines of monks and nuns toward the abbot from the entrance of the baldachin. Stamping slowly ahead, with her face looking stern, her eyes kept staring at the statue of Goddess of Mercy. From that moment on, her life would be forever changed. Reaching in front of the abbot, she knelt down and bowed to him and then the statue. A nun holding a tray with a pair of scissors and a comb was strolling on the same path Lin Dan had just gone through. Once in front of them, she knelt down and raised the tray over her head.

The abbot chanted, "Amida Buddha, benefactor Lin Dan has successfully passed the three-day test and now is ready to become one of our sisters and a follower of our great Goddess of Mercy, let's give her a helping hand."

He picked up the pair of scissors and the comb from the tray and started cutting Lin Dan's hair off. With her beautiful long and straight hair scattered on the floor, her mind was numbed and ceased to function. Since in her teens, she had been proud of her shining, long and straight hair. Indeed, it had won praises and envies of both men and women. But now all of it was coming off. She struggled hard to prevent the tears from coming out of her eyes.

Cutting and combing until all of Lin Dan's hair was off and her head had become starkly bald, the abbot put down the cutting tools and announced, "Namomitabhaya Buddha, the Goddess of Mercy, under your watch, we have just finished helping a new sister to be born again." All of them knelt down and bowed to the statue again.

Lin Dan was given a brown-colored nun's dress, a Buddhist sutra and a Buddhist name called Jingxin, or peace of mind. Every morning, the brass bell would chime at four, then she had to get up and sit cross-legged with some monks and nuns at the baldachin, recite the Buddhist sutra and chant eulogies to the Buddhist God for two hours. Others were practicing kung fu in the backyard. Then they had breakfast. After that, she would do the cleaning work, and some would take turns to go fetch water with buckets for another two hours. And then they would meditate and pray at the baldachin until noon. After lunch, she would join them to study the Buddhist sutra for three hours. Then, for two hours, she would learn martial arts. Shortly after dinner, they resumed reciting and chanting and bowing for an hour. Finally, they practiced kung fu again before going to sleep.

During these patterned activities every day, she was reminded herself, repeatedly, to forget everything and everyone she had known in the past. She wanted the evil out of her heart and become the genuine sister of the Goddess of Mercy.

Life was simple and pure. The sentimental things in the past—such as happiness, excitement, sadness, love, hatred, worry, despair, desperation and cravings—all of these emotions, feelings and prospects that a human possessed were gradually vanishing. Although pictures of the past kept flitting through her mind from time to time. And amazingly, her memories of the loved ones, friends and enemies were beginning to fade. Like the meaning of her religious name Jingxin, her mind was becoming more peaceful day after day. *Soon, I would become a hermit,* she thought, *everything and everyone in the past would be forgotten and everyone known in the mundane world would forget about me too. Thanks to my Goddess of Mercy, and Amida Buddha.*

*   *   *

Chen Jing was excited watching the giant red sun emerge slowly from the horizon. The clouds, the mountain, the rocks, the trees, the spiderwebs and the dew hanging or perching on the leaves of plants were all tinted in gold. She was jumping and yelling. The weariness inflicted from climbing uphill over an hour since the early morning had been forgotten. They hadn't seen sunrise for a long time since becoming adults, and it was the first time they had seen it from the ridge of a mountain. It was astonishingly breathtaking. Chen Yong tried to echo with his sister, but she could detect that he was absentminded, noticing that he often glanced at the temple, which was looming among the forest only a few hundred feet ahead.

Approaching the temple, they spotted some monks and nuns sweeping the floor, but Lin Dan was not there. Clasping his hand, Chen Yong hurried over and asked them if a girl name Lin Dan, who had a damaged face, was there. They were stunned by the question, especially that it was asked by a man wearing a traditional wedding gown. Looking at each other, they didn't know whether they should respond. They knew the girl was there and their religious belief prevented them from lying.

A monk finally said, "Benefactor, please wait here for a minute. Let me go in and check if she is the one you are looking for."

Hearing what he said, Chen Yong was happy. He was positive that his lover was there. He couldn't wait to see her, and he was confident that he could persuade her to go home with him.

After waiting for twenty minutes, the same monk accompanying the abbot stepped out of the building, but Lin Dan was not with them. Chen Yong leaped over and queried, "Where is my wife Lin Dan?"

"Amida Buddha, Benefactor, I heard that you are looking for the girl named Lin Dan and you said she is your wife, is it correct?" the priest asked with his hands clasping.

"Yes, it is. Where is she now?"

"Benefactor, that girl does not exist anymore. She has been born again here. Her new name is Jingxin, and she doesn't want to see you. In fact, she doesn't want to see anyone known in the past, including her relatives and friends."

"But Abbot Master, she is my wife. I love her and have missed her so much. Please, be kind to help me."

"I understand, but it was her decision to be here and her decision not to see you. It's the karma and destiny, accept it, Benefactor."

Chen Yong was so desperate, he stepped forward and knelt right in front of the abbot and bowed, mumbling, "Buddhists are supposed to be kind and gracious and their job is to help, guide and save people, not to hurt and split them. Please, help my wife to come back to me."

The priest was caught off guard, bending down to try to get him up. He said, "Please get up, Benefactor, and please understand that she came here to seek help and to be sheltered from the secular world because she had suffered so much. My heart sank by just looking at how terrible her face was. So I did my best to help her and save her from suffering more. She has gone through the admittance ritual and has become one of our sisters. She has now got onto the preliminary stage of maintaining a peace of mind, like what the meaning of her name is. It is hard and unfortunate for her to be interrupted now, Benefactor, please leave, for her sake."

Chen Yong remained impervious. He replied, "I understand it all and thank you for helping her. Everything, including her coming here has been wrong since we were forced to separate by a vicious and corrupt government official. But he has been arrested recently and my wife's face is repairable by modern medical technology. It is time for us to be reunified."

"Amida Buddha, your graciousness, what a terrible grievance, and what a good job you have done to rectify it. Now please help them to be together again," the priest chanted, his hands reaching to Chen Yong's shoulders. "Benefactor, please get up and wait here, let me go in and persuade her to see you. But whether she wants to see you or not, it will be strictly her decision and the karma between you and her."

"Thank you so much, Abbot Master, I understand, but I will remain kneeling until she comes out and agrees to come with me."

The priest muttered some kind of incantations again and headed back to the temple.

*   *   *

As a morning routine, Lin Dan was washing her clothes in a little pool of a brook with two other nuns. They were chatting about the meaning of the words and phrases in the Buddhist sutra and reviewing the names of the sequences of actions of the martial arts. They were prohibited to talk about their past or anything involving their relatives, loved ones, friends, sex and intimate relationships, except their daily tasks, study, and god-worshipping affairs. Anyone caught breaking the rule would be fined to recite paragraphs of the Buddhist sutra and to meditate alone for days. Thus it was rare for any one of them to offend the rules. They lived purely, peacefully, and harmoniously. Yet she enjoyed the spiritual life and the environment here and thought she should have been here earlier. Occasionally, she viewed her face with the reflection of a pool of still water—the temple was not allowed to have mirrors. When the memory of the past started popping up in her mind, she disturbed the water immediately.

This morning, she was feeling as peaceful and pleasant as usual when a monk sprinted over and told her that a young man, with a traditional wedding dress on, claimed to be her husband and demanded to see her now. *Amida Buddha, how could he find me here?* She gasped.

"Tell him there is no such person here."

"But Jingxin, as Buddhists, we don't lie," the monk reminded her.

"Oh, yes, I just forgot. Then tell him to leave, I don't want to see him."

"But what do you do if he doesn't want to leave?"

Deep in her heart, she had really missed him and wanted to see him, but under her circumstances, especially being a nun, they would have no hope to be together again. There was no way back.

"Well, just tell him that I am no longer Lin Dan, my name is Jingxin, a sister of the Goddess of Mercy. Lin Dan has died, so has our relationship."

The monk nodded and hurried away. But half an hour later, when she was fighting hard to calm herself down, he returned and said that the abbot wanted to talk to her. It must be, she guessed at once, that she would be advised or even condemned for causing trouble for the temple.

Stepping into the abbot's room with an ill feeling, she explained immediately, "I have no idea how he has found me here, Abbot Father. I swear to the Goddess of Mercy, I haven't told anyone that I am here."

After bowing to each other with their hands clasped, the abbot said, "Jingxin, none of us have blamed you at all and we all know that you are a devoted sister here. But could you honestly answer me one question?"

"Yes, of course."

"Were you married before you came here?"

"Well, to tell you the truth, we did not register. The two of us had the wedding ritual privately before we were forced to separate."

"I see. Do you still love him?"

"I . . . I can't, I am a sister of here now and I am happy staying here."

"Amida Buddha, I believe you two still have the karma. He seems to still love you very much, and he said the government official who inflicted your separation has been arrested. And more, he said your face is repairable by the modern medical technology. Maybe you should return to the mundane world again. It is up to you, Jingxin, but I should let you know that he has been kneeling there to wait for you. He said that he will remain kneeling until you come out to see him."

Hearing that, her long squashed and depressed emotions suddenly erupted. Yes, deep in her heart she still loved him and wanted to be with him so much. She felt especially touched for his dedication and persistence. They would have, she believed, a very happy family together. She really wanted to see him and talk to him and hug him now. But her look, her face, her bald head, yet her ugliest appearance, how could she face him now? Not only that, there was no guarantee that they would not be forced to split again by another Li Ben-type official. Hesitantly, she finally decided to reject the idea of seeing her sweetheart.

"Abbot, Father, I have become a sister here. I will go nowhere but stay here for the rest of my life. Please tell him to go away. I have no intention to see him."

The priest frowned, he did not expect her negative answer. Indeed, he wanted to help them to be reunited, because it was one of the responsibilities for a Buddhist to help rectify wrongdoings and to help people form and maintain harmonious families.

"Are you sure, Jingxin? Don't be rushed, maybe you need some time, maybe a few days to make up your mind. Let me tell him to wait for your final decision in a hotel room in the valley for a couple of days. What do you think?"

"No, Abbot Father. I have made the final decision already. Just tell him to go," she replied adamantly.

"Amida Buddha, I will tell him then."

Getting back to the vestibule of the front building, the priest's heart ached seeing the man still kneeling there. How would he react if he were told that his lover didn't want to go with him? He would rather let him wait instead of telling him the bad news, until he was too tired and out of patience to go on. But he was too late, Chen Jing called on him and queried at once.

"What did she say? Why doesn't she come with you?"

"Amida Buddha, Benefactor, she contemplates to stay here and wants you to leave her alone."

"Really? Does she know that her lover has been kneeling here to wait for her?"

"Yes, I told her that."

"Can I go to see her?"

"Amida Buddha, Benefactor, according to our temple's rules, our brothers and sisters should not be bothered by anyone from the mundane world. Please understand."

"But this case is different, her husband is here kneeling and waiting for her. And I know her well enough that she is not a heartless girl, quite the opposite. She is the most warm-hearted, kind and passionate woman I have ever met. Why has she become so stubborn? I don't understand."

"I won't leave until she comes out to meet me," Chen Yong cried with saddened heart.

Shaking his head, the priest sighed, "It's all about the feelings and sensations that often causes trouble, Amida Buddha." He turned, heading back to the building.

"Wait, Abbot Master," Chen Yong croaked. "Please tell her that I don't mind about her bald head and her damaged face because I love her so much."

The abbot turned around and nodded, disappearing into the edifice.

*   *   *

Kneeling down in front of the statue of the Goddess of Mercy, Lin Dan kept praying to calm herself down. She collapsed. Sobbing uncontrollably, images of her past flashed through her memory; her lover, her parents, friends and bad guys kept reappearing in her mind. With her hands clasped, her legs and her entire body started shaking. It became unbearable. Her mind was no longer in peace. She realized, finally, that she could not be isolated from the outside world, nor could her mind be completely peaceful. She could not live reclusively forever and did not belong to a temple. The hardest thing for her now was how she could face herself and her lover with her blemished face and her hairless head. She did not have the courage, nor did she know what to do. Suddenly, in dizziness, she heard the priest call her name and felt his hands grabbing her shoulders and lifting her up. She turned around facing the priest.

"Jingxin sister, I can see now that your mind is not here. You cannot devote yourself completely to the Goddess of Mercy because you can't sever yourself from the past. You don't belong to the temple but to the mundane world. You came here because you need a shelter. Am I right?"

"Please, forgive me, Abbot Father, I can't say that you are wrong. I am new here, it will just take some time to forget the past. I have been working hard on it. Today, this happened so suddenly that it caught me off guard. I have nowhere to go if you don't let me stay here," she pleaded.

"Jingxin, I understand, but even if you would manage to stay here for long, the memory of the past will come to haunt you from time to time. Especially after what has happened today. Besides, your loved ones, relatives and friends will come here often to persuade you to come back to them. Thus the chance for you to devote yourself here completely is very slim. And we don't want to see your stay here to cause so many people in the mundane world to suffer so much emotionally. Why don't you go see him now, he is still kneeling there and waiting for you."

"But I just can't see him now, my face and bald head will get him frightened."

"He said he does not mind about your appearance at all."

"Maybe he doesn't mind, but I do. I can't let him see how ugly I am now. It will be a disaster," she mumbled.

"I can see now you are still in love with him."

"I can't be," she blurted out, but regretted saying it immediately.

"Face it, Jingxin, don't try to escape. This shouldn't be a shelter for your shameful feeling forever."

"I wish I could. But please, let me stay, Abbot Father."

"I have no reason to drive you out, but your staying here is meaningless."

"I'll try my bet to fit in here, give me some time."

The priest sighed and retreated back to the baldachin, leaving her there alone. She resumed kneeling and praying, trying to calm her boggled and confused mind.

*　　*　　*

Chen Yong, determined to go on as long as it needed to have his lover's mind changed, kept kneeling for hours and refused to have lunch. There was a saying, "There was gold on a man's knee," or man shall not kneel. He ignored his sister's call and the gossips and chats of the temple's disciples and the onlookers, nothing would stop him from bringing back his lover. In the late afternoon, his limbs went numb and he started to shiver uncontrollably. The on-lookers were getting more crowded, many of them praised and chanted in support of him. He closed his eyes and bit his lips, and continued to kneel.

Seeing his brother's predicament, Chen Jing begged to the monks and nuns to bring her to see Lin Dan. A nun finally accepted her request. Following the nun, she passed through groups of people, stairways and buildings, and finally entered the baldachin. A baldheaded woman in a brown dress kneeling in front of the statue of the Goddess of Mercy was conspicuous among the tourists and Buddha worshippers. A nun stepped over and whispered to her. Lin Dan turned her head around, Chen Jing was terrified. The lovely and gorgeous girl she was so familiar with had become utterly unrec-ognizable. Her ghostly ugliness could only be seen in movies. She felt deeply sorry for her.

Approaching her, Chen Jing cried, "Dan Dan, it's me. I am so sorry to see you like this."

But Lin Dan stared at her for a few seconds, then she muttered, "Amida Buddha, Benefactor, you've got me wrong. I don't think we have met before."

"It's Chen Jing. I am sure you remember me as a friend and Chen Yong's sister. As a nun, you are not supposed to lie, Dan Dan."

"I don't know what you are talking about, Benefactor," Lin Dan replied, stood up and hurried away.

Watching her disappear out of the building, Chen Jing was disappointed, but she fully understood why she behaved like that. With the painful past experiences and a deformed face, she could not afford to be hurt again. But yet, at least, she had the courage to be alive. To change her mind, they had to be patient, or something drastic had to happen, Chen Jing determined.

Retreating back to where her brother was, her heart plummeted. It was about sunset now. She didn't know how much longer he needed to suffer before he collapsed. But she wouldn't try again to persuade him to abort it. He was stubborn, a rarity in modern society—a man so dedicated and devoted to his loved one. This kind of good man could only be found in fiction or movies and not in reality. She was so touched, feeling proud of being his sister.

The crowd around him diminished, as the dark canopy shrouded upon them. A monk carrying a bowl of rice and a plate of mixed vegetables on a tray approached him. He mumbled some religious blessings and left the tray next to him. But Chen Yong did not even bother to look at it, just kept on kneeling. With his eyes closed, his hands clasped, he looked as if he was praying as a pious Buddhism disciple. Chen Jing was sitting on a slate a few feet away quietly, watching him. In the early autumn the mountain breeze was getting cooler. She was shivering and asked a monk to get some clothes for her and her brother. When she received the blouses and tried to put one on her brother, her brother fell forward in his unconsciousness. She screamed, calling for help. A few monks hurried over and helped carry Chen Yong into the temple. Setting him on a wooden bench, the temple's doctor was summoned immediately. After a brief diagnosing, the doctor put a hotel towel on the patient's forehead and said, "After some rest, he would resume consciousness."

*　　*　　*

After running away from her lover's sister, Lin Dan went to the backyard to practice martial art, trying to get the intruding episode out of her mind. Inhaling and exhaling and moving her limbs and body slowly, she worked on the breathing slow motion martial art, an exercise that would help to get one's mind concentrated and serene. Her lover would go away if she continued to refuse seeing him, she believed. She had just finished the action named "two dragons explore the sea" and was about to begin "the ferocious tiger leaps on the mountain," when a monk yelled behind her.

"Jingxin, the man claiming to be your husband and kneeling out there has fainted."

"What? He fainted? My Buddha," she screamed hysterically, rushing down to the scene. While running, she prayed for his safety and damned herself for her selfishness. She would not have a peace of mind for the rest of her life if her lover became handicapped or even died because of her. Getting there, she cried and kept kissing his face, her tears dripping down incessantly. She muttered, "Please, wake up, A-yong, come back to me, please. I promise I will follow you home, please, forgive my selfishness."

Everyone there felt relieved, hearing what Lin Dan said. At last, this couple would get back together again, it would be a happy ending. They patiently waited while watching her regretful and sentimental reaction toward her unconscious lover. Their love was so pure and so real and had passed the toughest test that touched everyone's heart and soul.

When Chen Yong finally awoke, Lin Dan was overjoyed, holding his hand and calling his name. He, first, was startled to see his defaced lover, then was rejoiced. Forgetting his weariness, he got up and hugged her and kissed her. "Is this real? Am I in a dream?" he mumbled in doubt.

"Yes, honey, this is real, can you hear my breath? Can you feel my lips, my heartbeats?"

"Yes, I am so happy, honey. It's been so long. I've missed you so much. Tell me you won't leave me again."

"I promise I won't. I've missed you so much too. I was just afraid that my present ugliness would ruin my previous image that you had before. Thank you so much for your genuine love towards me. I love you, Chen Yong."

"I love you, too. You know what, your look now is no worse than I had imagined. According to the information I have and what I was told by the world-renowned American plastic surgeon, your face can be repaired thoroughly. I've brought all the brochures of their hospitals and the pictures I took with the doctors with me. You may want to take a look at them."

"But would it be easy to go there for surgery?"

"Yes, it is very easy because our company has several offices there, and I plan to set up a factory there soon. And you are my wife, what do you think?"

"Oh, that's wonderful. I can't wait to go there."

Watching and listening to them, everyone was not only happy for their reunification, but also admired them. With their hands clasping, monks and nuns around them chanted, praising and eulogizing Buddha and the Goddess of Mercy for their great love and mercy, and for bringing back this love couple together again. Chen Jing and the onlookers were deeply touched, their eyes were wet with tears.

It was dark now, they decided to stay in the temple overnight so that they could watch the breathtaking sunrise at a better location in the morning. During the entire night, they did not feel tired and sleepy at all. They kept talking, hugging and kissing. When dawn came and the brass bell chimed, monks and nuns swarmed there to give them a farewell ritual. They thanked them and bowed their way out of the temple.

Book Two
2000–2003

16

Having returned to Shenzhen, Chen Yong immediately applied for visas for himself and his lover to go to the United States. Considering that Lin Dan might need female companions during her months-long treatment, Chen Jing and her friend Wu Ting decided to go with them.

When they were ready to take the trip, Lin Dan's hair had grown over an inch long, she was no longer baldheaded and no longer needed to put on a hat. She had the happiest days yet in her life staying with her lover and friends, since coming back from the Song Mountain. They decided that they would have a wedding party after returning back to China.

Their flight would start at the Hong Kong International Airport. Two days prior to their air trip, they went to Hong Kong for both sightseeing and shopping. Traveling through the mountainous New Territory and the crowded Kowloon Peninsula. They were impressed by the orderliness and cleanliness of the former British colony. And it was a feast for their eyes when they viewed the panorama of Victoria Harbor and Lion Mountain on the other side of the harbor from the peak of the Taiping Mountain on Hong Kong Island. The harbor was like a huge and sinuous river lying serenely between hills and mountains, where the forest of concrete mingled with the jungle of nature, with seagulls and eagles flopping, hovering, gliding and chirping above. Now they understood why this tiny place had remained like a magnet for millions of people on the mainland. It was not only because of its history, prosperity and mysterious political system, but also because of the charm of its natural beauty. Chen Yong told his lover, they should be able to buy a villa and get settled down there if she wished.

Leaving the Pearl of the Orient, their flight took nearly fifteen hours to reach the San Francisco International Airport in the United States. Once they passed through the customs, they were picked up immediately by the employees of the Octopus Telecom's office stationed in Silicon Valley. Lin Dan and her friends were amazed that the temperature there was almost the same as that in Hong Kong, not too warm and not too cold.

Watching the enormous airport, the four-lane freeways and the orderly aligned houses here and there, they could feel the abundance of land in this great and wealthy nation, where the land-size was nearly the same as China but which had less than a quarter of its population. They admired and blessed the American's good fortune. And they were startled when told that the houses were built with redwood, a rare and extremely expensive timber used in making classic furniture in China, where all houses and apartment buildings were only built with clay and straws or stone, brick, cement and steel.

American's spacious and wealthy living environments were further proof when they entered one of the houses owned by their company in San Jose. They saw cars parking on both sides of the streets, but few pedestrians. This was quite different from their hometown where streets were mostly jammed with people, bicycles, and buses. When they entered the house, they were really impressed. Running in and out, they found the house had enormous front yard and backyard with a swimming pool and various fruit trees interspersed around them. Inside it was roomy and air-conditioned, the floors were carpeted, the sinks and bathtubs connected with both cold and hot water pipes. They were told that it was only one of the typical houses in America.

In China, very few people would have this kind of living condition, no matter how wealthy the nation had become, because it was over populated. Yet they believed, with its nearly perfect rule of law and the judicial system, the law-enforcing system, freedom and democracy and the wonderful living condition, the United States was one of the best places to reside on earth.

The next day, they visited Chinatown in San Francisco. The overcrowded and filthy Chinese community in this strange land reminded them of their hometowns in China. Except that the language being spoken here was Cantonese instead of their dialects or Mandarin, the Chinese official language. After spending half an hour struggling to find a parking lot, they had lunch there, but the food was not their cup of tea. They realized the dishes in the restaurants there were mostly prepared for the Western tourists.

After touring the downtown area, the Fisherman's Wharf, the Pyramid, the Coit Tower, and the Golden Gate Bridge—the preliminary image of America had implanted into their minds and they adored it. In the evening, they went out to a bar and then a disco to observe and experience a part of American nightlife.

The next morning, Chen Yong took his lover to register in the San Francisco Hospital. After carefully examining her face, the chief plastic surgeon, Dr. Edward, told them it would take about a month to complete the surgery because the damaged tissues on her face had to be removed first and then it required to transplant some pieces of good flesh and skin from other parts of her body, and the chance of a thorough recovery was very high—but there was no guarantee. However, he explained that even if the surgery did not carry out very successfully and some scars remained on her face, her appearance would still look much better than her present condition. Lin Dan and Chen Yong happily signed the surgery agreement with the hospital.

During her operation, the surgery room was thoroughly sanitized and germ-proofed, no one except the doctors and nurses were allowed to enter. After Lin Dan was anesthetized, the doctors started their magical chiseling and repairing work on her face and body. It took nearly half a day to complete the operation. Except for her eyes, Lin Dan's entire face and half of her body were bound with bandage.

In the first week, to avoid infection from happening, she was in the intensive care ward. No one was allowed to visit her or have body contact with her, except the doctors and nurses. She could only see and talk to her lover and friends through a closed circuit TV and the intercom. She thanked them for their support and encouragement and told them that she was feeling better every day.

She was delighted when they finally were allowed in to visit her and carry her out to the lawn in a wheelchair. While enjoying the sunshine and breathing the fresh air, she chatted and sang with them happily. In the following two days, her lover and friends were there on time to see her and take her out. On the third day, her lover had to have a business trip to Europe. Then as a routine, Chen Jing and Wu Ting came to meet and care for her. To their surprise, Dr. Edward said it was his birthday and invited them to the birthday party that would take place in his house that evening.

She was unable to go, but Chen Jing and Wu Ting were thrilled. Dr. Edward picked them up after work. They smelled the salty air and heard the roaring noise of the surging waves, and found that his townhouse perched on a foothill and faced the ocean.

"It's a beautiful house, doctor," Chen Jing exclaimed.

"Thank you. Yes, I really enjoy living here. I bought it five years ago," the doctor said, pushing a button. The garage door opened upward slowly, with a little cracking noise, and his car rolled in. Entering the house, they found a huge living room and a kitchen on the first floor, and three bedrooms on the second floor.

"It's so roomy, who else lives here?" Chen Jing was curious.

"I'm the only one living here," the doctor replied. In his late thirties, Dr. Edward told them he had dated twice before, but had ended the affairs because of the wildness and naughtiness of the Western girls. He admitted to them that he had admired the Chinese culture and wanted to date a Chinese girl, but had not found the right one yet.

Taking out the meat and pork ribs from the refrigerator, the doctor said he had ordered some food to be delivered from a restaurant. But in a meanwhile, he was going to grill some barbecue pork and spare ribs before his guests arrive. He mumbled he would have preferred to cook them Chinese dishes instead of the same American cuisine. Hearing that, Chen Jing asked if she could try. He was elated and told her that whatever was needed could be bought from a nearby Chinese grocery store. Then they jumped into the car and rolled out of the house. Twenty minutes later, they were back with all the needed cooking materials.

As the guests arrived one after another, Chen Jing's Chinese dishes, the spare ribs with black bean sauce, and sweet and sour pork, along with the delivered food, were ready to serve. Dr. Edward announced that the two Chinese dishes were cooked by the two special guests. After tasting them, everyone ranted and praised the food and said that they had never tasted such delicious Chinese dishes. Someone asked if one of these two special guests was the doctor's girlfriend. The doctor and the two girls did not deny it but responded that they were his patient's friends. With their broken English and gestures during the dinner, Chen Jing and Wu Ting talked fervently with the doctor and the other young male guest. After desert, the dance party began. The doctor invited Chen Jing to dance with him immediately, while the other young male and Wu Ting had become partners simultaneously. The guests were impressed by their nearly flawless dancing performance.

That night, while having fun, they made some new friends, learned more about American culture, and picked up new words and phrases in English. From that night on, Chen Jing with the doctor went out very often. Wu Ting with the other young man, David, an engineer, joined them. And soon, they became lovers. Lin Dan was startled when they first told her, but she congratulated them, wishing them happiness. But they had no idea if their parents and friends in China would accept the fact that their daughters had dated foreigners, because deep in many older Chinese people's minds foreigners were still barbarians. They were not able to communicate with them due to the language barrier.

* * *

Chen Yong returned to look after his lover periodically between his business trips. He regretted being so busy to spend so little time with her. But Lin Dan understood it and thought, *I will travel with you wherever you go after getting out of the hospital, honey.* She was happier day after day because her ordeal would be ended and a new chapter of her life would begin.

Nearly a month after she was admitted into the hospital, the magic moment of unbinding the bandages on her face finally came. The hospital organized a celebration for her with photographers taking photos. But no one knew how well her face had recovered yet, although the cuts on her body had healed nicely. Everyone, especially Lin Dan and her lover, were both happy and nervous. They prayed with their hands clasped, and she mumbled some phrases of the Buddhism sutra she learned while on the Song Mountain. Although she was no longer a nun, Lin Dan and her lover had decided to believe in Buddhism.

Lin Dan was sitting in a chair in the middle of a stage in a hall of the hospital, a huge picture of her before the operation was positioned next to her. Dr. Edward announced the beginning of the bandage unbinding, then layers of the bandage started loosening as he cut and unbound her face. Lin Dan's heart was pounding as she watched the bandage falling from her face. A mirror sat in front of

163

her, while photographers were busy taking pictures. When it came to the final moment of revealing her face, everyone stopped breathing and just stared at it without blinking. Lin Dan felt her heart was coming out of her mouth, she was panting uncontrollably.

With his left hand holding a cotton ball soaked with alcohol to clean away blood stains, the doctor's right hand slowly pulled down the last layer of bandage from his patient's face. Lin Dan exclaimed merrily, seeing her smooth and creamy face that began reemerging. She leaped up to her lover, hugging and kissing him, with tears washing down her face. An explosion of cheer and laughter erupted from the crowd, and the cameras kept flashing. The word "congratulations" in both English and Chinese mingled with the rejoicing boisterousness. It was a kind of magical work that achieved this brilliant result as the state of art in reshaping and repairing the human body.

Lin Dan thanked Dr. Edward and hugged him and took pictures with him. He reminded her not to take it too seriously because they might become relatives, and then winked at her. Hearing that, Chen Jing's face flushed and, at once, Lin Dan and her lover congratulated them.

Much better than expected, Lin Dan had recovered remarkably well. While Chen Jing and Wu Ting had dramatically picked their windfalls in finding their mister-rights, their America trip had resulted in not only a healing but also a romantic, rejuvenating and horizon-expanding journey. How wonderful. They were all in a high mood and in great spirits. Dr. Edward and David decided they would go to China to have the wedding party together, if their lovers succeeded in persuading their parents to accept them.

In the following week, they toured the scenic spots around the United States. They went to the Grand Canyon, Las Vegas, Florida, and New York. Wherever they went, they took lots of pictures and used their camcorders to commemorate their rejoicing moments in this great nation. Now, it was time for them to return to China.

*   *   *

Chen Yong's brother, Chen Song, the general director of the planning and development department, one of the three pillars of the Octopus Telecom, could have been married if there was no such custom that younger siblings should not get married before their older ones. For years he had been dating a pretty fashion model, one his company had once hired for shooting advertisements. They were ready to get married anytime, but needed to wait for his older brother and sister to get married first. Should a family break this traditional custom, people believed, it would not only show little or no respect to the elder siblings but also would bring bad luck to the marriages of all of the siblings of that family. So they had to wait.

Shortly after their return from the United States, he was happy to learn that his sister had dated an American doctor and it sounded as though they had committed to each other already. And to their surprise, his parents had no objection on his sister's dating a foreigner. Now with the solidly presumable imminent marriage of his older sister and brother, the obstacles of his marriage would soon be removed. He was happy.

He was proven to be not only a technocrat in his brother's company but also an excellent organizer, planner, and manager. Many of the company's strategies and tactics that he proposed, established, and carried out had significantly helped the firm's development and rapid expansion. He had been dubbed the ''Magician'' in the information technology field.

During the absence of his sister and brother, he was actually in charge of the entire company. His remarkable capability left no room for blunders and mistakes, and the company remained in full operation effectively. Yet the company's tentacles had reached nearly every corner of the globe. It had dug and squeezed open and enlarged the market occupancy rate in Asia, the middle-east, Africa, Europe, and America. They also challenged the world's telecom giants in all directions and in full scale. He had been playing a key role for his brother's firm in this bloody IT battle. He often made visionary decisions, such as when CEOs of other companies were still hesitating whether or not to accept the new concept of the third generation mobile phone, the Octopus Telecom, under his command, had already invested and begun the research and design processes for both the network and the phones. It had remained an unknown whether it would be the critical turning point for companies in this business. But from the company's development history, he would be the likely winner—so would his firm be upgraded and stronger than ever. Time would tell.

*   *   *

Having learned that Lin Dan had returned from her surgery trip from the other hemisphere and her damaged face had miraculously recovered thoroughly, her former colleagues, friends and relatives were overjoyed and decided to give her a welcome home celebration. When she appeared in the party, everyone was applauding, exclaiming and shouting her name. A little girl emerged from nowhere and handed her a bouquet of red roses and carnations, and hugged her.

"Dan Dan, big sister, do you remember me?" the little girl asked.

Lin Dan bent down to kiss her cheek, while slowly shaking her perplexed head. "Who are you, dear? I really don't know."

"My name is Ling Ling, the one you picked up from the rubbish dump, remember?"

"Oh, Ling Ling, my love, I've missed you so much, and look at you! You have grown into such a cute girl," she exclaimed, holding her up against her bosom.

"Welcome home, we all love you very much, Dan Dan, big sister," she chanted.

"Thank you all and I love you all," she raised her voice to a high-pitch tone so that everyone could hear. "Brothers and sisters, without your love and support, I wouldn't have made it and stood here today." She bowed to them. Everyone applauded, shouting her name again, surrounding her and hugging her.

Chen Yong announced good news to the crowd that his sister's boyfriend, Dr. Edward, and Wu Ting's boyfriend, David, would be coming to China next month, so, he and Lin Dan, his brother and his sweetheart—four paris of them—were going to have a group-wedding party, together. And everyone in the headquarters of the company was invited to attend. A roaring of glee and ebullience exploded with chants of congratulations, exclamations and yelling. It reverberated throughout the hall.

Yes, it was a season of celebration. The profit of the company soared as the business expanded, so did the income of everyone—the shareholders of the firm. Everyone was happy and grew fonder of the company, and they could see a brighter future was yet to come. Now their leaders, the brothers and sister, were all getting married at the same time. How wonderful. The joyful atmosphere permeated the entire company.

17

When everything was ready and the weddings about to take place, Chen Yong suddenly received a call from the director of the audit bureau, saying that his company had allegedly committed tax evasion crime and wanted to meet with him.

He shivered. It could mean a beginning of his ruin. The news reports about the devastation of private business owners and entertainment celebrities who were accused of committing tax evasion in recent years were still vivid in his mind. Especially those who were on the top-ten list of the richest people in the nation, which had been estimated yearly by the *Forbes* magazine, the world-renowned financial publication. Sadly, many of them had ended up not only being locked up in prison but also stripped penniless, or forced to exile to Western nations. The most recent one was named Yang Ming, who started his business in vegetable farming and flower planting, then wetted his feet in goods trading and real estate development. Soon he became a billionaire and was invited by a neighboring communist nation to head its newly established economic zone. But his conspicuous and ambitious move angered the state leaders, and he was accused of abusing the farmlands as well as tax evasion. As a result, his properties were confiscated and he was sentenced to fifteen years in prison.

Another one named Cheng Dagang, who founded an automobile mill in the northern part of the nation. It grew rapidly under his leadership. The mill soon cooperated with auto giants around the world, and it manufactured not only its own brand of trucks and cars, but also partly made and assembled famous and classic name brand vehicles like BMW. Automatically, he was on the list of the wealthiest persons and became an obvious target for the anti-tax-evasion campaign, and was blamed for usurping government properties. Smartly, he escaped out of the country before getting arrested, but his firm was taken over by the provincial government.

However, the one that attracted everyone's attention, old and young, male and female, was the nationally renowned actress and later a multibillionaire businesswoman, Miss Wong Jing. It was top news and the hottest gossips topic around the nation when she was arrested for allegedly committing tax evasion. As a famous public figure, the government was reluctant to put her on trial, but they kept her locked in prison for over a year until she sold off everything she had owned, including her companies, to fill in the holes of the astronomical figures of debt being charged for dodging income taxes. Her case served the purpose of "slaying one to warn the rest," a traditional way of handling things. As a result, the government's coffer swelled with both individual and corporate income taxes paid by the frightened people that year, especially by private business owners who were afraid of being audited someday.

From time to time, there were many similar cases being reported of rich people caught and destroyed for not fully paying their income taxes. Yet the tax audit had become a double-edged sword that rested just above the heads of the richest citizens. It was scary. Chen Yong felt the chill on his backbone, although he believed his company had fully complied with its tax obligation in recent years, but if some corrupt and wicked government officials decided to pick on your past—there was no way to escape. He wondered what they were after. Money? The ownership of his company? Whatever that was, it was ominous. He waited for the upcoming storm nervously.

*　　*　　*

Fong Jo, the director of the audit bureau, arrived at the lobby of the headquarters of the Octopus Telecom with two other men shortly after nine in the morning. They demanded to see Chen Yong immediately.

Chen Yong hurried down with the company's chief accountant. They didn't bother to shake hands but, rather, got down to the subject directly without going through the normal VIP etiquette.

"Chen Yong, we have checked through your company's taxation record and found that your firm only started to pay a fraction of the income tax in the past few years. How do you explain?"

"Well, as far as I am concerned, my company has fully paid the taxes due in recent years. We have our own record here," Chen

168

Yong replied, signaling his accountant to show the company's record to him.

But the director pushed that away.

"Save it, we don't want to see your fictitious bookkeeping. What happened during the previous period, our record shows that your company did not pay any taxes at all?"

"Because our firm had just set up and we struggled so hard to survive in this business and, of course, it hadn't made any profit at all in the first few years, that is why."

"You're lying, according to the information I have, your firm has been making profits right from the beginning."

Chen Yong was struck dumbounded. It was true that his company had made little profits in the first few years, but they were used to buy more equipment for new project research and development within the same fiscal year usually. So it resulted in showing no profit in the book for that year. Yet he was not sure whether what the company had done was legal or not, maybe that was the mistake his company had made—for not finding it out. But he was willing to make it up if it was not a law-abiding act.

"But each year we spent our profit on buying new equipment for more and better output. Would that be classified as part of the expenditure for that fiscal year? If not, we can always make it up, can't we?"

"Of course not, it's too late now. We believe that you did it deliberately for the purpose of evading taxes."

"No, Director Fong," Chen was panicking and denied it at once. "We have never thought of doing such a terrible thing. If we had, we wouldn't have paid the taxes fully in recent years."

"We don't care what you think. We evaluate what you do. You'd better come with us. We will do a thorough investigation about your company's tax evasion," Fong Jo snapped.

Chen Yong shivered, he knew he would be detained from that moment on. Realizing that his company had grown too fast and too big, he, the chairman, had attracted too much public attention and that might fit into the role for "slaying one to warn others." He regretted for being too ambitious. One just couldn't be too famous or too rich in this society, because it would provoke "red eyes," or jealousy from others. He didn't know how long he would be detained and how serious the charges he would face.

He told the accountant, "Tell A-Song and A-Jing to take care of the company and not to worry about me, I will be fine because I have not committed any crime but just some kind of negligence, that is all."

The accountant nodded and said, "Take care, Master Chen. We will talk to our company's lawyer."

Chen Yong was escorted out of the door toward the audit bureau's waiting minivan. Before getting into the van, he turned around and looked at his company's headquarters' thirty-story marble and glass-paneled building. It was the symbol of his IT empire, the dream of a teenager that had come true through hard work, wisdom, and luck. He smiled, life was meaningful, and Buddha had not been treating him badly. The only thing he regretted was the interruption and postponement of his wedding party and the romantic marriage life afterward. But he could wait, both of them could wait, the love between them had been deeply rooted into their hearts, and they had been waiting for long anyway. Like a saying said, "Good things require patience." Buddha had been fair and merciful with them, he just couldn't ask for more. His reverie was interrupted by the howling of the audit director.

"Get in the van, Chen Yong. What are you thinking about?"

*   *   *

Lin Dan, who waited anxiously for the upcoming wedding party and with her mind occupied with blissful feelings every day, was heartbroken when she found out that her fiancé had been detained by the audit officials. Feeling despaired, grim and helpless, she started to blame her fate again and wondered if she had brought back bad luck to her lover. Desperately, she went to visit him with the company lawyer, along with her fiancé's brother and sister. But they were not allowed to see him. Not until their lawyer protested and threatened to sue the audit bureau was their request granted. However, their meeting was strictly under the audit officials' surveillance. Except the mutual consolations, there was not much to say. From holding his hand and looking into his eyes, nevertheless, Lin Dan could read and gain the courage needed to survive this crisis from her lover. The willpower to fight with ill fate and rescue her lover and his firm began growing in her heart. She held his hand tightly and declared loudly and dauntlessly, "I'll get you out of here, honey." And he nodded assertively.

The next day, more to her desperation, she was informed that her lover's brother and sister were detained as well. Her mind was racing fast, emotionally. She called the lawyer at once and demanded he to go to visit them with her. But when they got there, they were told that the three siblings had been arrested and transferred to the city's detention house. Struck by further bad news, they felt depressed and hurried over there. After verbally fighting with the warden for hours, they were finally allowed to meet with Chen Yong. He told Lin Dan with the tone of seriousness and urgency that, during their absence, the Octopus Telecom would utterly rely on her, that she would have to manage the entire company on her own.

On the way home, the depressed Lin Dan felt the heavy burden of responsibility pressing on her. She could hardly breathe. Unlike the little firm that she used to manage for her lover, Octopus Telecom was the gigantic international IT monster. She couldn't imagine if she were capable of running it without being wrecking it and getting herself destroyed.

At company headquarters, and with the help of the lawyer and the chief accountant, Lin Dan summoned all of the various department directors to a meeting and addressed them.

"As you all know, our company has been facing an unprecedented crisis since our firm has been targeted for the recently nationwide tax evasion crackdown. But as far as I am concerned, our company does not have a severe problem on this issue but some little historical clouds. Once they are cleared, we will be back on normal again and our beloved chairman of directors and founder of this firm, Mr. Chen and his brother and sister, will return back here intact. I can assert you for that."

She had no idea how that assertion could be entertained, nor did she know if her lover's company would survive the crisis. It was just her spur of the moment.

"In the meantime, during their absence, they want me to be in charge of the company. It is too heavy and too difficult a task for me, but I have to do it for the well being of the firm and us all. I believe though, with your help and our hard work, our company will not only survive but will also thrive. Let's work together the best we can to meet the challenges now laying in front of us. We can make it, can't we?''

Starting with a few responses, loud applause spread across the room. The roaring positive replies from all of the directors of the Octopus Telecom reverberated in the conference hall. Lin Dan was delighted and thanked them.

To stabilize their customers, they started making phone calls and putting ads in various newspapers, stating that their company was functioning as normal as usual under the leadership of an acting chairwoman. The company's objective of enhancing both the international and domestic market occupancy rate had not changed one bit.

From early morning to midnight every day, Lin Dan read through tons of documents ranging from technical materials to planning and development and personnel structures of different branches located all over the globe, including numerical contracts with various firms. All this was her preparation in order to get familiar with the company's business and operation.

When making an important decision, she consulted with directors, department managers and technical experts. Judgments and decisions were made by the wisdom of the firm's elites. It worked remarkably well, and it was nearly error-proof. Doing this, miraculously, boosted the staffs' morale and a sense of belonging. As a result, the company's business, after a little dip, began picking up again.

The counterparts as well as rivals in the IT business marveled at Octopus Telecom's performance, as they waited anxiously to see the expected fall of the trouble-bound empire. Lin Dan, the acting chairwoman of the company, had instantly become a star in the IT field. Her stunning looking photos and her mysterious background had been printed in major newspapers. She often had to turn down interviews to avoid interrupting her work. But on the other hand, unfortunately, she had been exposed to the sex maniacs among the corrupt government officials and become the image of their fantasy.

*   *   *

Chen Yong and his siblings remained locked in prison without trial for almost three months. Lin Dan visited them every week, but

172

there was nothing she could do to get them out. She had advocated paying the government millions of yuan for the make-up taxes in exchange for their release, but it was rejected. The authorities would do the thorough investigation. Under her instruction, the company's lawyer had proved their innocence and demanded they be released. Both the court and the wardens ignored him.

Rescuing her lover and his siblings had become her core issue, besides keeping the company functioning. Once an opportunity emerged, she would make calls and visit both local and provincial government officials in order to make connections leading to freeing her loved ones. But since the issue had become public and conspicuous, no one dared to offer help.

One day, sitting in her office grimly and helplessly pondering about the issue, an idea struck her mind. She decided to pay a visit to the director of the audit department, who held the key to the issue, she had figured out. She thought about calling him to make an appointment, but decided to scrap it.

Arriving at the audit department, and to the audit officials' surprise, a clerk dashed to report to their director. The director immediately came out to meet her. With his fleshy and obscene smile, he led her into his office. He gestured her to sit down on the sofa and then locked the door. Sitting next to her, he said, "My god, you are gorgeous. I have expected your coming for quite some time. Now what can I do for you?"

How could you expect me to come? She pondered cautiously. *Did he plot the scheme? He sounded very much like I should have been here earlier.*

"You know pretty sure what I come here for, don't you?"

"I could guess."

"Well, then, to make it straightforward, I need your help in getting my fiancé and his brother and sister released."

His smile faded into an expression of seriousness. "They committed financial crime and that needed to be punished. I don't think I can help them," he said, shaking his head.

"Really? But I don't think it is a crime, instead, I would say, it is just a sort of negligence, the court will see to it. The fact is, our firm has been one of the largest taxpayer in the city for the past five years."

"Then let's wait and see, but I can assert you that they are not going to get out of the prison for quite some time," he bluffed.

He was right. If there was no trial for them, they would have nearly three quarters of a year to go before they could be given a chance to stand in court, according to the current rule stipulated by the nation's justice ministry. They would rot in the dim and stinking prison by then, not to mention the following sentences awaiting for them. She would have to yield and do something in his favor in order to turn the table around.

"Director Fong, I believe you are a very capable person with the power you have and you are very kind that you will help me, won't you?" she asked in a tone of nearly begging.

Here came the crack finally, he was elated. It was time for the home run, as she was now just like a piece of meat lying on the cutting board just for him—a butcher—that he could trim it which-ever way he preferred.

He got closer to her. "It depends on you, whether I can help you or not. You know what I am talking about, don't you?" He smiled again with a evil grin.

"I don't understand what you are talking about, can you be more specific?"

He stared at her for a few seconds, then said, "It's very simple and easy, all you need to do are two little things. The first one is to offer an honorable title for my boss at your company. I am talking about the vice minister of the IT industry, Li Qiang. And, of course, he would get the corresponding pay for no less than fifty thousand yuan per month from your company. He deserves it. Do you know how much he has done to protect the domestic IT industry from being beaten up by international giants? Your company has bene-fited from his work tremendously. Don't you agree?"

She pondered for a few seconds then nodded and asked, "What is the other 'little thing' then?"

He moved closer to her, so that their bodies were touching each other and his breathing was more like panting. He placed his hand on top of hers and said, "I loved you the moment I saw your photo in the newspaper. My god! The real you is even more beau-tiful."

Lin Dan flinched, withdrawing her hand. "I'm sorry, I have a fiancé. Please, director, be respectful."

He laid his arm across her shoulder and held her tightly and whispered, "I know, I just want to have fun with you for a few times before your fiancé gets released. Okay?"

Lin Dan struggled to get herself free from the hold of the man about her father's age. "No!" She blurted out. The memories of being a mistress of the corrupt officials flooded in her mind. It seemed that her fate had been linked with those lustful and evil men. It was not fair. Why should a woman be a sex slave to those men who were presiding as pillars of the society? Was there something wrong with her fate, or her beauty, or our society? The mixture of rage and grievance and the desire for vengeance that had accumulated since she was out of high school reached to a climax. Wanting that sad experience to stop repeating again, and to end her tragic fate, she snatched a ceramic cup on the table and threw it to him. The cup hit right at his private part, he screamed. Lin Dan hurried to the door and unlocked it. Opening the door, she asked, "Do you want me to call the ambulance, Director Fong?"

Moaning with pain, and with his hands holding his private part, he shook his head. He didn't want to inflict anymore embarrassment. Lin Dan declared, "You will get them released," and strode out of the door.

Having returned to the company, Lin Dan discussed it with the company's lawyer. He suggested her to report to the Central Disciplinary Committee just like she did before. But she refused the idea at once because it would take a long time to get her loved ones released by going through all the complicated investigations. Instead, she decided to call the deputy minister of the IT industry.

It was easy enough for her to find out the deputy minister Li Qiang's office phone number since the IT ministry had contacted the company before. She dialed the number and asked to talk to him, when his secretary answered the phone.

"Did you say that you are the acting chairwoman of the Octopus Telecom?" Li Qiang's low-pitched standard Mandarin accent droned on the line.

"Yes, it's correct, and my name is Lin Dan."

"Oh, I am delighted to talk to you, Lin Dan. I have seen your pictures in the papers and heard much about you. You've been doing an excellent job. You are a real heroine. But according to a saying, 'You would not come to the temple if everything is fine with you.' Please, honestly tell me if there is anything that I can do for you?"

"I call to inform you that we have granted you the title of a honored manager of the administrative department of our company, and the salary of that position is sixty thousand yuan per month. I hope you will accept the offer."

It was an astronomical number for a ministerial-level government official who usually made around twenty-five hundred yuan a month. It was yet a peculiar phenomenon in the nation that government officials had tremendous power but received little pay. It was perhaps the reason why so many of them were not afraid of the would-be punishment but rather chose to take chances. Li Qiang was just one of those who were trading their power for money.

"Oh, that is too big a gift for me. Anyway, thank you very much. I really appreciate it. Is there anything that you want me to do? You are my boss now."

"Yes, I want you to get the chairman of this company, Chen Yong, and his brother and sister out of prison right now. If you need to come down here, please do so."

"That would be easy enough, just a phone call would do it. Let me do it after this."

"But I am afraid that there is a problem as well. I hurt the director of the audit department, Fong Jo, accidentally, because he wanted to abuse me sexually."

"Really? That bastard. Don't worry about it, I will take care of him. And your fiancé and his brother and sister will be released tomorrow."

Here came the naked truth, extortion. That was all the melodrama of arresting her loved ones had plotted for. Lin Dan was so angry and vowed to revenge. The hatred towards the corrupt government cadres, who had repeatedly nearly ruined her life, deepened. "Someday," she muttered, half-childishly, "I will become an angel to fight with these wicked devils." She wondered what she would do after her fiancé returned to the company. There was no reason for her to stay in the supervising position in his firm; and yet she had little interest in the commercial business after trudging through hell in life. Instead, what she believed was the urgent need of an effective anticorruption mechanism or, at least, a well-managed organization that could supplement the existing state-run one.

She pondered and measured the possibility of establishing and heading one such organization of her own. But she couldn't imagine how she would face and resist the counterattacks launched by these powerful financial criminals. She would be destroyed by them easily and relentlessly. She sighed. It was for the feeling of powerlessness and the treacherous living environment she was in.

18

The next day, an announcement issued by the audit department of the city was printed in the *Shenzhen Daily* stating that the investigation of the Octopus Telecom's tax evasion had been completed and the suspected crime and violations inflicted by this firm were unfounded. Therefore, the founder and chairman of directors and his brother and sister, two of the chief directors of this company, were not guilty of the crime and were released unconditionally. The audit department apologized for the inconvenience and the damages on their personal and company's reputation.

In the afternoon, the director of the audit department, Fong Jo, held the releasing ritual for them and apologized to them personally. He bowed to them obsequiously, an utter change from the arrogance he had toward them when he first came to their firm and ordered to arrest them three months ago. They were startled by his turned-around attitude.

Lin Dan savored the joy and sweetness that resulted from her initial counterattack with the greedy officials. Now her loved ones were released, it was the time to take care of these financial criminals, she determined. Shortly after her wedding with Chen Yong, Lin Dan withdrew from working in her husband's firm. Instead, she established a detective firm named AVD Detective Agency. AVD was the abbreviation of angel versus devils. She got Liu Ming and many other nationally-renowned detectives and some PLA veterans and informants residing all over the nation to work for her. The detectives had connections she could use. She did not intend to make a profit. The firm posted a huge deficit, but she was not slightly moved by it at all. She believed the money was well-spent and worth every penny of its value.

Through her detective-informant net, Lin Dan discovered that the monthly pay of the honored administrative management position at the Octopus Telecom for the deputy minister of IT industry was split into two portions: Sixty percent went into the deputy minister's savings account, while the balance was deposited into Fong Jo's personal bank account. That was what the audit head received from carrying out extortion. He will not get away with, and must be punished, including him and his greedy accomplice. Lin Dan was determined.

*   *   *

With money extorted from various firms in the city, Fong Jo indulged in affairs with young and beautiful women. He bought an apartment in the expensive downtown area, which he used as a sex pad with girls he brought back from karaoke nightclubs or beauty salons where he visited several times every week. Unlike many others, he preferred his sex partners to be fresh one-night stands, because he was not interested in having mistresses.

One evening shortly after midnight, he stumbled home drunk with a tall and beautiful girl on his arms. He didn't know that from the moment he left the karaoke nightclub, two men had surreptitiously followed him back to the apartment. He felt annoyed when two burly men squeezed into the elevator with him and the girl. He was too drunk and sexually preoccupied to be alert. The two stocky men left the elevator with them. Once he unlocked and opened the door to his apartment, the husky men pushed them into the living room. Immediately he was gagged and bound, and was lifted and placed on the bed with his pants removed. One man sat on his chest tightly and held him down. The other man took out a cutter from the duffel bag and started the invasive operation between Fong Jo's legs. He gurgled in fright and struggled to move his body, and he became hysterical. Within minutes, his testicles were removed, and blood gushing from the cut. The ball cutter bandaged him quickly. After cleaning their hands, they posted a poster on the door of the apartment from outside that read: "This is the consequence of being corrupt and womanizing." They left the place at once, leaving the door ajar. Their mission was completed.

News that the audit department head got castrated because of committing corruption and womanizing spread all over the city, and then around the nation via the Internet and mobile phone message exchanges. Some condemned it as some lawless purging

179

conducted by ruthless bandits. Many others praised it as example of heroic traditional criminal punishment. To some, it sent out a warning signal to criminals of the same kind.

There were various rumors circulating around the city about who had carried out the punishment, but no concrete evidence leading to any proper conclusion had been found. The police, in the meantime, were not really interested in finding out who might be the culprits. However, under the pressure of the media and citizen gossips, Fong Jo was investigated and prosecuted. His accomplice, Li Qiang, also faced the same fate. All this was a result of a clandestine report given to the Central Disciplinary Committee made by the AVD Detective Agency.

*   *   *

Lin Dan carried out her vengeance not only to the greedy sex maniacs working in the local government, but wherever they emerged throughout the nation. A group of such officials in Fuzhou was also the targets of the AVD Detective Agency. One of China's major coastal cities and the capital of Fujian province, Fuzhou was known as a base for illegal emigrants headed to such western nations as the United States, Canada, various European countries, Australia and Japan. They were notorious for smuggling oil and other expensive foreign brand commodities, and of having numerous affairs with women. All with money they obtained illegally.

The smuggling ring, organized by a Hong Kong-returned merchant, later joined heads with customs and various departments of the city. It was the biggest unit of this kind in the People's Republic of China since it was established in 1949. The estimated value of smuggled goods handled by this ring was worth more than ten billion dollars. In order to seduce high-ranking government officials to work for him, the Hong Kong-returned merchant built a tenstory edifice called Red Mansion. The entire Red Mansion exterior was painted in red. The interior held a roomy theater, which often showed pornographic movies smuggled in from Hong Kong; a karaoke nightclub; a sauna facility with a swimming pool and massage rooms; the luxuriously decorated hotel rooms, were used primarily for conducting sexual activities. Hundreds of gorgeous girls in their teens or twenties were recruited from all over the country to work

180

there as sex slaves. This hotel-style brothel was not open to the public, and only available to powerful government cadres or key merchants involved in smuggling activities. They were selectively invited to come indulge in sexual sprees there.

However clean a government official was, once entering and staying in the Red Mansion, he would come out with a filthy mind. As a result, nearly the entire leadership of Fuzhou's government, from top to bottom, was rotten.

The Shenzhen-based AVD Detective Agency decided to strike at the head of the snake first. Their very first target was Mayor Liangg Jian, age fifty-four, had been married, and had two sons. Both sons were in their twenties and worked as managers in two different trading companies linked to the smuggling ring in the city. Local detectives hired by AVD were working frantically. They bugged his office, followed him whenever he went out of the government office building, and found that he visited the Red Mansion almost every other evening.

One early evening, on the way to an expensive seafood restaurant after getting off his car, Liangg Jian bumped into a stunningly beautiful girl wearing a green flimsy blouse and a short skirt. His chauffeur wanted to intercept for the mayor's safety reason, but the petrified mayor stopped him. He had never seen such a beautiful girl. Condescendingly, he apologized to her. "Please excuse my awkwardness, Miss," his voice cracked in his dry throat, while ricocheting at her angel-looking face and curvaceous body. "But may I treat you to dinner as a compensation and an apologetic gesture for hurting you?"

"Oh, you? I have seen you on TV several times. Yes. I remember now. You are our mayor, right?" she exclaimed.

He nodded, smiling. "Now, may I?"

"Yes, of course, it is my honor to have dinner with our mayor," she said excitedly, extending her hand to hold his. He placed his hand across her back, then down to her waist immediately. They walked to the VIP room together. His chauffeur then returned to the car and waited there. The mayor ordered a bottle of Maotai, the so-dubbed Chinese XO, and the most expensive dishes the restaurant could serve. On the menu ahead was a shark's fin soup, lobster with black bean sauce, and stewed abalone and scallops with cream and garlic sauce. When all the dishes were served at the table, the mayor told the waiters and waitresses to leave them alone then locked the door. While eating, the mayor's hand busily roamed all over the girl's body, placing avid kisses on her cheeks and mouth. The girl protested at the beginning but completely enjoyed it later. She tried to get him drunk. It was dark, when they finally finished dinner—and the mayor had reached his peak of horniness. With one hand gripping one of her breasts while hugging her with the other, he asked her to follow him to his villa. She refused it at first, but as he continued to beg to her, she reluctantly accepted. She went to the toilet and made a phone call before they left.

When they got to the villa, the sexually hungry mayor stripped off her blouse and could not wait to have fun with her. But she insisted he should take a shower first. He wanted to take it with her, but she refused. While Liangg Jian was taking a shower, she opened the door and hurried to make a call again. A few moments later, two men hiding in the villa sneaked in. When the mayor came out from the bathroom, the two men lunged at him forcefully and placed a chemical patch on his mouth. He fainted in seconds. They lifted him to the bed and proceeded with the emasculation.

*　　*　　*

Their next target was the party secretary of the Fuzhou municipal government, Chang Lei. His position was equivalent to, and sometimes higher than the mayor, because the Communist Party was the only ruling party in the nation.

Since the mayor had become the laughingstock among the officials and the citizens after what had happened, it aroused the alertness of the men of the same kind. They paid special attention to pretty girls trying to entrap them for whatever reason, either publicly or privately. Yet they believed the Red Mansion was the safest place for them to have sex outside of their marriage. The party secretary, Chang Lei, was one of them. He went to the Red Mansion often in the evenings, as the detectives of the AVD Detective Agency had observed.

One Friday evening, Chang Lei went to the Red Mansion as usual after dinner. Passing through the gate, he was greeted by two lines of girls standing on either side of the red carpet in the lobby. He was asked whether he would watch a porn movie or take the

182

sauna first. Most of the times, unlike many others who would go for the sex right away, he preferred to watch the movie first, a sauna after, and then the massage. The sex part would always be the last.

He was ushered to the theater by two new beautiful girls hugging him on each side after saying it would be the same as usual. To please these powerful and greedy womanizers, the Red Mansion often recruited new girls and relieved the older ones. Chang Lei requested fresh girls for whenever he came, and he always had the best ones reserved for him. These two girls were going to accompany him and serve him for the entire evening. They were trained and required to be absolutely obedient to these VIPs.

While watching the porn movie, the aroused man kissed and hugged and moved his hands all over the girls' breasts and vaginas like a hungry beast. He almost reached climax several times before he finished watching the porno film with the two sexy and beautiful girls. Next they would take the sauna together. Once getting to the sauna room, he couldn't wait to strip away all the girls' clothing. While caressing and licking their breasts, the girls were undressing him. Except intercourse, the three naked animals were hugging, watering, frolicking, soaping, caressing and kissing each other. They enjoyed all kinds of sexual activities one could imagine. Chang Lei wished the time would pause forever.

After all the excitement, it was time for him to take a little rest and enjoy the full-body massage. Prone on the massaging bed, he closed his eyes. The two girls tenderly pressed, rubbed, and caressed nearly every inch of his body. Although they were a bit awkward, it was good enough for him to enjoy such service. It was as if he were being treated as if he were the emperor. The main purpose of this part was to get him calm and rested, so that he would be ready for the coming thunderstorm of the next phase.

Finally, they entered a luxuriously decorated double room, where there was a king-sized bed setting against a full-wall mirror. The girls carefully locked the door, and then helped him to sprawl on the bed and undress. When he turned around and tried to get on top of a girl, his mouth was gagged with a patch. He gurgled for a few seconds and then lost consciousness. Hurriedly, the girls began the operation between his legs. After cleaning their hands, the two girls left the room and closed the door. On their way down to the lobby, they met the manager. "Where are you two going? Have you finished serving secretary Chang?"

"Oh, not yet. But you know, it is embarrassing. His thing doesn't get hard. So we are going out to buy some magic oil from the sexual aid shop a few buildings away from here," one of the girls replied.

One of the most significant changes in the nation since adopting the Reform and Opening policy was the people's attitude toward sexual activities. As a traditionally conservative society, the subject of sex in the past had been unofficially taboo in people's conversation, especially during the Cultural Revolution in which whoever mentioned the subject had to do self-criticism. But now the sexual aid shops display and sell condoms, aphrodisiacs, artificial sex organs, and toys were available everywhere throughout the country. Few people would feel embarrassed going in and out of those shops to browse and buy items once condemned as decadent Western products. Prostitution, at the same time, had been rampant nationwide, despite the periodical waves of crackdowns. But the truth was that the police did not bother to take action against this no-victim crime.

The manager smiled, "Well, that's the law of nature. Man just can't be as strong as a tiger forever, you know. Go get it as quickly as you can, don't make Secretary Chang wait too long."

"Yes, Manager."

They hurried away.

Shortly news of what had happened to the party secretary and the mayor of Fuzhou caught the attention of the CDC. It started the investigation and unveiled how serious the corruption and smuggling problem in that part of the nation was, and took action to smash the unprecedentedly large and well-organized criminal ring. Members of that ring stampeded, the head and a number of them escaped to Canada.

Realizing that the collapse of that nation's largest smuggling ring was attributed to the ones who carried out the castration, the CDC wanted to praise and cooperate with them, but found no clue of how to contact them. They placed advertisements in the newspapers and magazines, stating that they really appreciated their heroic actions and wished to work with them in the battle against corruption, but had never got any responses.

Chen Yong did not know exactly what his wife had been doing. He only knew that she was running a detective agency which was not founded for the purpose of making profit but utterly for her own interest. That's what he was told when he tried to persuade her to abandon that rare and peculiar idea and help him run his business. She refused, saying that her life experiences had changed her a great deal and that she was no longer interested in doing commercial business but would rather help people and the society. He agreed to let her do whatever she liked to do as long as it would make her happy, because he loved her so much. And he did not care how much money she would spend on whatever she was doing. Money was no longer the main issue, he had plenty. His happiness was with his wife, after all.

One day, while browsing the news at the website sohu.com, he was marveled by the news of all the corrupt officials who were also sex maniacs had been gelded. Like many others, he applauded such heroic actions. Had such actions been taken earlier, he and his wife would not have gone through such a hell of hardships. Although they were not quite justified and encouraging, such lynch-style actions were necessary in a society where it was in a social transition period and its rule of law and judicial system were far from perfect, he believed. But he wondered who had the guts to carry them out. This was not the kind of job an average citizen could handle because it required tremendous willpower, willingness for rule of law and justice, money, and possibly the support of some powerful person. Anyway, our society really needed this kind of person to rectify the social illness and distortion, he thought.

That evening he chatted with his wife about that news he had read. Lin Dan pretended to be startled by it and asked what his opinions were. After learning his views about it, she felt relieved. At least, he agreed with what she felt as well. She wondered how he would react if he found out what she had been doing. But it was not the time to tell him, she thought. In fact, all employees she hired for the ADV Detective Agency had to go through an oath-taking ritual and would be working like blood-line brothers and sisters. They swore not to tell anyone outside of the company, including their relatives, about what they were doing every day. And they got very high pay once hired. Yet no one had leaked out anything about her vengeance against the wicked officials, as far as she was concerned. That was good. She didn't want to think about the consequences of what she had been doing should it ever leak out. She was just a fighter, an avenger, conquering the wickedness and evilness of the society.

Chen Yong had no idea of all that. He didn't know that the woman he had just married was no longer the same as before. he still remembered vividly how astonishing he had felt and how much he had admired her, when she told him how she had gotten him and his siblings out of the prison. Yet the news of the audit department chief's castration remained a puzzle to him. He could have figured it out by linking the case of Fong Jo and the recent ones in Fujian province, but he was too busy for it.

*   *   *

AVD Detective Agency had created a storm of fear for those who committed this same kind of crime with the same punishment nationwide. They were more alert than ever. In some cities, they organized together to counterattack the possible attempted attack on any one of them. At the same time they paid reporters and lawyers to write articles to the newspapers to condemn such lynch-style actions as a felony committed by lawless-minded hooligans, and demanded that the crackdown be taken immediately, despite the citizens' overwhelming support. But law enforcers were reluctant to take action because all the victims were criminals inside the government. None of the innocent persons were involved. They helped a great deal in the anticorruption operations as well. So most of the law-abiding police officials throughout the nation just kept their eyes closed in these cases. The repercussion of Lin Dan's vengeance to the greedy and lawbreaking officials was, indeed, more positive than negative. It had won the support of most of the innocent people in the nation. Only the ones who had the "demon" in their hearts tried hard to put it out, but in doing so provided the profile for AVD detectives to spot them.

Ma Li, the governor of Yuennan province in the southeastern part of the nation, renowned as the home of minorities and the kingdom of flowers, was a typical high-ranking corrupt official and a womanizer who had traded his power for both money and sex by helping various companies—both domestic and international—to win business bids. He ordered the provincial police department head, Zhong Ping, to investigate who had carried out the castration on the so-called public servants. Zhong Ping sent two police officers to Shenzhen, then to Fuzhou to do the investigation. Upon their arrival, the AVD detectives learned of their mission through their nationwide informant net. They kept their eyes on the investigators while informed colleagues in Yuennan checked out who was behind the scheme.

The AVD detectives soon found out that the police chief was a crafty official who bribed the governor to get his position two years ago, and he had worked closely with his constantly money-and-sex-hungry boss after that. Often, Zhong Ping would arrest or give trouble to those who had any conflict of interest with the governor. They both shared the same appetites in common—money and sex.

There was a rule being made: An investment or construction project that involved the use of more than one hundred million yuan must be approved by the governor, while the lesser one must obtain permission from the police chief. These two powerful men used this rule as a magic wand for moneymaking, and their animal desire-releasing orgy after that. Many investors and companies had to bribe through them with large amounts of cash and sometimes beautiful girls to win their business bids and to get their projects approved. And under the same sky of the evil kingdom, no one dared to complain.

Enjoying the privileges attributed to their swelling wallets and the satisfaction of their beastly desire, they were afraid to become the next targets of the male private part busters. They learned about the recent horrified incidents listening to the news. They decided to act first, preemptively, before they could get to them, to root them out, if they could. They felt better and safer after sending out two of the most capable and loyal police officers to venues in the costal provinces where the previous emasculation took place, to conduct the hunting. Their weekly routine sex spree, which mostly took place in the governor's villa, remained unchanged.

One night, Ma Li and Zhong Ping were chauffeured in his car to a karaoke nightclub to have fun. While they were having fun inside, his chauffeur remained in the car waiting for them. At around one o'clock in the early morning, they drunkenly stumbled out of the nightclub. The chauffeur helped them get in the car, but they were too drunk to recognize that the chauffeur had been replaced. They began to snore immediately when the car moved down to the street. Darting through the early morning traffic, which was relatively light, the car headed toward the city border. It passed clusters of buildings and villages and shrubs, then entered a dust road. Rounding curves and spreading gravel, it stopped in front of a hut. Four burly men waiting inside the hut came out and brought the two drunken yet powerful men into the hut and proceeded with the castration operation. Leaving the two castrated men there moaning, they drove away when it was done.

A month later, these two powerful men were rounded up by the CDC, as the news spread around the nation, and were executed. This was the work done by the AVD Detective Agency. The whirlwind of Lin Dan's vengeance swept the nation, and shocked and frightened all the wicked officials positioned in various levels of government. They vowed each to find out who engineered and carried out these humiliating and lethal attacks.

*   *   *

One day, Lin Dan was in her office discussing with her assistants some juicy information just gotten by her colleagues about the director of the transportation department of the Gueizhou Province. The place was famous because of a historical convention of the Communist Party which took place during the Long March, in which the Red Army traversed over six thousand miles from its original base in southern China to a new base in the northwestern part of the nation to avoid being besieged and attacked by the national troops. Mao Zedong was elected as the chairman of the Communist Party during that convention, which laid the foundation of victory for the communist revolution within the nation.

The information showed that the head of the transportation department of the Gueizhou province, Hong Jing, a relative of one of the nation's top leaders, had been stealing state funds. He did that by inflating the project costs with contractors who gave him a large percentage of the fake expenditure. He accepted bribes from road construction companies bidding to win contracts from the provincial government. And like many other corrupt officials, Hong

Jing had the habit of womanizing. He not only had a mistress, but often had one-night-stands with prostitutes or Three-accompanying girls from the nightclubs—all with money obtained illegally.

Rage burned inside her. Lin Dan ordered to take care of him immediately, but was warned by her colleagues of possible retaliation by the man's powerful relative. She hesitated at first, but the memory of her painful past and thinking of those evil men who abused their power to harm the interest of the state and innocent citizens, it made her heart ache. She couldn't bear any longer. She slammed her little fist on the tabletop and blurted out, "Get him." She was dauntless and capable, an invincible female warrior.

The detectives in Gueizhou Province received the order and took action in the following days. Unlike other notorious officials who were mostly executed, the emasculated Hong Jing was first deposed from his job and repelled from the Communist Party. Then he was prosecuted and sentenced for only ten years in prison, a lenient result of his powerful relative's interference.

Lin Dan began to feel the danger and fear of treading on a minefield. She could visualize being hunted, retaliated and murdered by those powerful, wicked, and vicious men, the so-called pillars of the socialist society. But it was too late, there was no way back.

She noticed now that she was three months pregnant, unexpectedly. She would be a mother soon, a sweet dream of her childhood. Yet she felt confused and lost. She was supposed to be a dedicated wife and mother, fully taking care of her husband and raising decent children of their own, a thousand-year tradition for women. Instead, she was tracing, plotting and murdering men as her daily tasks. How sick, but the satisfaction and excitement of getting rid of the bad guys from the leadership of society had made her feel much better and it had urged her to go on. *I am the angel, sent by God to fight with the devils. I must keep on going until all of them are eliminated.*

Chen Yong reveled when she told him that she was three months pregnant. Caressing her stomach, he bent down and placed his ear on her belly trying to detect any noise caused by the embryo inside. She was laughing at his foolishness and awkwardness.

"There is no baby inside yet, in only three months, honey."

"I am going to tell Daddy and Mommy that they are going to have a grandchild soon," he mused. "Oh, by the way, you should probably stop working now, honey."

"It's still early, I can hang on for at least a few more months," she replied right away, giving no chance for objection. She didn't want to be interrupted with what she had been doing.

"I don't really know exactly what you have been doing every day, you have been too absorbed in it that we seldom have time to talk and take leisure trips together. Would it be the time to hire someone to take care of the business for you, honey?" he grunted with the tone of protest.

"Yes, I will, just give me a few more months. And I am sorry for not having spent enough time with you, honey," she said, guiltily.

He hugged her and kissed her cheek. *She's so beautiful and lovely, as long as she is happy, I do not mind what she does.* "It's okay, honey, I just want you to relax and take good care of yourself, especially now that you are pregnant."

"Thanks for your understanding, honey. I promise to you that in less than five months, I will quit."

*   *   *

After thirteen years' exhausted negotiation with many economic powers in the world, 2002 was an exciting historical year for China. It was finally accepted into the World Trade Organization. And through a decade of bitter struggle competing with other major athletic countries and having failed twice before, China lastly won the privilege to host the 2008 Olympic Games. The entire nation plunged into a sea of joy because the WTO entry would guarantee a boom in international trade, foreign investment, hi-tech, sophisticated management skills, and high-quality services for the nation and its citizens. The hosting of the world's highest-level and prestigious athletic games would enhance the nation's popularity and the citizens' confidence and would bring in more business. These were top news in the newspapers, radio, and TV broadcasting. Citizens in major cities were letting off firecrackers and fireworks, beating drums and gongs, performing lion dances, holding rallies, dancing and singing in celebration. Everywhere, the nation permeated the aura of festivity.

The entry of WTO was another milestone for Octopus Telecom. While it continued to develop and manufacture both stationary and mobile phone network equipment, it began to produce mobile phones with its own brand name. Shortly after entering the market with its superior technological advantage, it found that manufacturing and selling mobile phones was another great potentially lucrative business, and it enjoyed the exponential growth rate as the number of mobile phone users climbed up repidly nationwide. However, it was only the beginning, the about-to-be-born third generation video mobile phone network system development had reached the final stage for practical use. This meant the network would create a mega-huge market for the new generation mobile phone manufacturer. With two thousand engineers working on it day and night, Octopus Telecom was ready. All it needed was the license to make and sell them, and it was going to get it. Chen Yong was sure about it.

*　　*　　*

Lin Dan had become the goddess to her followers. They were loyal to her not only because of the high pay she offered them, but because of the common hatred toward the despicable corrupt officials and the will to eliminate them. They felt awesome for her dauntlessness and selfishness, and worshipped her gradually as they gained victory after victory in their sacrosanct work. They vowed to follow her and encourage her as they discovered that they had encountered counterattacks from their preys, both hidden and exposed. She was touched and felt grateful when they promised to her that they would protect her and the AVD Detective Agency with their lives if necessary.

Despite of the fear and worry, she was becoming addicted to work. The more rotten government officials her agency exposed and punished, the more relieved and satisfactory she felt. Under her instruction, whenever and wherever a bad official was busted, her agency would notify the CDC at once. This was to ensure that a full and complete investigation and punishment would follow by the government's anticorruption organization. She was stunned by the number of the rotten officials her agency had taken care of since its establishment in just a little more than a year. Yet the number of them her agency had taken care of was merely a little cube of the iceberg, as far as she was concerned. The statistics

191

showed that nearly ninety percent of the dug-out-corrupt-officials were more or less involved in womanizing by spending illegally obtained money. How decadent and evil they were. They should all be eliminated.

Remaining underground and well hidden and highly effective in crashing the wicked financial criminals, the AVD Detective Agency had been hunted by the bad elements of the government and the CDC. While the bad bosses wanted to get rid of their new nightmares, the CDC contemplated to cooperate with it.

An clandestine underground organization called Green Dragons formed in major cities by a group of high-ranking corrupt officials who were occupying extremely important positions in the central government. Its objective was to uncover and annihilate the scary underground gelding organization. All members were secretly picked, well-trained, and experienced spies or police officers or PLA veterans who were loyal to their masters completely by their extremely high pay offer. They swore to commit suicide in case of getting caught or faced the risk of exposing their masters. They got in work immediately.

The Green Dragons had their own informant network throughout the nation. And they were not cheap for those who could provide valuable information. Soon they found that some detectives in almost all large and medium cities, who belonged to the same organization, had been frantically doing clandestine research and investigation on some government cadres. They were excited and reported it back to their big bosses immediately. But they were told not to take actions in fear of exposing themselves as they were not quite able to completely root out their rivaling organization yet. Instead they were instructed to keep track of them and find out where the headquarters was and who led it. There was still a lot of work to be done before they could round them up, their bosses warned.

At the same time, the highly alert professional detectives of the AVD Detective Agency all around the nation noticed that they had been followed and spied on by some skillful unknown people in the field. Lin Dan was informed and she attended to it at once. She showed no panic this time because she had anticipated it long before she started her vengeance. After widely consulting with branch heads, she listed out instructions and procedures for her subordinates to deal with the situation. Her strategy was not to confront with the opposition detectives directly but to unveil and attack their bosses whenever was possible. She was sure that whoever was in charge of that organization must be more powerful and more corrupt than all of the bad guys her AVD had dealt with before. But they had to be very careful from now on. A foreseeable fierce counterspy battle between the two hostile underground organizations was imminent and unavoidable.

*   *   *

Wu Ping, the director of the CDC, was listening to a report that his committee had just failed to spot an anonymous informant. Like many times before, the informant notified this state anticorruption body of the name, position, the record of crimes committed and the city in which this official had just been gelded, so that the aftermath punishment against that greedy womanizer could be carried out by the state. It had remained a puzzle to the committee how such a fairytale type of thing, found only in stories that took place in the ancient times, could happen in the twenty-first century? It had been a great help for his committee in the campaign against corruption, although it was not encouraged from the legal point of view. It would be more effective and more efficient if they could find the organization and persuade them to work with the government. But, still, they had no clue how to contact them. It was obvious that they neither wanted to be found nor intended to work with the state law enforcers. This indicated that they lacked the confidence in the government, since their targets were the bad government cadres. But they could be easily harmed by the bad guys, who had tremendous power in the government. They had tried many times to locate the surreptitious informant, but all of their attempts had failed.

Wu Ping was sitting in his chair behind his desk pondering what to do for the next attempt in contacting the fairytale heroes. He had already ordered action against a newly informed "eunuch." His secretary came in and handed him a written report, and he frowned after reading it. It said that some of his subordinates got wind that some high-ranking officials in the central government had recently organized the counterattack to the brutal ball busters. Like a hunting hound, he smelled both the trace of prey and upcoming danger. The big fishes finally came up to the surface from the deep water. It would be a good opportunity to catch them, but their invisible partners were at great risk. He had to find them quick. But the problem with this state-owned bureau was that most of the staff were not as devoted to what they were doing as he was, they did not work hard and efficiently, mainly because they did not get paid well, the same story for all other state employees, including the corrupt officials.

He was one of a few exceptions in the state's only anticorruption organization. Born in an extremely poor farming family in the middle of China during the late 1930s, he participated in revolutionary activities during his teens and joined the Communist Party in the early 1950s. Having trained in the communist theory classes and participated in various political movements, he had been a devoted and active member of the party in the following decades while remaining clean with a simple lifestyle. Now he was a member of the Communist Party Central Committee, one of a few hundred top leaders in the one-party-ruled nation. He was a highly respected leader and was not afraid of being retaliated by the decadent criminals within the government and the Communist Party. Indeed, he was their constant nightmare. He didn't work for money but what he believed. He had been stunned by the enormous number of financial criminals since the Reform and Opening and worked hard, trying to eradicate them before they could eat too deep into the government body. But he often felt too lonely and too weak for his bureau to fight with such a myriad of devils. The recent emergence of the civilian fighting force against the evil elements of the government had served as a stimulant for him. He was not alone! They would be like soldiers sent by God to work with him side by side, if he could find them and persuade them to work with him.

*   *   *

Most of the corrupt officials positioned in the central government did not directly involve themselves in the power-money trade, but did so through their sons and daughters and in-laws, and with some exception with friends or partners. These groups of sons and daughters and in-laws of the powerful central committee members

194

were well known as the "Prince Gang" or "Princess Gang." They usually worked in state-owned enterprises, if not in the state or local governments, as CEOs or general managers or department managers. Some of them even had their own businesses, mostly in commodity trading or real estate, regardless of their abilities.

The highest-ranking organizer of the Green Dragons was Hong Long, a six-decade-old revolutionist, a member of the Communist Party Central Committee, and father of the busted Gueizhou province transportation department head, Hong Jing. With all of the evidence pointing against his son, Hong Jing would have been sentenced to death, or at least to serve in prison for a lifetime, instead of a ten-year lenient treatment, without his illegal interference. But he was far from satisfactory, he couldn't bear the humiliation inflicted to him and his family. After talking with his long-time avid and arrogant and criminal-prone friends, he decided to form an underground organization with them to counterattack those who had got his son and friends' relatives in trouble. They were determined to revenge and root their enemies out. Through decade-long connections with many of their previous subordinates scattered around the nation in various fields and government departments, they were able to organize this evil force, the Green Dragons, quickly. Searching and hunting and sifting through all the information gathered from the Internet, the archival and reports from some local police departments and their informant nets both within the gangsters and criminals and the legal detectives, they soon had the preliminary outlook of their enemies. But they hadn't yet found out who the leader was and where their headquarters was located. So they decided to uncover it first before taking action.

Weeks had passed and they still remained in the dark. Unable to bear any longer, Hong Long ordered the arrests of their rivaling detectives, so that they could torture them for the badly needed information.

Working painstakingly day and night, the AVD detectives found out that their rivaling organization's name was Green Dragons and was led and controlled by a few powerful members in the echelon leadership of the party. They were unable to directly pinpoint who they were. Although they had learned that Hong Jing's father was one of them, and they had the reason to believe it, they hadn't been able to prove it. Lin Dan could feel the imminent danger after talking with branch leaders. She warned all of her assistants and detectives to be careful and ordered them to move to new places immediately. She moved her headquarters to a new building as well and used a false name for her organization, which was Happy Family Consulting Agency, pretending to do business intended to solve family affairs. Yet they had stopped hunting and investigating the corrupt officials for the time being, instead, she urged her followers to find out who the big heads of their rivaling organization were as soon as possible, and to watch their every move. She knew that it was going to be bloody violent when the moment of their showdown came. Their enemies meant to kill her and her followers the day the Green Dragons was founded. Yet the only way to topple them was to dig out who was behind them and to inform the CDC. But it was extremely difficult, and they were running out of time. Judging the situation, the idea of cooperating with the CDC reappeared in her mind again. But she really hated to work with the government. *Not yet, unless I have to,* she thought.

*   *   *

Hong Long was puzzled when informed by his followers that they had lost track on his son's ball busters, who suddenly disappeared from their eyes in all cities. His order to arrest some of them to torture for badly needed information was unable to carry out. He was so mad that he slapped the person, Tin Hang, who reported it to him, hard.

"How could it be, did any of you spit around? Find them out for me in three days, I don't care how you do it," he roared.

"Yes, Master Hong," Tin Hang replied, bowing out of the office.

Slumped into his chair disapapointedly, Hong Long telephoned the police department heads in some cities ordering them to comb residential areas for unregistered individuals. But they all knew that with the nearly free-flow of extra laborers from the rural areas into the cities, such armies of unregistered residents occupying most of the low-rent residential apartments in every major metropolis, combing such environments was like looking for a needle in the ocean. But it was an order that they couldn't defy, if they wanted to keep their positions. They decided to handle the job perfunctorily, knowing that all their mad boss needed to do was to make a few phone calls to destroy their hard-earned careers.

He fully understood the difficulty of finding his prey now, but he had to keep pushing his men on this matter. His feeling of being humiliated and the hatred toward his son's private parts busters had been growing day after day. The only way to ease his feeling was to dig them out and kill them all. He had the excuse to it, after all, for cracking down on the illegal castrators.

Something made him worry about the combined forces of CDC and his prey. He would have to abort his vengeance plan if that happened. It would put him in the situation of fighting against the entire state's law enforcers, since the CDC had the superior power over nearly all departments of the state, including the police department. He and his men had to act quickly before the sky collapsed on them. He had to find out, actually, if that had already taken place.

"Little Du," he yelled at the door.

"I'm here, Master Hong. What can I do for you?" Little Du appeared a few seconds later and replied, timidly.

"Pass my words to Lei Jun to have the reception room of the CDC bugged, quickly."

"I'm afraid that it is too difficult, Master Hong. It not only has guards, but also—" Little Du explained, mildly. But before he was able to finish his last sentence, Hong Long slammed his fleshy fist on the table and thundered, "How dare you! This is not even your task, and you are already trying to thrash our brothers' morale? Tell me, just who do you work for?"

Little Du shivered, regretting what he had said. He shook himself and begged, "Of course, Master, you are the only one I work for in my life. Please excuse my stupidity." He bowed repeatedly.

"Do what I just said then," he threw a wooden penholder at him and barked.

"Yes, Master."

*　　*　　*

The remaining AVD's detectives worked frantically but more cautiously in the capital, the place where they believed the headquarters of the Green Dragons to be. Their sole task was to find out who had organized and led that evil force. The other detectives had to hibernate themselves for a while in order to avoid confronting with Green Dragons.

Still, it was extremely dangerous for those who worked in the capital, knowing that the Green Dragons were determined to hunt and kill them all. Sun Ming and Chai Zhong, detectives of the AVD, one day were tracing the juicy material they had gotten two days ago for a further exploration with a couple of gangster informants who had connections with the "Prince Gang." After paying them a large amount of money they demanded, in a dilapidated house in the old and slum-like residential complex, four members of the Green Dragons appeared with knives in their hands. They fought off and ran for their lives and jumped over parapet after parapet, and alley after alley, trying desperately to get away from them. Not until bumping into two police officers patrolling the street by feet did their pursuers retreat. They told the police officers that they were both detectives investigating a family affair for their client, but were discovered and pursued by those men. The cops warned them to be careful and let go of them.

Hong Long exploded when briefed about what had taken place that day. With his hands griping on Tin Hang's shoulders and squeezing them as hard as he could, he hit his victim's private part with his right kneecap—a new habit he had recently developed for revenging what had happened to his son. Tin Hang screamed with excruciating pain.

"How did you screw up such a great opportunity to catch them? You idiot. Why didn't you send more men to surround that place?" He kicked him again and thundered.

"Please excuse my mistake, Master," Tin Hang begged.

We could have tortured the two men for all the information we need if we had caught them, Hong Long thought. But that opportunity had been shattered with the recklessness and brainlessness of his followers. Time was not on their side. He went over all the imperative actions that needed to be taken in his brain. He roared abruptly, "I give you one last chance to make up your stupid mistake, Tin Hang. Now get our men to visit all of the informants in town, and pay double to those who can provide valuable information, and report them to me immediately. I will handle all the operations from now on. Do you hear me clearly?''

"Very clear, Master Hong," he replied.

"Go then.''

"Yes, Master.''

19

A girl appeared in front of the CDC headquarters building and requested to see the director to report a serious corruption case. After talking on the portable phone and checking her ID, the security guard escorted her to the elevator. In the reception room of the office, the CDC director, Wu Ping, greeted her by the door. When he was about to guide her into his office, she said she needed to go to the toilet.

A few minutes later, she screamed and called for help in the toilet. Rushing out with her face pale and her white skirt stained with blood, she told the men and the receptionist running toward her that she had been bitten by a big rat in the toilet. They hurried to the toilet and were stunned to see blood spots splattered here and there, but found no sign of the rat. While everyone was frantically searching around for the rat, the girl swiftly pulled out a listening device from her handbag and quickly installed it into the phone sitting on the receptionist's desk. Then she sneaked back to the elevator and pushed the down button. Crying, she ran toward the gate of the building. But she was stopped by the security guard.

"Don't go away. We watched what you did to one of our phones on the TV screen," a guard growled.

The girl's face whitened, her right hand dug into the handbag and probed out a small paper bag of powder. Tearing open the bag, she swallowed the powder at once. She fainted immediately and fell on the floor. Blood was dripping out of her mouth, nose, eyes and ears. She was dead instantly. The security guard was astonished. Every move of the girl had happened so quickly. He glanced into her handbag and saw a couple of torn little red-ink bags in it.

Learning that, the CDC director was puzzled.

What the Green Dragons had been doing worried Lin Dan. Sun Ming and Chai Zhong, her detectives in the capital, were almost caught and hurt. As her fellows were watching, many of their informants had been goaded to work for the Green Dragons. Still, they hadn't received any information indicating that Hong Long was leading the Green Dragons. Nor had they had any evidence to prove that he was involved in his son's corruption schemes. *Something must be done now. We just can't wait and do nothing before getting killed,* she thought.

Pondering for a while, she telephone the branch leader, Jia Liang, in the capital. "A-Liang, it's Lin Dan. I wonder if you can organize some brothers to ambush and capture one or two of the members of the Green Dragons, so that we can interrogate them for the information we need."

"Yes, I have thought about that too. It's a good idea."

"But you have to plan it perfectly well and be very careful. I don't want any of our brothers to get hurt," she stressed.

"Yes, ma'am, I'll plan it perfectly well, and make sure that none of our brothers get hurt."

"Please, keep me updated for any new development."

"Sure, I will."

"Thanks, Liang."

The detectives of the AVD in the capital disguised themselves almost everyday when they went out to execute their missions. They put on fake beards or wigs or darkened sunglasses or various costumes and, sometimes, they even changed the shapes of their figures, depended on the needs of their tasks. Today they pretended to be motorcyclists, waiting for customers at various places in the crowded streets. It's a way for many of the unemployed men to make a living by giving convenient rides to others with motor-tricycles. Although it was not legal, the local government did not bother to ban it due to the serious unemployment problem. Yet their eyes kept ricocheting around for the possible appearance of their target. They had found out that a member of the Green Dragons had often loitered there. In order not to be interrupted with their mission, they would only take short-distance rides and refuse the long-distance rides by asking ridiculously high fares to the clients.

In late afternoon, their prey appeared. Jia Liang, through his mobile phone, talked with his brothers in other locations, telling them to come over at once. He then beckoned to the other two to park their motorcycles while following the man in around fifteen feet away. He stepped into a grocery store as the man turned his head. Some distance ahead, his brothers watched the scene closely, ready to make corresponding moves at any time. Searching carefully around with his small but brisk eyes, making sure that he had not been followed, the man quickened his steps. But his trip had been within the eyes of the AVD detectives. Darting between the crowds on the sidewalk, the man stopped abruptly at the herbal tea shop at the corner and pulled out a one-yuan coin and handed it to the owner.

"The usual," he muttered, sitting down on a stool.

While sipping the tea, he studied the environment and every-one standing or passing by on the street rather meticulously. A few minutes later, he got up and went into an alley next to the shop. It was within their calculation. Two of Jia Liang's brothers had been placed there, one was pretending to sell boiled corn sticks with a plastic bucket, the other one was sitting on a little wooden bench in the middle of the alley as a self-employed shoe shiner. They took glances at the man as he slowly roamed along lighting a cigarette. They knew that he often went to an apartment upstairs to play marji-ang in the late afternoon until midnight.

Watching the man turn left to the stairway, Jia Liang decided to delay taking actions. He told the two brothers on duty in the alley to keep their surveillance there until the man ended his gam-bling orgy for the day and came out.

Shortly after midnight, the man humming a song and seem-ingly walking on air, stepped briskly down through the alley again. It was realized instantly to the two AVD detectives waiting there that the man had been lucky on the marjiang table. They called their boss immediately.

"A-Liang, the snake has just come out. He's walking toward the street, happily. Looks like he's got luck tonight."

"Not anymore. Follow him out, both of you. We are all waiting on the street," Jia Liang replied to his mobile phone.

When the man gaited out of the alley, a couple of prostitutes came to him and held his arms and said, "Let's have fun tonight, honey."

"I really want to, but I don't have that much money," he re-plied.

Several middle-aged men sitting on the motor-tricycles ignited the motors simultaneously and moved closer to him, touting for the potential business. The closest one said to him with a tone of obsequiousness, "Master, where are you going? Let me give you a ride."

The man studied him for a second then got on and told him the address. The motor-tricycle roared into the darkness. Five minutes later, when the man discovered that he had been taken to the wrong place, the driver replied that he was taking a short-cut. His motor-tricycle stopped abruptly in front of a shrub a minute after. The man sensed danger and was about to jump off when a patch gagged onto his mouth and he fainted immediately. The man was stretched out on the floor of an isolated house on a little hill. They searched him thoroughly before he regained consciousness and found two little paper bags of poison from his pockets. They knew then, the man had not had the chance to commit suicide before getting caught.

They interrogated him in the early morning. The man was named Tao Langgei. He remained silent during the interrogation, regardless of what his interrogators asked. What puzzled Jia Liang and his brothers was, however, the man pretended to be unperturbed when they placed wads of cash on the table and pushed right in front of him. They said that the money could be his so long as he was cooperative with them. Unbelievably, there was nothing they could do with him. They were not allowed to hurt him, as they were told by their boss. Without getting anywhere, they adjourned the interrogation. Before they had time to bind and lock him up, the man suddenly bumped his head to the wall, attempting to commit suicide. But he was held back right in time by Jia Lang. Except for a small mound on his head, no life-threatening wounds had been inflicted.

In the afternoon, to their surprise, the man requested to make a phone call to his married sister to take their chronically ill mother to the hospital tomorrow morning, a job he had been doing regularly every week, and tomorrow was the due day. That opened the opportunity to crack down his defense. Jia Liang was elated. He handed him his mobile phone immediately. Taking the phone, the man returned a smile. He called several times and was disappointed because no one answered the phone. Jia Liang consoled him and told him to call later. And then they started talking.

"What kind of disease does your mother have?" Ja Liang asked gently.

"Kidney failure."

"That can be replaced by a donated one. I know a few who have had that operation."

"I know, but we can't even afford her weekly treatment. Indeed, it was partly paid by—" he stopped abruptly and his face turned grim.

Jia Liang could guess who had been aiding his mother's treatment. "Your boss, right? But that doesn't solve your mother's problem in a long run."

He nodded, with his head slumping forward then down. "In fact, it is the only reason why I risk my life to work for them."

"I feel sorry for you and your mother. I tell you what, we will pay for your mother's operation, if you agree to it."

"Really? For what?" Tao Langgei exclaimed, staring at Jia Liang with a doubtful expression on his face.

"Nothing, just want to be your friend," he smiled.

"But I and my mother will get killed if my boss finds out," he muttered, the grimness reappeared on his face.

"Don't worry, we will protect both of you," Jia Liang assured him.

"But how?"

"After giving your mother an operation, both of you can stay here. This place is very safe."

Tao Langgei looked out from the window, plunging himself in deep thought. "I took an oath with them when I agreed to work for them. I just can't break it," he muttered bitterly.

Jia Liang patted his shoulder and said, "It depends on who you have pledged to. If you do it to the bad guys, it is not worth it. By the way, do you really know who you are working for? They are the corrupt officials, the criminals."

"Really? To tell you the truth, except for my boss—the team leader—I don't really know who leads the Green Dragons. We grass-root detectives aren't permitted to know."

Jia Liang was struck by what he heard. He pondered for a moment, then said, "Yes, for the sake of our citizens and for your mother, let's work together to get rid of them."

"Okay. I wouldn't have worked for them if I knew they were corrupt government officials."

"Until now, you are innocent, for not knowing the truth. It isn't too late for your awakening. Let me arrange a hospital for your mother's operation first, then we talk about our plan."

"Sounds good to me."

Tao Langgei's mother was not going to have an operation until another three weeks later, according to the hospital's schedule. As instructed by Jia Liang, he returned to the Green Dragons and pretended that nothing had happened to him. His job was to help trap his team leader, Dong Bell. But the next two days, he had disappeared, and Jia Liang lost contact with him. When Jia Liang wondered what had happened to him, his brothers found out that he had been killed by the Green Dragons.

Jia Liang mourned, feeling the pain of losing a born-again brother and a very valuable spy. He pondered how the Green Dragons had found out the loyalty shift of their man. Anyway he had to be very careful in handling such things from now on. He phoned and reported it to Lin Dan immediately and suggested a change of the tactic.

From what Tao Langgei had told them, his team leader, Dong Bell, lived in a newly constructed thirty-six-story apartment building complex. His luxury apartment had a camera and an alarm installed by the wrought iron gate in front of the wooden door. More than that, all of the windows were barred with stainless steel. When he came in and out of the apartment, he always had a couple of burly men accompanying him too. Jia Liang went there to take a look. An idea appeared in his mind.

The next morning, Jia Liang and one of his brothers registered as phone technicians coming in to repair the wiring problem in the office of the security guards there. Climbing on the stairway on the second floor, they went to the electric room. Ja Liang unlocked the door with a specially designed key. His brother took cordon outside of the room, he then quickly began working on the phone lines on the electronic panel. Minutes later, he located the two wires connecting to Dong Bell's apartment. He knew obviously that one was connected to the man's home phones and the other to his computer for Internet service. He hooked a crocodile clip of an electronic meter to the wires to check if the phones or the computers were being used. Then he disconnected one wire and put on a bug with it and reconnected it. He did the same to the other wire skillfully. When it was done, they locked the door and left at once.

The eavesdropping provided a lot of valuable information from Dong Bell's communication between his boss and his men on both the Internet and on his home phone.

"Master Hong, I can't wait to tell you that nearly all informants, both public and underground in the capital, are willing to work for us. And our enemies have been forced to cease functioning in the rest of the nation."

"Don't be complacent, idiot. We have not gotten rid of one single one of them, and we are running out of time. You have to keep your eyes open everywhere, and try to dig them out as quickly as you can, Bell. I give you one week to make some progress. You know what the consequence is if you fail to do so."

"We are doing follow-ups, and our boys are all over that place where our traitor got hooked up. Soon, Master Hong, we will get them."

"Don't be stupid! You think they will continue to have their operations there, waiting for you to catch them? Try to track them somewhere else."

Their conversation had proven that they were desperately tracking down their rivaling detectives, and Hong Long was the paramount leader of the Green Dragons. Jia Liang informed it to Lin Dan immediately. It was quite a breakthrough. But it was still far from what they really needed. The most difficult thing to do, they knew, was to prove that Hong Long had involved in corruption. But the task would be too tough and too risky for them to handle since their lives had been threatened by this powerful man and his followers. Obviously this was something that could not be done by themselves alone.

*　　*　　*

She really didn't know how long she could keep on doing this. What started and sustained her on carrying out the vengeance was the grudge toward those corrupt officials, it fostered throughout her past experiences and the will to revenge for what she had suffered before.

206

Her belly had grown bigger and bigger as her baby's due date got closer. Touching the budging belly each time, she started visualizing herself as a mother, holding and feeding her baby with her breasts. Yes, she really wanted to be a dedicated mother with her love completely devoted to her own child. The hatred toward the rotten officials had hindered and deprived her time and sensations from devoting herself in loving and caring for her husband wholeheartedly. Now she really didn't want it to happen to her child. She reconsidered the idea of letting her AVD Detective Agency merge with the CDC, so that she could retire from fighting with the trash of the society. Pulling out the CDC brochure that she had once gotten from the director of that government organization, she dialed the phone number.

20

As an experienced spy, Dong Bell had the habit of checking his phone lines and connections periodically. As usual, one day, he and his men traced the phone lines from his apartment all the way down to the electric room of the building. They were amazed when they saw that his two phone lines had been bugged. Dong Bell stopped them when his men tried to pull the bugs off. Instead he told one of them to go fetch a box that had various kinds of electronic components. As required by his profession, he had learned the knowledge of electronics and was fond on repairing and assembling electronic devices. He picked up a little resistor and a capacitor from the box and connected them to one bug, and did the same to the other. He knew from doing that, it would create noises on the signal received. And he figured out that the perpetrators who had installed the bugs would come back to fix it.

Hiding themselves there and waiting for a couple of hours in the evening, Jia Liang and his brother appeared with flashlights. While they were fixing it, Dong Bell and his men whacked them as hard as they could with logs and pipes. They were crippled instantly, their eyes and faces were bruised and swollen, and blood coming out of their mouths. They gagged and bound them and put them into the linen bags, then took them into the elevator. Once down, they carried the two heavy bags out of the building and loaded them onto a minitruck. Dong Bell reported their catches to Hong Long from his mobile phone right away. His boss was overjoyed, telling him that he would be there immediately to interrogate them.

The truck scurried ahead, passing crowded neon-lighted and dimly lighted streets. Unlike many vehicles running in the streets, it was patient not to honk, lest they be stopped by the traffic police—although the chance for that to happen was very slim. It finally came to a complete halt right in front of the wrought iron gate of a two-story brick house, which was surrounded with an eight-foot barbed compound. As Dong Bell yelled and gestured, the security guard pressed the button of the automatic control, and immediately the gate screeched open to both sides. The truck rolled in and the gate closed back right away. They unloaded the two bags and unbound them. Their captures were writhing with pain. They were kicked while being pushed toward a cottage in the backyard of the house. The door of the cottage was wide open. Through the dim light, they could see that a mean-and-rude-looking old man, with a lighted cigarette clipping between his right-hand fingers, was sitting in a chair behind a table. They were pushed in and forced to sit on a stool in front of the man's table, facing him.

Dong Bell got in and bowed to the man and said, "Master Hong, they are here." Then he pulled the gags off his captures' mouths and sat down next to Hong Long.

"Jia Liang," the man blared, "the only way for you to get out of this house alive is to cooperate with us. Do you understand?"

Jia Liang raised his head slowly and looked at the man through his swollen-shut eyes, and said nothing. His assistant seemed frightened, squeezing his eyebrows and tightening his bruised face.

Knowing that they would not reply to whatever they asked and wanting to please his boss, Dong Bell slammed his fist on the table and barked, "What is the name of your organization and who is in charge of it?"

Again Jia Liang remained silent. But his assistant started to feel uneasy, and kept glancing at their interrogators every now and then. Dong Bell got up and leaped over and slapped Jia Liang's wounded face hard, and growled, "Open your goddamned mouth."

Jia Liang screamed with the unbearable pain and said, "Why don't you just kill me, one way or the other, you will not get anything out of me."

"I don't let you die easily. I will make you pay for what my son has suffered, unless you cooperate," Hong Long threatened.

"You bastard, social trash, do whatever you like," Jia Liang retorted.

Dong Bell slapped Jia Liang again, and Jia Liang cried painfully and fell off the stool. Then he grabbed the hair of his assistant and pulled his head up and thundered, "What the hell is your name?"

The man stared at him with fear and moaned uneasily. Dong Bell spanked him and roared, "Say it, you damned son of a bitch, otherwise, I will kill you." He pulled his hair harder. The man croaked with pain, "Lu Zi."

"Lu Zi?" Dong Bell howled. "What is the name of your organization, and who leads it?"

Lu Zi hesitated. Jia Liang struggled to claw over and knelt in front of him. "A-Zi, don't tell them."

Dong Bell kicked at Jia Liang as hard as he could, and he uttered a painful cry and fell down with his back on the ground.

Hong Long slammed the table again and thundered, "How dare you, Jia Liang. I give you one last chance to confess before we kill you in a slow and extremely painful way."

Lying on the floor and moaning with his eyes closed, Jia Liang remained unperturbed from what his interrogator had just said. His mind started to drift to the past. Like his boss, he had been a victim of the greedy government officials. He used to work for a state-owned enterprise as a manager of the security department. The company closed down due to huge embezzlements committed by the heads of the firm, who had escaped out of the nation with most of the firm's cash with them in the fear of being discovered. They left all employees with no job, no welfare, and no pay. Until recently he had worked as a self-employed detective. The AVD Detective Agency provided him an opportunity to vent his indignation toward the sick guys in the government while making a living. Until he got trapped and caught by his enemy, he had been so absorbed by his work and loyal to his boss. His reverie was interrupted by the roaring of his captor.

"Jia Liang, you confess or not?" Hong Long howled.

Sitting up slowly, Jia Liang tilted his head up a bit and said, "I confess. I regret falling into your trap which deprives my opportunity to fight against corrupt officials."

"Shut up." Dong Bell slapped him back down onto the floor.

Hong Long clapped his hands loudly three times and droned, "Let's begin by roasting a man's testicles."

Three men outside of the cottage replied and came in immediately. Two of them carried ropes in hand, one was holding a tray with cotton balls, and a can of gasoline. Grabbing and pressing Jia Liang on the ground, they took off his clothes and bound his limbs on two stools. In his protest, they wrapped his private part with layers of cotton and then poured some gasoline onto it. Hong Long got up and examined it, then he threw a lighted cigarette stub on it. Instantly, a column of fire was generated between Jia Liang's legs, the flame nearly reached the ceiling. A burning smell of gasoline, pubic hair and human flesh mingled and spread all over the cottage. Jia Liang screamed hysterically, his body kept wiggling and convulsing violently between the stools, but unable to get free of the bondage.

Lu Zi was frightened and gasped with his mouth opened to the utmost limit, his eyes were bulging and looking dead.

While the burning was going on and their victim screaming heartbreakingly, Hong Long and Dong Bell and their men were chuckling, dancing, and indulging themselves in the beer-drinking orgy. Hong Long walked over and poured some beer into Jia Liang's mouth and said, "This is only the preliminary vengeance for my son and many others who have suffered from being castrated. We will catch all of you and your boss and do the same. Now let's celebrate our future victory in advance."

Jia Liang gurgled and fainted. The cottage was permeated with the smoke and the pungent smell of burnt human flesh, gasoline, and alcohol. Lu Zi was weeping uncontrollably. Dong Bell stumbled over drunkenly and grabbed his shirt right at the chest and pulled him up. "What the fuck are you crying for, since everybody else is so happy here?" Then he crammed a can of beer into his mouth and ordered, "Drink it, dumb ass."

Lu Zi choked by the jumble of tears and beer, began coughing.

"If you don't cooperate with us, this is the example for you, Lu Zi," Hong Long warned.

The burning died down. A layer of ash covered Jia Liang's crotch. His hip and belly had burned to utter dark and brown, with blisters bulging all over.

"Now it's time to serve our distinguished guest, Lu Zi, a precious meal of roasted penis," Hong Long said, gazing at him.

With his left hand holding a plate and his right hand gripping a knife, one of the men strode next to Jia Liang's body and crouched down. He laid his sharp knife against the lower part of the unconscious man's roasted private part and sliced at it abruptly. The dark and awful-looking penis was cut off from Jia Liang's body, blood gushing out from the wound. Jia Liang uttered a loud cry, his body convulsed a few more times, then he was dead.

Lu Zi covered his ruined face and eyes with his hands, sobbing. Dong Bell roared behind him, "Stop crying, here is your late-night snack." He handed the ugly and grisly looking little libido right in front of his face. Seeing it, Lu Zi shuddered and turned his head aside at once. "Eat it, or do you want to confess now?" Leaving no time for him to reply, Dong Bell grabbed the man's hair and tilted his face upward with his left hand, and his right hand picked up the charred penis and stuffed it into his mouth. Lu Zi shrieked with fear, struggling with all the energy he had to get rid of his captor's grip and Jia Liang's roasted penis out of his mouth. Croaking, he threw up all the food he had eaten that evening.

Vomiting uncontrollably, Lu Zi was unable to reply to what his interrogators asked. Hong Long was furious. He roared, "Take off his clothes and do the same for him."

Before the men reached him, Lu Zi yelled urgently, "Stop it, I will tell you whatever I know about our organization."

Hearing it, they looked at each other and smiled. "Then we are listening," Hong Long said.

Clearing his throat, Lu Zi told them everything that they wanted to know. In the end, they exchanged glances and whispers. And they all believed what he said and decided what to do with him.

"We hate traitors, don't we?" Hong Long asked.

And they replied unanimously, "Yes, of course."

Then he asked them again, "What do we do with them?"

"Kill them."

"Then you know what to do with Lu Zi, right?"

"Yes." Two men secured Lu Zi immediately and gagged him. They didn't want people living nearby to hear his screaming in the middle of the night. And they repeated what they did to Jia Liang to him. Then they began a new round of celebration deep into the night for getting the most important information needed for their vengeance. They plunged themselves into another orgy of beer-drinking and late-night snack eating, despite the presence of the two newly murdered corpses.

*　　*　　*

After two rings, the receptionist of the CDC answered the phone. "Hello, Central Disciplinary Committee. How may I help you?"

"May I speak to the director, please? I have something very important to talk to him."

"May I know who is calling?"

"Yes, my name is Lin Dan. I've been there before."

"Lin Dan? Oh! I remember you. You reported a big case that took place in Shenzhen and stayed here for several days before. I know then that whatever you report is important for us. Hold on for a minute, let me transfer your call."

Having waited for a few seconds, she heard a man's voice at the other end, "Lin Dan, how have you been? Nice to hear you again."

"I'm fine, and I hope you have been doing all right. I am calling to confess to you that—" She hesitated for a second then went on, "I am sure you have heard about that some corrupt government officials have got castrated, right?"

"Yes, although it is illegal, it helps us a lot in the battle against corruption. Whoever does that should receive credit for it. By the way, do you have any idea who has been doing that, because I want them to work with us?"

After another second of hesitation, Lin Dan replied, "Indeed, yes."

"Who? Tell me, please," Wu Ping exclaimed and could not wait any longer to hear the answer.

Taking a deep breath, Lin Dan pronounced articulately, "To tell you the truth, it is me and my people."

"Really? You aren't joking? You are such a weak and lovely girl, how could it be?" he cried skeptically.

"I know, it is hard to believe, but that is what we have been doing for the past year. I am prepared to receive punishment for doing all of that. But before you do that I want to inform you one last time about the highest-ranking corrupt officials we have yet encountered and are unable to deal with. This is the reason why I call you as I want to cooperate with the state's anti-corruption force."

Still shocked in process what he had just heard, Wu Ping cleared his throat and said, "I have to tell you that, it is too big of a surprise for me. I am appalled. Anyway, if that is the case, you have been doing an excellent job. Indeed, we have been looking for the possible cooperation with whomever is responsible for those heroic actions badly. I have never thought that it would be you. I don't think you should be punished for doing good things for our nation and its people. But that is not what I can decide, but the judicial system and the ones who run it. I will do whatever I can to defend you. But it will not come to that until months, even years from now. Now let's discuss our cooperation and the case you have.''

"Do you know who Hong Long is?''

"Yes, of course, he is one of the senior central committee members of the Communist Party. And as far as I can remember, his son got emasculated by your people due to the fact that he had committed a series of corruption and womanizing crimes. He was disciplined by our committee and sentenced by the people's court for ten years in prison.''

"And he deserved a much more serious punishment," Lin Dan cut in. "Instead, he received a lenient sentence because of his father's interference, right?''

"I guess you are right. That's what I sometimes feel powerless about. Why do you mention him? Is he involved in corruption as well?''

"That's something I need you to find it out. But I can tell you that he has found and led an underground organization called the Green Dragons, one of its purposes is to revenge and counterattack us and protect the corrupt officials. Our lives have been threatened, and I feel too tired and too weak to fight with them.''

"Really? How dare he. He shows no regret of what his son had done and no gratefulness for getting a lenient treatment for him. I will talk to the chairman of the Communist Party and begin investigating him soon, very soon. Thanks for your information. Now tell me your plan for our cooperation.''

"I would like to place my detective agency to be under your command. My agency has about two hundred detectives working in all major cities in the nation. Although it is a financial burden, it is worth every penny the state will spend on it because they all work dedicatedly and effectively.''

"That sounds wonderful, but how about you? Are you going to work with us?''

"No, I am going to retire to be a mother and a housewife.''

"What a waste of talent, and a good and brave heart," he sighed. "I tell you what, I will fly over to talk with you about it in detail and take care of the merging stuff. Thanks for calling. Lin Dan. I have really missed you.''

"I've missed you too, Director Wu. Please do take action as soon as possible. I am afraid that it is already too late, the Green Dragons have been hunting us madly. I look forward to seeing you soon. Bye.''

"Don't worry about it. I will work on it right after our conversation. Take care, bye!''

*　　*　　*

In her seventh month of pregnancy, Lin Dan began to feel the move of the baby in her stomach. She told her husband about it and he was overjoyed. Every night before going to sleep, Chen Yong knelt down next to her and placed his ear on her stomach, listening, feeling, reporting, yelling, and laughing at every discovery of the kick and wiggle inside. Then they chatted on for hours what the upcoming life would be with the arrival of a newborn baby and bet on whether it would be a boy or girl. Both agreed they would accept either sex happily. Beginning a month earlier, instead of making love, they only caressed each other, lest it would disturb or hurt the developing baby.

Once in a while, the merry would-be-father Chen Yong would sneak out of the office and go to the nearby supermarket to buy some diapers and milk powder. He'd bring them home and stock the baby room, along with toys and cradles and beds.

They had placed advertisement in various newspapers to recruit a nanny for their oncoming baby. Several respondents had actually been interviewed. They sorted out a couple whom they believed were healthy and proper for their baby.

Lin Dan seldom went to her office. Instead, she had physical examinations in the hospital often. Within two months, she figured, she would be completely retired from fighting with the corrupt officials and be a full-time mother and housewife. She had promised to her husband it would be so, and the talk with the CDC director had paved the way.

On her way back from the hospital after the routine pregnancy physical examination, Lin Dan received a stranger's phone call telling her that he was an informant who had dug out extremely important information about the leader of the Green Dragons. He

215

would not tell her anymore about it until they met face to face. Getting his name and address, she told the chauffeur to drop her down there. When they reached the place on the outskirt of the city, they found that it was a kind of a deserted and dilapidated house crouching on the lower part of a foothill with bush and shrubs all around. Feeling a sense of danger, she told the chauffeur to back up. Right at the moment, a tall and ferocious-looking man came out of the house.

"Is this Lin Dan? Nice looking car and you are so beautiful." The man praised, his throat went dry.

"Yes, are you Jong Pong?" Lin Dan rolled down the window and replied. "You can tell me now."

"It's me, ma'am. But you are with a man, please come down here with me or tell him to go away for a while, and I will tell you the information.

She whispered with the chauffeur for a few seconds then stepped out of the car slowly, avoiding any bumps to her bulging belly. The man was beckoning her to come closer. Suddenly four burly men came out of the thick bush right behind the car. Before the driver was able to shift the gear, the men got into the car and pulled him out. Jong Pong budged over to Lin Dan, grabbed her arms as if he were a hawk clawing on a little hen.

She cried, "Who are you? What are you doing to a pregnant woman?"

"What are we doing? We want to have fun with a beautiful girl like you," the man chuckled obscenely, pulling her toward the house. And her chauffeur was being dragged by the men right behind her.

"Stop! My baby! Oh! My baby!" she cried.

"Why the hell do you care about your baby, since you can't even care about yourself," the man howled.

Once getting into the house, Jong Pong pushed her onto the ground. The other men were whispering and laughing sordidly after they threw the driver down at a corner and bound his limbs. "Let me have fun with her first. This is the most beautiful piece of chick I have ever seen so far, my god," one said excitedly.

"No, let me do it first," one protested.

"I go first, I am the oldest."

"Ha, shut up, all of you. Don't touch her yet until we find out what Master Hong says, okay?" then he pulled out a mobile phone from a pocket. After pressing some buttons, he spoke into the phone, "Master Hong, we have caught the bitch. What do you want us to do with her?"

"Do nothing, just keep watching her. I will be there in ten minutes," Hong Long said succinctly.

Lying on the floor, she blamed herself for getting trapped. *This is not my true self, but the baby, it must be it. The baby has been making me drowsy and tired, and I retired from vigilance recently, and now my brain has not been functioning normally,* she thought. Her hand reached to her stomach. The baby was kicking. Her husband would be so happy to listen to it and feel it with his face and hands if she were with him now. How sweet. She smiled while caressing her stomach with her hand feeling the move of the baby, forgetting the deadly situation and environment she was in. She suddenly gasped and was frightened by hearing a man say, "Look, she is flirting with us. Let me go for it. I just can't wait." The man was moving toward her.

"Take off, A-Fei," Jong Pong ordered, pulling the man back.

At that moment, they heard a mechanical rumbling approaching the house, and then the noise went abruptly dead. "Master Hong has got here," the man, taking watch outside of the threshold, reported.

Accompanying by his chauffeur, Hong Long strode into the house. He shot a glance at Lin Dan and her chauffeur and then sat on a stool reserved for him. Studying her thoroughly, he was stunned by her beauty, wondering if he could keep her as his mistress. But that idea quickly vanished in his mind, knowing that she was married to a famous entrepreneur and she had battered his reputation and destroyed his son's life. She would have to pay, the hatred toward her rekindled.

"Sit up, bitch, and look at me," he roared.

Knowing that it wouldn't do her any good to disobey him, Lin Dan struggled to sit up slowly. She looked at him and saw no sign of recognition. The man was in his sixties and looked mean and stubborn. She was sure that he was the leader of the Green Dragons, Hong Long, most likely, since she had heard one of the men called him Master Hong minutes ago. This old and malicious-looking man was going to take revenge for what his family and son had been suffering. Unless there was a miracle, there would be no escape for her. She shivered, nervously waiting for the man's move. But she wondered how they had found out her information and got her trapped. There came the man's first grunt.

"Lin Dan, first I have to admit that you are a good-looking bitch, and you have tons of wealth and prestige by marrying a rich businessman. But why the hell do you want to bother and destroy those who work so hard for the nation and the citizens, and just want to get back a fraction of what they had contributed? Why?"

That was a senseless and irresponsible and egotistic accusation and question, it was not worth replying. But she knew, in facing these men who had little sense of rule of law and justice, silence would inflict brutal reactions. She decided to brush his silly comment aside and pretend not to know what he was saying.

"I really don't understand what you are talking about and why do you bully a pregnant woman like this. You will get arrested and punished for hurting innocent citizens. But if you want some money, I can tell my husband to give it to you, provided you do not hurt me and let me go. And I promise to you that I will not report this to the police."

The men were laughing. "If you are as innocent as what you say, you would not have been trapped here," Hong Long snickered. "Don't try to fool us, we got everything about you from your men in the capital, bitch."

She shivered. If what he said was true, some of her detectives in the capital had been captured and, at least, one of them somehow betrayed her despite their near absolute loyalty. She felt sad, not only because she had been betrayed, but because that people who worked for her had suffered or been killed. As far as she was concerned, her detectives would not give up their loyalty toward her easily. The Green Dragons must have treated them badly. She regretted implementing the plan of merging her organization with the CDC too late, otherwise the tragedy could have been avoided. Yet she really wanted to know how many of her detectives had been captured and how badly these men tortured and hurt them in the capital.

"You have committed a new crime against the state and the citizens for hurting my people. How many of my detectives in the capital did you cripple or kill?"

"We only took care of two, and we will get the rest after we take care of you."

She knew the exact meaning of "being taking care of" by these vicious criminals. "Who did you kill?"

"Your lovely Jia Liang and Lu Zi. But does it matter who we kill first, they all are going to die anyway. It is our vengeance for what you have done to our relatives and friends," Hong Long confessed.

The sad news struck her hard. Jia Liangg was such a nice, honest, loyal and hard-working man. She had just talked to him a week ago. How could such a decent man be brutally slain? She felt so sorry and depressed with a sense of guilt, as if she had murdered him. Yet her vengeance battle toward the wicked officials had caused the deaths of innocent and decent people, not to mention the capture of herself, her baby, and her chauffeur. She wondered if it was worth fighting, although she had gained victory after victory in this battle, the price was unacceptably high. Her reverie was interrupted abruptly by the man's groan.

"Pretty bitch, you will be killed quite comfortably, or you can spare your life and, of course, your baby's, if you tell us about the members of your organization in detail, including the names and the cities they have been working in."

"Don't be ridiculous, I have resented my naiveté and loathed your insanity and brutality for causing the death of innocent people. Do you think I am that heartless to let it happen again? Wake up, men. Stop murdering law-abiding citizens and breaking rules and laws. Give yourselves up to the law enforcers. Believe me, you will be much happier without the greed and hatred in your minds."

"Shut up and don't try to act like a goddamned Western missionary. You've physically hurt and destroyed my son's life and many others' lives, bitch. Nor do you qualify to teach us and tell us what to do," he retorted. "Just answer my question or you will regret for failing to do so."

"And you will regret for your stubbornness and lack of remorsefulness."

The man got up and slapped her heartily, and warned, "Stop teaching me, confess now."

Moaning for the pain, she muttered, "The only confession I want to make is that I regret not being able to dig out your material and report them to the Central Disciplinary Committee."

"And have my testicles cut off, ah."

"Yes, if you are both a womanizer and a corrupt official."

"You're good at cutting a man's balls off, ah? Now demonstrate it to us how you do it," he said, beckoning to Jong Pong. "Pull that man over and take off his clothes."

Crying and floundering in protest, Lin Dan's chauffeur was dragged over with his clothes taken off right in front of his hostess. Jong Pong was holding a pair of scissors and said, "Now show us how you get him gelded."

Lin Dan felt ashamed and mortified, while the men around her were laughing loudly and obscenely, urging her to proceed. Her chauffeur was being lashed, sobbing, and looking at her in terror. Holding a pair of scissors, her hand was trembling, she could not dare to look at his private part. She dropped the scissors onto the ground and clasped her hands and closed her eyes. She began mumbling some Buddhism sutra quotations. The recollection of the short period of reclusive life and the past came flooding into her mind.

Starting from being a mistress of a local corrupt official, her bumpy life before her marriage was very much linked to her gifted beauty. The saying, "beautiful women often have ill fates," was amazingly true for her. She would have yet been living peacefully and quietly in the temple, if she were not moved by the craving of love that had deeply rooted in her heart. Or she could have been living simply and happily as a housewife with a man if she were just an average-looking woman. It was her fate, the fate that there was nothing she could do about it, but the divine being. She felt sorry for her husband, her relatives and friends, who would be saddened and hurt from missing her. She imagined the ugly scene of her lying in a pool of blood with a contorted face caused from pain and the wound in her chest still gushing, and her baby kicking in protest with being murdered before entering this world. She shivered and screamed and then sobbed.

There came a sudden strike to her face, and she fell onto the ground with excruciating pain and terror. She awakened to face the horrible reality again. "Do it now. Stop playing tricks, bitch," Hong

Long, the ugly old man chided, pulling her up. Taking that opportunity, she picked up the pair of scissors quickly and plunged it into his chest. The old man screamed heartbreakingly and fell onto the floor heavily. But a knife penetrated through her heart from the back. She uttered a last horrified and disillusioned croak, and then crumbled backward.

*　　*　　*

Kneeling in front of Lin Dan's grave for hours, Chen Yong's physical and emotional sensors within his brain and body ceased functioning. He was starkly numb, with no feeling of sadness, fatigue, or hungriness. The only thing that remained working within him was the craving of a miracle, like the one that took place when he was kneeling in the temple for the hope of bringing back his lover.

The telecommunication empire that he had struggled so hard to build with the help of his lover suddenly became meaningless to him.

Epilogue

By the year 2004, Deng Xiaoping, a man who was extremely short physically even by Chinese standards, had been passed away for seven years. He was fully charismatic with a quick and visionary mind and a warm heart among the leaders in China's modern history. The thoughts he had left behind and the framework that he had helped build laid a solid foundation for a foreseeably wealthy, strong, democratic, peaceful, and respectable nation on earth.

Today, after implementing his policy of Reform and Opening for a quarter of a century, the nation's GDP has leaped five fold. A country that used to be lacking in everything, now has an abundant supply throughout the nation and has become a world factory that produces the most number of mass-market products. This included: mobile phones, color TV sets, air conditioners, washing machines, refrigerators, microwave ovens, toys, garments, shoes, clocks, and watches. Indeed, China has become a major world supplier of daily commodities. And yet, as the world's fastest growing economy, it has shown no sign of slowing down.

Most important, the ideological controversy about whether China should go on the road of socialism or capitalism has been silenced and vanished. The echelon leadership that used to be divided into reformers and hardliners, now has consolidated uniquely to lead the nation for a better tomorrow. Practicing capitalism with characteristics of socialism has achieved enormous success in this former radical communist country under Deng's influence.

As the first and the largest special economic zone established under Deng's instruction, Shenzhen has stunned the world with its remarkable pace of progress. The little poverty-stricken fishing town has now become an internationally renowned modern city and one of a few major industrial manufacturing bases in the nation in just twenty-four years. And it is still leaping forward impressively.

However, being in the social transition period and without a fully established and implemented judicial system and the rule of law, crimes have been rampant in Shenzhen and the rest of the nation. The ubiquitous phenomenon of corruption is like a malicious tumor growing and expanding inside the governmental body, eating up its health and threatening its life. A proper and effective treatment to deal with it has not yet been found, despite the progress made by the anticorruption movement within the government. Indeed, the reported cases of the busted corrupt officials are just tips of the iceberg.

May God bless this ancient cradle of civilization.

About the Author

DAVID TSUI was born and grew up in a village in southeast China. His education was interrupted and ruined by the Cultural Revolution when he was in the third grade. He was a farmer until he met "The Educated Youth"—the former Red Guard during the ten-year turmoil—who were sent to the countryside to be "Reeducated" by the farmers from Guangzhou, the capital of Guangdong province. He attempted to leave the "Bamboo Curtain" with them one night by swimming the entire night across the bay between the mainland and Hong Kong, but he was captured and detained in prisons on the mainland for many months. Having stayed in the British colony for four years after his successful escape, he immigrated to the United States as a refugee in 1980. At the age of twenty-six, he started to learn English by attending evening classes after his exhausting restaurant work. Three years later, he struggled to make up the high school courses and went on to college. He received a bachelor's degree in electrical engineering when he was thirty-three: He returned to his hometown to teach English in 2001. He resides in San Francisco and is currently working on his new book.